# THE
# WIDOW
# BRIDE

## BOOKS BY CAREY BALDWIN

*Her First Mistake*

*The Marriage Secret*

*Second Wives*

THE CASSIDY & SPENSER THRILLERS SERIES

*Judgment*

*Fallen*

*Notorious*

*Stolen*

*Countdown*

Prequels

*First Do No Evil* (*Blood Secrets Book 1*)

*Confession* (*Blood Secrets Book 2*)

# THE
# WIDOW
# **BRIDE**

## CAREY BALDWIN

*bookouture*

Published by Bookouture in 2024

An imprint of Storyfire Ltd.
Carmelite House
50 Victoria Embankment
London EC4Y 0DZ

www.bookouture.com

ISBN: 978-1-83790-976-6
eBook ISBN: 978-1-83790-975-9

*For Erik, Kayla and Lumi,*
*you light up the world.*

# PROLOGUE

My chest aches as I watch her.

She reaches a too thin arm to open a cabinet and winces, then pulls down cups and boxes of tea, prattling on about chamomile versus orange spice, whether or not she has cookies to go with them. Eventually, we sit down across from one another at the kitchen table with piping hot cups and a box of animal crackers.

Her face is devoid of expression—a smooth mask.

She's never going to confide in me.

*I have no choice.*

Even if it angers her, even if it embarrasses us both, there's no way around it. The only way to get her to tell the truth is for me to go first. "I know everything."

Her lips turn white, matching her pale complexion.

"I won't let you do this on your own. I'm here to help," I whisper, keeping my voice too low for the microphones to pick up.

She brings out a beauty queen smile. "If you've found out my secrets, that means you've been spying on me. Obviously, I don't need to recount the story to you, and your being here is slowing me down. Please leave."

"I know you're angry with me. We can work through that later. The important thing is to get you to a safe place. Now that we're not playing games, we don't need to sit and chat over tea. I promise not to slow you down. Let me help you."

"I don't want your help." She climbs to her feet, still with a phony smile for the cameras, still speaking in a hushed voice. To anyone watching it would appear we are having a lovely time.

"Two people executing a plan is better than one. It will maximize your chances. I'm not going to take 'no' for an answer. I know you're only trying to protect me. Well, guess what? I can handle *him*."

"You don't know how brutal he can be."

"I do, now." I want to hug her and hold her and cry with her, but we don't have time for any of that. "I suggest you pack a small bag with the bare essentials. Like you said before, he's probably not watching us live. But we can't waste any more time. Give me your keys. I'll pull your car off the street into the driveway."

"But I need a car."

"We'll take mine, and then I'll leave it with you. I can grab a ride-share home. He might have a tracking device on your car."

She fakes another laugh for the cameras. "I should've thought of that. Thank you. And when he comes home and finds me gone, if my car is in the drive, he'll watch the security tapes. He'll see us laughing together and think we've gone out for drinks. That will buy me a few extra hours."

I grab my gut as if doubling over with laughter. "I just realized he'll see you packing a bag."

"No cameras in the closet. I'll pack in there. Then, from the app on my phone, I'll turn off the cameras and doorbell feed. We'll run like hell out the front. Once we're in your car, I'll turn the cameras back on. That will look like a momentary glitch in the feed. If we smile just enough, we might pull it off. I *might* be able to get away."

# ONE

## NOW

Good thing Rosalyn Monroe Hightower had stopped by to check on her late brother's widow. At two o'clock in the after-noon, she'd found Melanie still in bed, and the house, to put it nicely, in disarray. At first, Mel claimed to be feeling perfectly fine, but from the pinched look around her eyes, Rosalyn deduced she was having one of her headaches. Mel soon conceded it was so, and Rosalyn decided to stick around and make herself useful until her sister-in-law felt better.

So far, Rosalyn had straightened the living room and the study and put on a load of laundry—next up, the kitchen.

What time was it now?

3:00 *p.m.*

Mel had taken headache pills, and, by now, she ought to be improved.

Rosalyn slid her fingers over the bumpy, worn leather band of her watch, lifted her wrist close to her ear, listened to it tick-ing, and breathed in the scent of leather—an oft repeated act that sometimes tortured, and other times comforted her. The watch was an old, wind-up Timex their father had given to her late brother, Philip, on his eighteenth birthday. A week later, while mowing the lawn under a hot Arizona sun, Dad had a heart attack and died.

Philip had worn the Timex every day.

Later, her brother had become a wealthy man, thanks to a simple, yet brilliant invention—The Chuckle: a portable phone charger disguised as a slender, stylish buckle you attach to your belt or shoe.

But despite his newfound wealth, Philip had never upgraded his watch. And even though Rosalyn possessed half a dozen timepieces of her own, she'd coveted Philip's Timex because it'd been a precious gift from their father.

Then, three years ago, on Rosalyn's twenty-ninth birthday, Philip had set a small, awkwardly wrapped box beside her dinner plate. When she'd opened it and discovered the watch inside, she'd been furious with him for believing she'd ever accept such a gift under the circumstances.

Earlier that same week, they'd received news that, in spite of aggressive treatment, Philip's cancer had progressed.

*You're already giving away your most cherished possessions? I won't be party to that!*

But Philip had remained calm, pressing her to take the watch, insisting he wanted to enjoy seeing it on her wrist while he was still alive.

Reliving the feel of her brother's fingers fastening the watch around her wrist, she inhaled sharply. It had been more than a year since Philip died, and now it was Rosalyn who wore the Timex every day.

She shook out her shoulders.

She'd promised Philip she'd look after Melanie, and at the moment, that required her to stop brooding and get busy in this kitchen. Because the watch was old and fragile and definitely not waterproof, she undid the clasp and slipped it into the pocket of her frayed jeans. Then she turned on the faucet, blinking as hot water gushed over the dirty dishes in her sister-in-law's sink. Mechanically, Rosalyn rinsed and scraped and loaded the dishes, and when she was done, she wiped down the countertops and checked the fridge.

A lemon, an orange, a head of cauliflower—all molded. An empty milk jug. Three lovingly prepared meals sent over by Rosalyn last week—still in Saran Wrap and obviously untouched.

How had Mel managed to pile up dishes if she wasn't eating? Take out? While she was tossing the ruined produce into a garbage bag, Ros heard footfalls overhead.

"Mel? You up?" She quickly washed and dried her hands, clasping the watch back onto her wrist as she climbed the stairs to Melanie's room.

"Mel?" She knocked at the door.

"You can come in... unless you've got a plate of food in your hand."

"I ordered a grocery delivery for tomorrow, like you agreed I could, but, no, I come in peace."

"Swear you're unarmed."

"I promise." She'd force feed her sister-in-law if she could, but Melanie wasn't a child, and Rosalyn understood that if she treated her like one, Mel might not continue to welcome her into her home. "How's the headache?"

"All gone."

Melanie was dressed—sort of. Her bright-blonde hair was brushed off her face and clipped with a barrette. She wore a tailored gold blouse that turned her lovely brown eyes coppery... and plaid pajama bottoms.

"Love the outfit," Rosalyn teased.

"Oh, come on." Mel grinned. "No one wears pants at home anymore. It's a thing."

Rosalyn breathed out, and her shoulders lifted. It was good to see Melanie smile. "You really are feeling better."

"I wouldn't say so if I weren't. So, you can stop fussing

over me."

"Sorry. I don't mean to be bossy."

Melanie puffed out her cheeks. "I never said you were bossy. I love you, and I appreciate everything you do. But I'm okay. I don't need babysitting."

"I know that. But you looked pale earlier, and I just wanted to make sure you didn't need anything."

"It was sweet of you to stop by, but you really didn't have to stay." Melanie sank back onto the bed and stretched her feet out in front of her. "Please tell me you didn't do the dishes again."

Mel needn't feel badly about Ros rinsing a few plates. It was no trouble and hardly worth discussing. "Now that you're feeling better, we could go to a movie or shopping. Looks like you could use some pants."

"Nice pivot, but I'm going to take your dodge as a 'yes'—you've been cleaning up."

"Just a little. I won't do it any more if it bothers you."

"If I had a nickel."

Mel was right about this. Rosalyn needed to back off, give her space. According to her husband, Ashton, she was "enabling" Mel to wallow in her misery. But to her way of thinking, grieving over the loss of one's husband shouldn't be characterized as wallowing. And looking out for her brother's widow shouldn't be characterized as "enabling".

"I promise I will never load another dish into your dishwasher if you put on pants and come out and play with me. In fact, I won't even require pants. I think the plaid PJs are a good look."

"Don't you have a husband stashed somewhere? Won't Ashton be home in an hour or so?"

These days, Ashton often worked late and then grabbed a bite to eat on the way home. Besides, he knew how important it was for her to keep her promise to Philip to look after Melanie. "He won't mind."

"Well, anyway, as much as I'd love to, I can't."

"Big plans?"

"Believe it or not, I have a hair appointment in half an hour." Mel punched Rosalyn's arm playfully. "Don't look stupefied. I want to look nice for the neighbors."

"You're kidding."

"Not about the hair appointment."

And then, Melanie hustled Rosalyn back down the stairs and out the front door.


Melanie's joking remark, and the way she'd rushed her out, had Rosalyn so distracted she nearly stepped into the path of a white Tesla barreling down the street in front of her sister-in-law's house.

"Hey!" Heart pumping, she raised both arms and shouted, but the Tesla whizzed by so fast, she doubted the driver had seen her admonishing gesture—or cared. What kind of a person drove like that in a residential area? There might very well have been kids crossing the street.

*Thank goodness there weren't.*

As she climbed into her Jeep Cherokee, her pulse settled down, and her thoughts returned to her conversation with Mel.

Blocks later, she was still puzzling over her remark about wanting to look nice for the neighbors. It seemed an odd quip, and something about the expression on Mel's face made Ros wonder if she really did want to impress someone. A man, perhaps.

That would signal remarkable and unexpected progress.

Then, suddenly realizing that she'd inadvertently accelerated a little above the speed limit, she tightened her grip on the steering wheel and let up on the gas. She prided herself on being a safe driver, unlike that jerk in the white Tesla...

*Focus.*

Tuning in to the sights and sounds around her, she shifted uneasily in her seat.

What was that weird rattling?

She muted the radio, which had turned on automatically when she'd started the car, and then strained her ears, intent on identifying the sound.

Naturally, as soon as she started to pay attention, the noise disappeared.

It hadn't been too long since they'd had the car serviced, and the mechanic hadn't found anything out of the ordinary.

*There it is again.*

*What is that?*

A seat belt jostling around?

She glanced in the rearview mirror, but a horn blared, causing her to jerk her attention back to the road. Apparently, the BMW behind her thought driving the speed limit was a crime. What was with her fellow drivers today?

She pulled into the slow lane to allow the car to pass.

Another blast of the horn, and she felt her body tensing, her face growing warm.

The last thing she wanted was to get into a road rage situation.

*Oh, man.*

Now the BMW was pulling up beside her, the driver still laying on his horn.

Her pulse bounded in her throat. The blaring stopped, and she heard the noise again, this time loud and clear. It sounded like a baby shaking a rattle. Daring to take her eyes off the road for a second, she turned her head and saw something in the backseat of her car... a *snake* hissing, rearing its head.

She jerked the steering wheel and, as the car spun out of control, the rattling grew nearer, more ominous, amplified a thousand-fold by her fear. The car came to a screeching halt— the rattling came closer.

# TWO

## NOW

Rosalyn clenched the door handle; yanking, shoving, fingers numb, thoughts racing. Her tight chest would not allow her lungs to fill, but she huffed and huffed, forcing them, at last, to expand.

*Open! Dammit!*

The door was jammed. The handle flopped uselessly in her hand. From the corner of her eye, she saw the thick, slimy body of the snake, now coiled in the passenger seat, its tail vibrating, filling the car with the terrifying sound of an imminent strike.

*Open!*

She heaved her shoulder against the driver's door, and, miraculously, it flew open. Then someone grabbed her by the arms and dragged her out of her car. Her back slammed against the asphalt, spiking pain up her body.

Her rescuer kicked the car door closed.

She jumped to her feet, amazed that her legs still worked.

"Snake! Watch out!" she screamed at the man's back.

He turned, and she squeezed her eyes shut, then opened them again. "Blake!"

"Stay back, Ros."

"There's a snake!"

One side of his mouth lifted wryly. "Glad you finally noticed. It's trapped in the front seat of the car. Why don't you head across the street, and I'll open the back door. Hopefully it will go on about its business, and then we can check you out."

How could he be so calm? But lucky for her, he had a good enough head on his shoulders to drag her out of the car and imprison the snake.

"Take a breath. You're safe now," he said.

She bent over and grabbed her knees, retched, and a small amount of yellow fluid leaked out of her mouth.

*I'm safe.*

Her heart let up its pace. "Thank you. Thank you. Thank you. The door was stuck. If you hadn't opened it from the outside that snake would've bitten me for sure. Did you see it? I think it's a diamondback."

Blake approached and laid his hands on her shoulders. Despite his recent exertions, dressed in gray-and-white-striped seersucker chinos, an immaculately-fitted blue shirt, and designer penny loafers, he looked like he was headed for a men's magazine photoshoot.

Wishing she hadn't paired her dingiest white T-shirt with her loosest, most comfortable jeans, she combed her fingers through tangled auburn hair. "We should call someone. There's no reason for you to take a chance trying to get the snake out of the car on your own."

He pursed his mouth, considering. "That's definitely an option. But I think I can pull it off. The sooner we get it out of your car, the better I'll feel. Walk over there, and I'll give it a go. I promise, if it looks like it's too close to the door, I'll bail."

Just minutes ago, it felt as if her life was over, and now, everything seemed perfectly fine. She was calmly discussing how to get rid of a deadly reptile, admittedly common to the Arizona desert, with Blake Tyler, her husband's old college roommate. Her breathing and heart rate had reverted to normal, and her mind had shifted into problem-solving gear. She backed away, and crossed the road, not taking her eyes off Blake. He went around to the back passenger side and gently opened the door, then turned and bolted to her side of the street.

They huddled there, for a good five minutes, until the snake finally slithered out of the car and down the embankment into the desert.

She needed to call Ashton, but suddenly realized her phone was still in the car. Even though the snake had fled, she wasn't ready to return to the scene of the crime.

Seeming to read her mind, Blake pulled out his cell. "Hey, buddy. Rosalyn's okay, but there's been an accident. I'll put her on and let her explain."

Ros took the phone and filled in her husband, surprised by how relaxed she sounded, and, indeed, by how calm she felt. "He's on his way." She passed Blake his phone back.

"We should wait in my car—it's hot out here. Do you want a water? I've got a couple of bottles with me."

"Thanks." She turned and followed him to a vehicle she'd never seen... until a few minutes ago in her rearview mirror. It'd been *Blake* in the BMW, tailgating her. "Where's your car?"

"Shop. This is a loaner. The whole time I was following you, I was thinking that if only I'd had my car, you would've known it was me and stopped." He handed her a water bottle that was labeled "Courtesy of North Central Tucson Luxury Vehicles".

She took it and gulped down half the bottle. "So, you were trying to get my attention. You saw the snake?"

"I pulled out behind you when you were coming from Melanie's place. I was about to turn a different direction when I thought I saw something through your back glass. It caught my attention because it was pressed against the rear windshield. I had to get closer before I could make it out, but as soon as I realized it was a snake, I followed and honked."

It had never occurred to her someone was trying to be a good citizen, to warn her of danger. She was so accustomed to all the bad news about crime and road rage, she'd instantly assumed the worst.

"I called you a few times, too," Blake added.

"I had my phone on *do not disturb*. When I'm driving, I only let Ashton's calls through. But I'm officially adding you to the list of permitted callers."

"I'm honored." He turned a concerned gaze on her. "Seriously, I'm just so glad I could help. When I think of everything Ashton and I have been through together... it would destroy him if he ever lost you. But let's not get maudlin. There's always antivenom."

She crunched her half-drained plastic water bottle in her fist. "Yeah. Good old antivenom."

"How the hell do you think that snake got in your car? Do you make a habit of leaving your windows down?" Blake asked.

"No way. I hate the idea of inviting in creepy crawly things like scorpions and spiders. I never thought about a snake getting into my car, but obviously I should have. Especially since I found one in our garage last week."

Blake frowned. "That's quite a coincidence. Was it a diamondback?"

She really didn't know. Luckily, she'd spotted it as soon as she'd opened the garage door, before she'd even pulled in. So, she'd stayed in her car and called animal control. Then Ashton had shown up and sent her inside through the front door. And even though he'd promised her he wouldn't go near the snake, he'd later admitted he'd grabbed a long-handled broom in the garage and "swept" it outside. "Ashton got a better look at it than I did. He chased it out and watched it go into the wash beside our house. I was worried it might come back, but he said it was a harmless king snake and canceled animal control. You think it's the same snake?"

"This one was definitely a diamondback. But if Ashton was mistaken about your king snake, and it was still hanging around your house, I suppose it could've found a way into the cabin of your Cherokee from the undercarriage or... maybe gotten in through the trunk."

She'd had the trunk open briefly when she and Ashton had loaded up an old rug to take to Goodwill—but that was over the weekend.

Her hand flew to her mouth.

Had she been driving around with a deadly snake in her car this entire week?

# THREE

## NOW

Detective Julian Van yanked off his tie and stuffed it into the inner pocket of his linen blazer. He enjoyed dressing well. He kept his fingernails buffed and his thick blond hair cut in a mid-fade with textured top.

Fifty should be no impediment to looking sharp.

It was his firmly held belief that taking care with his appearance showed respect to the varied individuals he encountered as a criminal investigator. But there was a line between professionalism and setting yourself too far apart from the person you were set to meet, and, in this instance, his silk tie crossed it.

This morning, the sun shone brightly in a blue sky sprinkled with pillowy clouds. A mild breeze lowered the temperature from borderline hell to bearable. It was far too nice a day for the task at hand—he'd come to update the grandfather of a young woman who'd been missing over a decade.

By now, he ought to have found Zoe Wessex.

Zoe, tragically, had fallen on hard times at the ripe old age of eighteen months. Her mother had overdosed on a cocktail of tranquilizers and booze, and baby Zoe had been discovered, dehydrated and half-starved, curled up next to her mother's corpse. After a weeks-long search, the authorities had located her maternal grandparents, Walter and Hannah Wessex, and handed Zoe over. Though the couple had little to offer financially, Walter and Hannah had showered their granddaughter with an abundance of love.

Unfortunately, love isn't always enough.

For years, Zoe blossomed under their care, but when adolescence hit, so did trouble. She fought her grandparents' rules with every ounce of her being, and, at the age of sixteen, she landed a job as a hostess at a restaurant and petitioned the court for status as a legally emancipated minor.

When Zoe moved out of the house, it broke Hannah and Walter's hearts.

But after being given her wings, Zoe flourished, surprising everyone.

She held down a job, paid her rent, and even turned up at Hannah and Walter's place for dinner once a week. She was rebuilding a loving relationship with her family, and then she simply disappeared.

Vanished into thin air.

When Walter and Hannah reported Zoe missing, the police took a report and made the standard inquiries. But given Zoe's emancipated status, they quickly decided the most likely scenario was that she'd changed her mind and decided to cut ties with her grandparents once and for all.

Unlike the rest of his colleagues, Julian wasn't one hundred percent convinced Zoe left of her own free will. If there was any chance she'd met with foul play, he couldn't let go of the case.

Hannah and Walter vowed to never quit on Zoe.

Julian vowed to never quit on Hannah and Walter.

Then, nine months ago, Hannah died, leaving only Walter to keep the faith—making Julian even more determined not to let him down.

Julian braced himself.

Returning to Walter with so little to offer deserved a gloomy day. He should've had to race from his car to the door of the run-down brick duplex with a high wind whipping his hair and black skies threatening. Instead, he trudged up the walkway, climbed the steps and lingered on the front porch with the sun warming his back and the scent of honeysuckle tickling his nose.

He rapped at the screen door, and it rattled on its hinges.

The inner door, painted in peeling blue, opened as far as its chain lock allowed, revealing a rheumy brown eye and a mop of oily gray hair.

"Walter, it's me, Detective Van."

After a few moments of fumbling with the chain, Walter Wessex opened the door, then commenced struggling to unlatch the screen. His hands, covered in fat, purple veins, trembled. His bent fingers, made slow by arthritis, eventually managed to pop the hook out of its latch, and the screen door swung open. "You're late."

Actually, he was ten minutes early. "So sorry. How are you, Walter?"

Walter shook his head in response, and Julian followed him into the living room. After coming in from the brilliant outdoor sunlight, it took a minute for his vision to adjust to the dim room —all the shades were drawn.

Walter directed Julian to a misshapen olive couch before falling into a golden armchair with the stuffing leaking out.

Julian sat across from Walter, shifting his backside to avoid being poked by a couch spring. Like everything else in the Wessex house, the cushions were worn out, but holding up as best they could.

Walter Wessex shook a few cookies out of a Chips Ahoy! bag onto a plastic plate, then pushed it toward Julian.

Julian was feeling Hannah's absence this morning as an

ache in his bones, and the store-bought cookies only made things worse. Walter's wife had always baked fresh cookies for Julian whenever he came to update them on Zoe's case. Their home used to smell like warm sugar and cinnamon. Now, the scent was tangy and not at all pleasant. "Did you get a cat?"

"He adopted me. Not long before she died, Hannah noticed a skeleton in a mangy yellow coat hanging around and started leaving tuna on the back porch. A'fore we knew it, the thing was mewing and rubbing up on us and asking for a different name than 'kitty kitty'. Funny thing is, Hannah hated cats. Never would allow one in the house, but all of a sudden she's insisting Whiskers is our responsibility. I think she didn't want me to be alone after she passed." His cheek twitched. "She'd kill me if I didn't offer you refreshments."

Julian bit into a cookie. It tasted stale and went down dry. "Thanks."

"Don't compare with Hannah's, do they?"

"Wouldn't want them to. I wish I had better news for you, but I'm afraid—"

"Nothing new. Case still cold. You're not giving up, but there's no new leads. Keep my chin up. I know the drill. But, Detective Van, you made a promise to me and my wife to find Zoe and bring her home, and I promised Hannah I would hold you to it."

"I promised to keep looking. To do all I could. I've done that, and I'll keep on doing that. You have my word."

The silence stretched between them.

It was time to thank Walter for the cookie and be on his way.

Going over the same old questions was unlikely to yield new information and more than once, the captain had warned him not to give the Wessexes false hope. But Julian considered the term *false hope* to be an oxymoron.

By definition hope comes without a guarantee.

"Tell me again about this business idea of Zoe's. The one she was so keen on before she disappeared."

"The second-hand boutique. It wasn't a pipe dream. She'd found a place to lease cheap, and she'd picked out a real clever name—Zoe's Closet. I still got a carload of used clothes she bought from the flea markets. She had an eye for finding a gem at the bottom of a rubbish pile."

"You kept the inventory?" Julian rubbed his fist in the corner of his eye.

"Don't give me that look. Detectives are supposed to be tougher than that. You can't get soft on me if you're going to find Zoe. I've known a long time Zoe's never going to open that shop. But Hannah couldn't let go of the hope we'd find her alive, and I promised her I wouldn't throw out the clothes until we had Zoe home—one way or the other. After all these years, I figure it probably won't be the homecoming we prayed for, but I *need* to find her."

Walter might look frail, with his bent frame and withered eyes, but he had a steel backbone.

"I won't quit on you." It was all he could offer. He'd keep looking until he found that young woman or took his dying breath.

"Good. I know Zoe wouldn't have just taken off and left everything behind. Not after putting money down on a space for the shop."

He narrowed his eyes at Walter. This was the first time he'd mentioned that Zoe had gone so far as to put money down. It was a minor detail, but still, it was new.

"Where did she get the money? Savings from her hostess job?"

"Yes. And... she had an investor." Walter bit his lip hard enough that a drop of blood appeared.

Had he meant to say that, or had it been a slip up?

*Are your frickin' kidding me?* Julian mentally counted to ten. "An investor?"

"Yup."

Julian's foot started tapping in time with his breathing. Who, besides family, would be foolhardy enough to give money to a young woman like Zoe? A high-school dropout, in and out of trouble—especially for a second-hand clothes shop? Unless, maybe, they expected a return on their investment that didn't involve the exchange of money.

Zoe had led a hard-knock life. The heartbreak of it was that she had been trying to cross over from the shady side of the street. But who knew what she'd been willing to offer to get to the other side. "What kind of a bargain do you think she struck with this investor?"

"Not the kind you're thinking."

Hannah and Walter had always been eager to defend Zoe's character—to the point Julian sometimes wondered if they'd held back details in order to protect it. "What's this investor's name?"

"I don't remember."

Julian didn't believe him, and not only because Walter was avoiding his gaze and covering his mouth with his hand. He'd said he didn't remember the investor's name, which implied he'd known it once. And if there was one thing Julian understood about the Wessexes, it was that they would never simply *forget* the name of that investor. They would have been shouting it at the detectives from the get-go... unless they thought it would somehow harm Zoe to offer it up. "What's going on, Walter?"

"You're just like the others. Still looking for a way to write her off. Still looking for evidence she left on her own."

"I'm looking for the truth. I'm looking for *Zoe*. Why are you holding back the name of this investor? Why haven't you mentioned this before? It's been ten years, Walter."

"I'm not holding nothing back. I told you everything there is to tell. I'm sure Hannah and me answered all your questions as best we could over and over again. I don't remember you or anyone else asking me about where Zoe got money for the store before right this minute. I guess it just didn't come up. You can go on now, and I'll see you next year."

There was an edge to Walter's voice, and a look of despair on his face that made Julian second-guess himself. Walter wanted to find Zoe. He would never intentionally hold back an important lead. "You mind if I look through the inventory—those old clothes—before I go?"

"You'll have to come back another day. I got a doctor's appointment, and I need to call a cab."

"I'll drive you."

"Don't bother."

"It's no bother. I've got the time, and we can stop for a bite after. I hate to eat my lunch all by myself. You'd be doing me a favor."

"I guess. As long as it ain't no trouble."

"Great." It occurred to Julian, then, that he could look through the inventory when they got back, but maybe it would be better to wait. It would give him an excuse to check in with Walter again, make sure he was okay. "I'll stop by another day and look through the things Zoe bought at the flea markets."

Walter raised his eyes to Julian's. They were less wary now. Either he wasn't the type to hold a grudge or he realized it wasn't in his best interest to cut ties with the only detective still interested in Zoe's case. "Tell me what you're looking for and I'll help."

Julian shrugged. "A gem in the bottom of a rubbish pile, I guess."

# FOUR

## NOW

Since Rosalyn's close encounter with a poisonous snake, things had gotten back to normal. Her car had been fully repaired, and her husband, Ashton, had *mostly* stopped hovering. He'd returned to his habit of spending an inordinate amount time with his best friend, although he must still be a bit rattled—*ha ha*—because tonight, he'd insisted on dragging Rosalyn to Blake's house with him.

She soon tired of the golf patter between the two men and stepped out onto the balcony to breathe in the red-sky beauty of an Arizona sunset. Then, suddenly, her attention became laser focused on a mysterious voice floating up from below the second-story terrace.

*Rosalyn.*

The desert sun, slipping behind the craggy slopes of the Catalina Mountains, threw dark shadows across boulders and brush, making it difficult to see, and even leaning across the railing didn't give her a good view of what was beneath her. There were too many blind spots.

*Rosalyn.*

"Who's there?" She leaned farther and farther, scouring the rocky terrain below until the blood rushed to her head.

Without warning, a cool hand whispered across the bare skin on the back of her neck, raising the hairs on her arms. Her feet lifted off the terrace, and, at once, she lost both her breath and her balance.

Her gaze froze on the giant, spiked boulders below.

As the weight of her body tipped her over the edge, a scream died in her paralyzed lungs.

Just in time, powerful hands grabbed her by the legs and yanked her back to safety.

Still shaking, she tested the concrete beneath her feet, then turned to find her husband, Ashton—flush in the face, a vein pounding at his temple.

Her breath wheezed out of her tight lungs. "Damn it, Ashton! You scared the life out of me. It's not safe to sneak up on a person like that."

"Also, not safe to dangle yourself off a balcony. You were this close to going over." He held up two fingers about an inch apart, then planted his hands on her waist. His body canted toward her. "Never do that to me again."

"Ditto. Seriously, do not ever sneak up on me like that." Her heart was racing, but the reassuring warmth of Ashton's hands at her waist, the way his dark pupils were swallowing the hazel in his eyes, and the fiercely protective look on his face, sucked the fight clean out of her. She'd now had a lifetime's worth of close calls in a single week, but that wasn't Ashton's fault.

"What the hell were you thinking?"

*Good question.* She should never have leaned over the railing like that. And she couldn't fault him for his raised voice. "I thought I heard someone call my name. In fact, I'm sure of it. Down there. Someone was running across the rocks."

"Probably javelinas," he said, in a lower decibel.

"You think it was wild pigs?"

"Blake's doorbell camera picked up a mother and baby last night, rooting around on his front porch. They knocked over that giant terracotta planter of his. Made a huge mess, and he's mad as hell. He said he called animal control, and they told him to chill out, that the javelinas were here first."

Wildlife sightings were expected in southern Arizona, even within the city limits, and they sometimes came right up to the houses, but... "Wild pigs don't talk."

"Not to put too fine a point on it, but technically, javelinas are not pigs, they're collared peccaries."

"Then collared peccaries don't talk." She couldn't help smiling—even with buckets of adrenaline churning through her system. Leave it to Ashton to know the most peculiar facts. "Do not try to distract me with minutiae. I'm telling you a *person* was hiding down there."

"I highly doubt it. If someone wants your attention, why conceal himself in the shadows? Conversely, if he's up to no good and doesn't want to be seen, why call out your name? And if it's you he's after, why look for you here, at Blake's place?"

She sucked in a breath. "Point taken. What types of noises do javelinas make? I suppose it could've been grunting, and my brain misinterpreted it."

"What's going on out there?" Blake called to them from inside, his big voice carrying easily on the breeze. "Get back inside. Ros, I made you tea. If you want, you can have a front row seat while Ashton gives me dating advice."

"Wow. I don't want to miss that." Ros followed Ashton through the open doors and into their host's study. It was elegantly appointed with an oversized leather armchair, a love seat and an imposing oak desk. The walls were painted a tasteful cream, which complemented the tawny wood-tile floor, in turn complementing the muted browns of the leather furniture. Blake's silver-framed diploma, from the University of Arizona, hung above his desk on an otherwise bare wall. An attractive, but not extraordinary, room—until you pulled back the curtains and threw open the French doors. That filled the space with natural light and revealed a positively stunning view of the Catalina Mountains. "I'm intrigued. Have you met someone you're interested in?"

Blake swept his hand out, motioning for her to take a seat facing his desk. On a marble side table, a cup of tea, along with a porcelain pot, awaited within easy reach. "You bet, and I'd love to get a woman's perspective."

"That's a surprise." Ashton and Blake had never included her in such matters in the past.

Since their college days, Ashton had been assisting *bumbling Blake*, as he liked to call himself, in his quest for love —with little success. Blake's bad luck with women was a puzzle to Rosalyn since on top of being good at getting rid of snakes in your car, he had blue eyes that sparkled when he smiled, thick, sandy hair that curled at the base of his neck, and a voice deep enough to make your knees quiver. But according to Ashton, around a woman he cared to impress, Blake couldn't find his words even if they were inked onto the palm of his hand.

"I don't know the first thing about being a wingman," she said.

"But you do know about women," Blake replied.

"Then I'm happy to observe, and I'll speak up in the unlikely event I have anything to offer." Over the years, she hadn't asked too many questions about Blake's love life, or tried to offer him counsel. Blake was Ashton's closest friend, and she didn't want to horn in on their special bond, even though at times she felt a bit neglected. It wasn't that she envied the close-ness between the two men—Ashton was her confidant, her soul-mate, so she didn't feel cheated in that department. It was rather the *time* she lost out on while Ashton and Blake hung out at sports bars, or on golf trips, and so forth. She wished Blake would hurry up and find his person, so she could spend more time with hers.

Settling back with her tea, she sipped, savoring the brisk taste on her tongue, the warmth wending its way down her gullet; and it wasn't long before she spotted a problem. Ashton's tips for winning over a woman were about as far off the mark as they could get. Thank goodness he hadn't tried to pull any of this nonsense with her or they might not have ever gotten together.

While Ashton and Blake continued on and on, going over the same stale territory, Rosalyn waited for an opening. She hadn't caught the name of the lucky woman Blake intended to court, but, like a thousand others, her favorite color was blue, her favorite movie, *The Hunger Games*, and her favorite singer, *Beyonce*. There were lines from a Shakespearean sonnet to be memorized, ones that Rosalyn was pretty sure a twelve-year-old could quote without missing a beat: *Shall I compare thee to a summer's day? Thou art more lovely and more temperate.*

There was never going to be a perfect moment.

*Time to speak up.*

"Okay, that's enough." Rosalyn set her teacup onto a cork coaster. "Ashton, this can't be your best advice on how to make a woman fall in love. Figure out what she likes and then pretend to like all the same things?"

Blake turned to her. "Thank you, Rosalyn. I've been saying for years that the Ashton Method doesn't work."

"I think I did okay." Ashton shrugged.

"It's not working for *me*. It's time I get a woman's input— Rosalyn, you're up."

"I'm surprised you two would come up with something like this." Shocked was more like it. The idea of her husband coaching his best friend to mislead a potential romantic partner gave her the creeps. She'd always assumed that Ashton offered Blake a practiced line here and there, to help him get a conversation started, but she'd never imagined he'd encourage Blake to pretend to be someone he wasn't. "If Blake wants an enduring relationship, he has to be his authentic self."

Ashton frowned. "Desperation isn't attractive."

"But vulnerability can be."

"I'm not desperate." Blake's face reddened.

"You're *vulnerable*," Rosalyn said. "And that's a good thing because it means you care. Instead of pretending to be someone you're not, instead of reciting sonnets like some cheesy Lothario, why not tell her how you really feel?"

"I wouldn't know where to begin. What would I say?"

"Well, I'm just spit-balling, but something like: *I love the way I feel whenever I'm near you. When I spot you from a distance, I can't stop myself from smiling*—assuming those things are true. If not, find something else that's *real* and from *your heart*, not Shakespeare's pen."

"I couldn't."

"Why not?"

"Because then, when she rejects me, she's rejecting the *real* me."

Apparently, Blake really did need help finding love, or at least a confidence boost. And she definitely owed him. "Isn't the flip side worse? When she falls for you, she's falling for someone you're not? Ashton, I don't mean to sound harsh, but I don't think you're giving Blake good advice. Maybe I can help after all. Who is this mystery woman? Someone I know?"

The look that passed between them said it all—she did know the woman—the *target*. She quickly quashed a ripple of misgiving. *Target* wasn't a fair characterization at all. Blake wanted to find love. He needed help. There was nothing wrong with rendering aid in this situation. Nothing nefarious about stepping up to help a friend, especially if she could persuade him to present himself honestly. "So, who's the lucky lady?"

Ashton cut his gaze away, making her wonder if they'd been deliberately avoiding mentioning her name this whole time.

Blake pulled his shoulders back. "It's Melanie. The honest-to-God truth, Rosalyn, is that I'm in love with your brother's widow."

# FIVE

## NOW

Rosalyn lifted her hand to shield her face from view. She didn't want the men to see her eyes welling.

One breath out. One breath in.

"Ros," Ashton said under his breath, "what's happening? You look like you don't feel well."

"I just need a minute."

"I'm sorry," Blake said. "You've got a knack for reading people, and I thought you might have guessed how I felt about Melanie by now. I should've given you some backstory, laid the groundwork. And I shouldn't have put it so bluntly. I didn't mean to upset you."

Blinking back her tears, she lowered her hand and pulled her elbows close to her sides to steady herself, embarrassed by her intense reaction. This was one of those moments when something had suddenly reminded her that Philip was gone. "You caught me off guard is all. I miss Philip so much, and talking about Melanie that way, like she's on the market..."

"Hang on. The last thing I want you to think is that I'm looking at Mel as a commodity," Blake said.

"I know. It just hit me the wrong way. The mere fact that

we're discussing fixing her up with you means Philip is... It just reminds me that I've lost my brother. But I understand, intellectually, that it may be time for Melanie to..." She couldn't bring herself to finish the sentence. Rosalyn would always be Philip's sister—there was no *moving on* from that. But the same wasn't true for a widow. Melanie could, and should, move on.

She touched the Timex on her wrist, wondering what Philip would want.

*Mel's happiness.*

Melanie had mentioned wanting to look nice for a neighbor, and Rosalyn had hoped that meant she was taking an interest in a new man. So, what was Rosalyn's problem with the reverse—a neighbor taking an interest in Melanie? And was it possible that Blake was the neighbor Melanie wanted to impress?

Ashton crossed the room and took a place next to her on the love seat. He kissed the top of her head, then poured hot tea into her drained cup.

She shook her head at the offering, trying to interpret the look on her husband's face. "How long have you known about this?"

The only thing more surprising than Blake declaring his love for Melanie, was that Ashton hadn't said a word about it to Rosalyn.

"That's my fault," Blake rushed to Ashton's defense. "I asked him not to say anything."

Irritation washed over her, which was good, because it pulled her out of her grief. "Ashton?"

"It wasn't my secret to tell." He grabbed her hand. "Try to understand. He's my best friend."

"And I'm your wife." They had a rule: total honesty. If anyone swore Ashton to secrecy about anything, he would say nothing to anyone... *except her*, and vice versa. Did his silence mean that his allegiance to Blake took precedent over marital intimacy? "How could you not tell me that Blake's in love with Melanie?"

Ashton locked eyes with her. "You're both making more of this than it is. He's not in love with her. It's an infatuation."

"I care for her, then. I admire her," Blake said.

Not long after Philip's death, Melanie had sold her home and bought a new house that happened to be across the street from Blake. And over the years, they'd been around one another numerous times because of Ashton and Blake's friendship, so he certainly knew Mel a little. But as far as Rosalyn was aware, apart from waving at one another, or an occasional conversation about misdelivered mail, Melanie and Blake didn't speak. Melanie even complained to Rosalyn that Blake acted aloof, and she thought it rude, seeing as how he was Ashton's closest friend. Rosalyn found it baffling and out of character. Blake was a very friendly fellow. So why was he standoffish with Melanie?

*Because he has a crush on her.*

Actually, he'd said the *honest-to-God truth* was that he was *in love* with her. He'd only backed it down to *I care for her* at Ashton's insistence.

Rosalyn freed her hand from Ashton's and turned to Blake. "I don't mean to interrogate you, but it sounds like you're saying you have deep feelings for Melanie. How can that be when you barely know her?"

"He admires her from afar." Ashton was explaining for his buddy again.

He seemed to be trying to spin things—whether for her benefit or Blake's she didn't know.

"It's medieval, and I've tried to tell him so. I think they'd be good together, but it's never going to happen if he doesn't step up. He's been infatuated with Melanie since college."

Blake's eyebrows shot up. "You can stop helping me now. Rosalyn is going to think I'm a stalker."

"He's not a stalker." Ashton shook his head as if that settled that.

She was getting a queasy feeling in her belly. She liked Blake, she truly did, and for years she'd been hoping he'd find his person. Not just because she might finally get her husband back—Ashton seemed to spend more time with Blake than he did with her—but because he deserved someone special. Just look at how he'd stepped up for her when she'd been in trouble. He'd made it out to be no big deal, but he'd risked getting bitten by a poisonous snake for her.

Still, she didn't love the way the men had been plotting to win Melanie over with smooth lines and pretenses.

Rosalyn remembered, in vivid detail, the moment she'd promised her brother to look after Melanie. It had been one of Philip's few good days between rounds of chemo. She'd driven him up a scenic byway in the foothills, and they'd found a perfect spot to view the sunset. As they'd watched in awe, the reds and golds had infused the clouds to the bursting point. Then Philip had pointed out that it might be the last time they shared a sunset together. She'd urged him not to say such things, but he would have none of it.

*Be realistic*, he'd said. *We have important matters to discuss.*

And first on his list had been his love for his young wife.

*Treat her like your sister. Look out for her when I'm gone. Promise me.*

She let out a long breath. "I won't help you win Melanie over with tricks and phony lines. But, if you want me to facilitate, say, a lunch date, all out in the open, on the up and up, I might consider it. And first, I need you to tell me the whole story. I had no idea either one of you knew her before she met Philip, and that seems really weird."

"That's just it. We *didn't* know her, and she didn't know us," Ashton said. "But Blake—"

"I can speak for myself," Blake said. "One summer, Melanie

worked at a bakery near the university. That's where I first saw her, and I thought she had the best smile, the prettiest golden eyes—warm, and sweet, like honey."

If he continued putting his feelings into words like those, he wouldn't need anyone's help to win Melanie's heart. "That's downright poetic, Blake. Did you tell her that?"

"I wish I had. Ashton and I used to go into the bakery sometimes, but she never seemed to remember us, and I couldn't screw up the courage to ask her name, much less flirt with her. Then, one day, we went in and she was gone. It crushed me that I'd lost my chance to get to know her. I couldn't believe it when, years later, Ashton told me the woman from the bakery was about to become his sister-in-law. I made him promise not to tell you about my college crush because that would've made it awkward for everyone whenever I was around."

"I suppose that's true." Her doubts were dissipating. Blake had been attracted to Melanie in his college days. She was gorgeous, so there was nothing abnormal about that. He'd never tried to impose himself on her—according to Mel, he barely acknowledged her even though they currently lived across the street from each other... "Ashton, please tell me you didn't engineer her moving into Blake's neighborhood because of this crush."

"You're misremembering," Ashton said. "After Philip died, and the house across from Blake came on the market, *you're* the one who insisted it would be perfect for Melanie."

"The way I remember it, you were the one who pointed out the house was on the market," Rosalyn said.

Ashton shrugged. "Could be. But it was definitely you who thought it would do Mel good to sell her house because it held so many memories of Philip. I have to say, I don't think the move has done her much good. She's still locking herself away from the world, and that's hard to watch."

Melanie rarely smiled anymore, and Rosalyn knew Philip

would hate that. Mel deserved to have someone in her life who truly cared for her. And who knew? Maybe that someone would turn out to be Blake. "I'll set up a lunch. Leave it to me."

"You won't tell her about college?" Blake seemed anxious now, bouncing his knee.

"You'll be the one to do that. If you want my blessing, you have to be upfront with her."

"Understood."

"And no rehearsed lines or pretending blue is your favorite color—unless it is. I'm glad you finally confided in me. I'm rooting for you both to find happiness." She rose, and, on impulse, gave Blake a hug.

A few minutes later, as they were saying goodbye on the front porch, she noticed the absence of the terracotta planter— the one the javelinas had destroyed. After learning of Blake's feelings for Melanie, she'd all but forgotten about the mysterious commotion coming from below his balcony. "Do you have outdoor security cameras?"

"Besides the doorbell cam? No."

That was disappointing. "I was hoping we could check the footage to see if it caught anyone down on the rocks below the terrace."

"Sorry. I don't want cameras inside the house *or* outdoors aimed at the balcony. I'm paranoid about someone watching *me*. You know this stuff is all in the cloud. It could be accessed by someone with criminal intent."

That seemed far-fetched but, then again, a lot of people these days worried about technology in the home.

"Anyway, I don't need more cameras. The doors and windows are alarmed, and I have a security company that monitors everything."

"But if someone was out there—"

"Javelinas, honey." Ashton threw an arm across her back. "No one was lurking below Blake's balcony waiting for you to make an appearance. And if they had been, unless their name is Romeo, they wouldn't have been calling yours."

At that, the men chuckled, and Rosalyn smiled politely, but she didn't relish the joke. It felt as if the two of them were minimizing her concerns. They might well be right. It could have been the wind distorting animal noises, but she'd heard something that seemed out of place. "You two can stay here if you want, but I'm going around the side of the house to see if I can find any animal tracks or footprints."

"I'll turn on the floodlights for you," Blake offered, his tone turning remorseful. "We'll all go. But I doubt whatever you heard left prints behind. There's nothing but rock below the balcony."

"Blake's right. It's useless to check for footprints. That terrain is not going to give up any information," Ashton said.

"We might find other telltale signs." Rosalyn planted her hands on her hips. "Is there some reason you don't want me to search the area? I would think the two of you would be interested in looking around, if not for safety's sake, then to prove me wrong, since you're so sure you're right."

Ashton's face flushed. "I can see this is important to you, so let's go see what we can find. We can take all the time you like."

Blake hit a switch on the wall near the door, flooding the porch and the surrounding landscape with light.

With the men trailing her, Rosalyn hurried down the steps. By the time she reached the area beneath the balcony, she was out of breath and pumped up to find some sort of clue that would solve the mystery: a piece of fabric snagged on a branch, a dusty handprint on the wall... "A cigarette butt!"

For a split second, her sense of triumph outweighed her anxiety, but then her pulse began beating in her throat.

Someone really had been out there.

*Watching.*

Blake strode to her side. He picked up the evidence, then

straightened, inspecting the crushed stub between his fingertips. "This cigarette butt has orange marks on it. My air conditioner was on the fritz last week and the woman who came out to repair it was here for hours. She left a pack of smokes on the counter, and she was wearing awful, orange lipstick."

"So, the cigarette butt is no smoking gun," Ashton said, stony-faced.

The joke took a second to land, but then Rosalyn smiled. She'd never been so glad to be wrong.

# SIX

## THEN

Most days I wake up happy. But this morning, I'd rate my mood four out of ten. A ten would be the day I broke my stepfather's nose and got kicked out of the house for good—my best day ever. A one would be the day that bastard drove Floyd to the desert outside of Tucson and dumped him because he claims he's allergic to dogs.

I know it was really because it cost too much to feed him. Just like it cost too much to feed me. But it doesn't matter now. Floyd sniffed his way back home, and Mrs. Verrado next door said he was smart and she could use a good watchdog.

Now Floyd lives with Mrs. Verrado, and I live on the streets.

We're both better off.

I miss my friends at school, and some of the teachers, but I can't go back because I'm only fourteen. In Arizona, I'm not legal to live on my own, and I sure as hell am not going from my stepdad to a foster home, which is what will happen if the teachers catch on.

Besides, I'm doing really good—really *well*—on my own.

I'm teaching myself all kinds of stuff and learning more than

I ever did in a classroom. I believe that's because I got a hunger —I *have* a hunger—for a better life.

I found a jacket in a dumpster behind some apartments, and the culvert (I looked up what they call those big concrete drainage pipes) I'm sleeping in stays plenty warm, even at night. February means March is right around the corner, and then the weather will be perfect so I can sleep in the park on the soft grass and get out of that lonely ditch.

There are people in the park.

I miss people.

Food hasn't been as big a problem as I expected. I'm not hungry all the time, like I was at home, because there's a lady behind the counter at McDonald's who sneaks me free burgers, and I get spare change begging on the street corners. I'm scared to go to the soup kitchens because I don't know if the do-gooders will call child services and get me locked up in foster care. Once I turn sixteen, I can be something called an emancipated minor. Then I can live out in the open.

I can get a job and my own apartment—I'm sure it won't be fancy, at first.

But once I'm legally on my own, I can get my high school diploma online, and then I can apply to college.

They have grants and loans and something called "work-study" programs for poor people, and I got—I *have*—a good sob story.

Meanwhile, I spend a lot of time at the library researching tips on writing a good college entrance essay. They say stories about overcoming hardship make the best ones, so I won't even have to fake it.

I can't go to the library during school hours because the librarian might figure out that I'm on the streets, but from three o'clock until close, I'm there, reading, surfing the internet, washing up in the bathroom.

I make an effort to stay clean.

It's part of my disguise.

Which is the reason, today, my mood is only a four out of ten.

My clothes have gotten pretty rough. I've got to steal some new ones if I'm going to keep fooling everyone. It's okay to look poor, but if I look *homeless*, the librarian will turn me in.

Man, I hate stealing.

If I get caught, I'll get something much worse than jail time.

I'll get tossed into *the system*—foster care.

I'm not going to live with strangers who don't want me.

My own family doesn't want me so why would strangers?

And when you're not wanted, you get beat—*beaten*.

I look down at my jeans. I can get by with them, because holes in jeans are okay. But my torn-up shirt has got to go, for sure, and my socks are worn down to a thread. I need socks because I walk a lot, and the blisters hurt bad—*badly*.

I close my fists and grit my teeth and slide into the store real casual.

I see a camera in the corner, but this is a local place, not a big chain store, and I don't think there's a security guard watching the feed.

The bad news is the place is practically empty.

There's only one customer besides me.

The good news is she's *beautiful*, and the counter guy cannot stop staring at her boobs. Her body is smoking hot in leggings that hug her butt. Her hair is long and wavy. She has dark, thick eyelashes that don't even look fake, and her lips are shiny and slick. I bet they taste like cherries.

I know I shouldn't, but like Counter Guy, I can't stop staring at her.

She smiles at me, and I duck my head.

When she turns her back, I creep over to the socks and stuff a package under my jacket. I think about nabbing some boxers, but they're not a necessity—I can go commando—so I move on to the T-shirts. I've got my eye on a long-sleeved orange one. I pick it up, unfold it and see it's got an Adidas logo on it. It's a size too big but it'll do. I fold it and lay it back down, take a step away. I wander over to the shoes. I'm practically drooling at the thought of soles without holes. I wait until the hot girl takes a pair of pants up to the counter, and, while she's checking out, I prowl back to the shirts. Lightning fast, I dart out my hand and sneak the orange shirt under my jacket.

I stick up my chin and stroll, bold as you please, toward the front entrance.

Holding my breath, I push my shoulder against the door.

"Hey, kid!" The clerk dashes out from behind the counter.

"Who, me?"

He jerks my jacket open and the *contraband*, that's my vocab word of the day, plops onto the floor.

"I'm sorry. I'm just a kid and I need socks and a shirt." I don't bother to lie, because that will only make things worse. For a second he just stares at me, and then I get this genius idea. He doesn't look like the type who would worry about where I'm sleeping at night. He'd turn me in for stealing, but not for being a kid with no family. "If you let me keep them, I'll work it off. I'll stay behind the counter when you go to lunch or need someone to watch the store. I'll come in anytime and hang out however long you want, and you can pay me with clothes instead of money."

The hot girl comes around, and, hands on those sexy hips of hers, checks me out.

This *emboldens* me—yesterday's vocab word—and I say, "I'm fourteen. If you're worried about child labor laws it's perfectly legal as long as I'm not working during school hours. But if you pay me in clothes and food instead of cash, I can work any hours you need, and you won't be breaking any laws." I'm not sure about the last part, but it sounds plausible.

He gets a deep crease between his brow, like he's thinking about it... then he jumps me.

My back crashes against the wall. We're nose to nose, now, and his sour breath makes me want to puke.

My heart is pounding and my thoughts are racing.

He's a lot bigger than me, but I've got good reflexes, and I'm strong as hell.

I could probably get free and punch him in the nose, like I did my stepdad, but then he'd call the cops for sure, and I'd wind up in juvenile hall or foster care, or worse—back home with my parents.

So, I hold my breath and wait for him to make the next move.

He's leaning against me, his body hot and sweaty. I can feel his heart jumping. He just stays there, mashing up against me, all weird and kind of panicky. It's like he's caught his crook, but now he doesn't know what to do with him.

"Let him go." The hot girl keeps her voice low, but her words have a hard ring to them, like hoops spinning around a steel rod.

Counter Guy mutters something and releases me. Takes two steps back.

I stand up straight and blow out a breath and cut my gaze at her. "Thanks."

"No problem." She doesn't even blink.

I turn to leave, and he grabs the back of my jacket. "You're not going anywhere, asshole. I'm calling the cops."

"Look, I'm just a kid."

"What if we pay you?" she asks.

"I'm calling the cops. It's for his own good."

"For his own good" is what my stepdad always tells my mom before taking a belt to my back.

"I'll make it right." She bats her long lashes with intent.

"I don't want your money." He shakes his head.

"That's good." Her tongue darts out and circles her cherry-red lips. "I don't have a lot of cash. But if you let him go and promise not to call the cops, I'll give you something money can't buy."

"I'm not a kid," I protest, even though I've just been insisting I am. I don't want her to see me as a child. She can't be much older than me—she just *acts* grown up. I can't let her do this. "Go ahead. Call the cops."

"Hang on." A disgusting twitch of a smile spreads over his face. "Let the lady talk."

"I'll show you my breasts," she says.

My face flushes. I'm shaking my head in a hard no, but I feel my body responding to the thought of seeing her topless. "Don't do it."

"Not good enough," says the creep.

"I'll let you touch them."

"I want a blow job."

"Let him leave, and then we'll go in the back."

"Deal." Counter Guy starts rubbing himself over his slacks.

My face gets hot and my fists clench. "No way. I won't let you."

She winks at me, as if to say she knows I can't do anything to stop what is going to happen next. Then she curls her index finger in a come-hither motion and Counter Guy walks up to her and grabs her between her legs. Her arm flies up and she smacks him across the cheek, then she curls her hand into a fist and lands a jab to his jaw.

He stumbles back.

Falls to the ground.

She comes around and kicks him in the side.

He groans and grunts, and, after a moment, he sits back up, bloody spittle spewing from his mouth. "You little bitch! Now, you're both going to jail."

She levels her gaze at me. "Grab whatever else you need, and then let's bounce."

*You are the most incredible woman.* I'm thinking the words, but they don't actually come out of my mouth.

"Hurry up before someone comes." She smiles.

"I'm calling the cops." Blood is dribbling down Counter Guy's chin.

"No, you won't. If you were going to, you would have done it already. Why haven't you?" She points to the camera in the corner. "Is it because that camera just caught you sexually assaulting a minor? I'm only sixteen."

*Tears* form in his eyes. Clear fluid leaks from his nose. He's literally sniveling. "Please, just get out."

"Don't worry. We will." She goes behind the counter and takes two giant shopping bags, one for her and one for me.

We fill them up with the most expensive stuff we can find—plus underwear and shoes for me—and then we march out the door with him still sitting on the floor, crying.

"You're fantastic." This time, I say the words out loud.

"I don't disagree." She takes me by the hand.

As we walk down the street, our arms swing between us like we're boyfriend and girlfriend. The air is crisp and clean and filled with sunlight.

"You can crash at my place if you promise to be good," she says.

"You're sixteen and you got—you *have*—your own place? How is that possible?" I try to sound curious yet casual, like she hasn't just rocked my world.

"I'm emancipated. My mother is dead, and my grandparents were suffocating me. You can surmise why I had to get out of there."

"*Surmise,*" I repeat, completely unable to conceal my intense interest.

"I'm not in school, but I teach myself stuff. You have to if you want to get anywhere in life. Surmise means—"

"To deduce or conclude. To suppose without having concrete evidence. How do you get money? Are you a hooker?" I ask.

She arches an eyebrow. "I'm a hostess at Cuts, and I make monster tips."

"I've never eaten there." *Obviously.* It's one of the most expensive steak restaurants in town. I know a lot about it, though, because the name came up when I was researching local companies that offer their employees college scholarships.

"Once we get you cleaned up, I'm sure I could get you a job there, washing dishes or busing tables."

"Cool." *No way!*

"I'm Zoe, in case you're wondering." She smiles at me in a way that makes it impossible not to smile back.

*Eleven out of ten.* Today is my new best day.

# SEVEN

## NOW

The ambience in the upscale seafood restaurant exuded luxury. A black marble wall featured a brightly lit cut-out with a massive wine collection. Ubiquitous crystal chandeliers threw twinkling light around a dining room filled with customers dressed in designer clothing. Most of the women had sleek, expensive haircuts, toned, tanned arms and dramatically bejeweled fingers. The men wore colorful ties and sports jackets.

The blasts of men's cologne, mixed with pungent perfume, that preceded many of the couples, provided Rosalyn advance notice whenever someone was about to pass by.

Melanie squeezed her hand under the table. "Isn't this fun? A double date. I feel like a teenager. And I haven't been to The Ocean's Table in ages."

Not since Philip died, Rosalyn guessed.

She squeezed back and then withdrew her hand, a knot forming in her stomach. She recalled Philip's excitement, the way he'd thrown his arms up, making big happy gestures, when he'd recounted his first date with Melanie. He'd brought Mel here because she'd mentioned she loved shellfish, and the build-your-own seafood tower tasted like a million bucks. Never mind it was thrice the price of other local establishments. For both those reasons, the cost and the memories, The Ocean's Table wouldn't have been Rosalyn's first choice for their double date tonight. But it had been Blake and Melanie who'd invited Rosalyn and Ashton, so it had seemed ungrateful to suggest another venue.

Besides, if Melanie was comfortable, Rosalyn should suck it up.

She couldn't expect Melanie to give up The Ocean's Table just because it had been the site of her first date with Philip. In truth, she shouldn't expect Mel to give up *anything*.

Melanie enjoying life again was *the point*.

It was why Ros had encouraged her to give Blake a chance, get out there and dip her toes in the dating pool, and it seemed to be working out better than she'd imagined. Over the course of the last three months, Blake and Melanie had become inseparable. As far as getting Melanie out of the house and back into the world, Blake had succeeded where Rosalyn had failed.

Still, she couldn't help wondering if this restaurant had been Melanie's choice or Blake's. Something about Mel seemed off tonight—she kept exclaiming how much fun she was having, over and over again, almost too eagerly.

"Oh my! I don't think I've ever had a tastier meal." Mel put both hands on her flat tummy. She was positively glowing, but maybe that was the sequins on the chic black top she'd paired with silk pants and the highest of heels... or perhaps it was the pinking effect three glasses of champagne had on her usually pale complexion.

"Fantastic." Ashton, who looked especially dapper this evening in a sky-blue sports coat and crisp white shirt, clapped Blake on the back. He always made an effort to look nice if they went somewhere fancy, and tonight he definitely didn't disappoint. "We'll split the check."

"No way." Blake shook his head. "We invited you. Tonight's my treat."

"That's not necessary, Blake."

"Sure, it is. You can pick up the tab next time."

When Ashton shrugged his reluctant consent, Rosalyn was secretly relieved. They weren't in irreversible financial difficulty —she'd sold a few freelance magazine articles recently, and, of course, there was her share of Philip's trust. But not long ago, Ashton had run into trouble with his online art business. One of the paintings he'd sold turned out to be a forgery, and he'd had to refund the money, plus compensatory damages, to a very angry buyer—not to mention the legal fees they'd run up fending off potential criminal charges.

Even though Ashton had taken every precaution, including having an independent expert authenticate the work, the fake had somehow slipped by everyone. The worst of it was that the online scandal had sown doubt in the minds of other customers, many of whom had pulled out of even bigger, pending deals. Although Rosalyn's share of Philip's trust was more than ample to bail Ashton out of trouble, the trustee kept her on a tight allowance. Ros had an upcoming appointment with him to request a release of extra funds. She'd have to plead hardship to convince him, and if the trustee found out they'd been dining out at pricey restaurants it wouldn't help her case.

Blake lifted his hand, signaling to the tuxedoed waiter who'd been hovering nearby.

The service here was always good, but tonight, they'd hardly been able to eat because of the excess attention the staff had showered on them. Blake must have slipped the maître d' an extra gratuity.

"I hope you don't mind, but I took the initiative and ordered individual desserts for everyone," Blake said.

He'd also preordered several appetizers, and she didn't think she could eat another bite. She'd finished her sea bass only because it was expensive and wouldn't reheat well. She'd been brought up not to waste food. "Is it too late to cancel mine?"

"Definitely." Blake motioned, again.

The waiter appeared. "Ready for dessert, sir?"

"Yes, thanks." He slipped something into the man's palm.

"I'll have another one." Mel tipped her empty champagne glass.

"Certainly, miss."

"I wouldn't advise it, darling. I've got plans for the evening, and I need you conscious for them." He softened his words with a wink and a smile.

Blake was clearly heavily invested in making sure the evening went according to his elaborate plans, and Mel did seem extra cheery from drink. But the remark didn't sit well with Rosalyn. Blake's generosity apparently came with a price— letting him take charge of everything and everyone. Rosalyn lifted her own half-full glass and said, "Another one for me, too."

Blake's eyes locked with Mel's and she shrank in her seat. What the hell was that look he was giving her?

"Two for the ladies it is," the server said.

Blake arched an eyebrow.

"Make it one. I've changed my mind." Mel fiddled with the napkin in her lap.

Earlier, Melanie had ordered salmon, and then Blake had whispered in her ear. Suddenly, she'd changed her mind. Then Blake had ordered the chef's special for two. Now that he'd made his disapproval of her alcohol consumption clear, Melanie had acquiesced again.

Rosalyn pulled her lower lip between her teeth, debating. The last thing she wanted to do was push another drink on Mel if she didn't want one. On the other hand, she hated to see Mel trying to please her date at the expense of her own desires. "Oh, come on. Dessert's not the same without a little bubbly to wash it down. Are you sure you won't join me, Mel?"

"Well, I suppose—"

"None for my lady. But we're ready for desserts." Blake reached across the table for Mel's hand, and she readily gave it to him.

*My lady?* Very sweet—but also very proprietary.

"He's right. I've had my quota for the evening," Mel said.

"Oh, please have one if you like, darling," Blake crooned, as if he hadn't just literally told the waiter not to bring Mel another drink.

*Now he's fine with it?*

Rosalyn was confused. His words said one thing, but the way he'd beamed his approval at Melanie once she'd said she'd had enough clearly indicated another. He didn't want her to imbibe more than she already had.

"No, thanks, I'm good." Mel gazed adoringly back at Blake.

"Cancel mine, as well," Ros said through a tight smile.

She stole a glance at Ashton, to see if he, too, felt uncomfortable, but he was sipping his beer in apparent oblivion. And then, the tension, which seemingly only Rosalyn felt, was washed away by a deluge of lively conversation.

Desserts arrived.

To his credit, Blake had correctly selected everyone's favorite, including chocolate lava cake for Rosalyn, although she had never ordered one entirely for herself. But it was, after all, Blake's money, and if he wanted to indulge everyone, there was no real harm in it. He seemed completely besotted with Melanie, and if he was over the top with his take-charge attitude, he was probably trying to compensate for his prior shyness. After all, he'd waited years to make his interest in her known. Too bad that in reforming his image, he'd gone from a reticent, unsure suitor to Macho Man. Hopefully, if the relationship continued, he'd feel more secure in his relationship with Melanie, and then he could go back to being the considerate, capable man Rosalyn knew him to be.

The man who'd been a loyal friend to Ashton for years.

The man who'd stepped in without a thought to personal risk and saved her from a deadly snake.

"Aren't you going to try your crème brûlée?" Ashton asked Melanie. "It looks so good."

She shook her head. "I'm too full. Would you like it?"

Blake and Ashton exchanged a glance full of secret meaning. Really, it wasn't subtle. Something was up.

"No, thanks, I've got my own apple crumb cake." Ashton looked like the proverbial cat who'd just gulped down the canary.

"Take just a bite or two for me, darling," Blake cajoled.

Melanie spooned pudding into her mouth, and another look passed between Blake and Ashton.

They both rose on their haunches, eyes fixed on Melanie.

Then Blake scooted his chair out from the table.

Her spoon made a tinkling sound as she stirred, and then hesitated—Mel's dessert suddenly became the center of the universe.

Rosalyn's cheeks heated, and her stomach flipped.

*Surely not.*

They'd only been dating three—

Melanie lifted the spoon for inspection. "What on earth?" She plucked out a shiny object—a big diamond solitaire, dripping in caramel and cream. "Oh, Blake!"

Blake dropped to one knee, moisture brimming in his eyes as he gazed up at Melanie. "I know I'm just a regular guy, and you're the most extraordinary woman on earth. But I love you with all my heart, and I promise you this: If you'll marry me, I'll spend the rest of my life working to become the man you deserve. Just say yes, darling, and make me the happiest guy on the planet."

# EIGHT

## NOW

What had she done?

The ground was still soft, the air musty from last night's rain. Rosalyn's sneakers squished in the damp grass as she trod the distance between the sidewalk and the graves. What had compelled her to come to the cemetery today? A quest for absolution or guidance or both?

It'd been hard enough to accept the engagement.

She'd been able to think of little else for the past two weeks, since Blake proposed to Melanie. And now...

If only Philip were alive, he'd know what to do. Without him, she had to rely on her own instincts, do her best to divine the path he would have her take. Rosalyn halted in front of her brother's headstone. "I'm so sorry, Philip. I was only trying to keep my promise—to look out for Mel the way you asked me to. But something's happened, and I'm worried I might have made a terrible mistake."

The red roses that filled her arms trembled in the breeze. Her muscles quivered from the effort it took to resist breaking into Philip's tribute box. Sometimes, doing the right thing is harder than lifting a car off a baby.

And today she doubted she could muster the strength.

When Philip died, Melanie had consulted Rosalyn regarding *almost* all of the arrangements for his burial, including the selection of a traditional marker with the simple epitaph:

*In Loving Memory of Philip Monroe*
*Beloved Husband, Son, Brother and Friend*
*Until We Meet Again*

But she hadn't told Rosalyn about the box she'd commissioned. Mel had paid an artisan to craft it from stainless steel, then plate it with beautiful Carrara marble and bolt it onto the base of Philip's headstone.

The first time they'd returned to visit her brother's gravesite after the headstone went up, the box had taken Rosalyn by surprise. She'd *pretended* to avert her eyes while Melanie unscrambled a built-in combination lock and placed what looked to be a letter inside. Though she'd only glimpsed the first two numbers before her sense of shame kicked in, and she'd squeezed her eyes shut, she'd seen enough to guess that the combination was Philip's birthday. So, in the time since his death, the box's contents had been protected by Rosalyn's sense of propriety, rather than by its lock.

Now, heavier matters than propriety weighed on her.

Many times, Rosalyn had verified the combination. Whenever she'd visited Philip's grave alone, she would dial in the numbers, open the box, and stare at the growing pile of letters. On several occasions, she'd gone so far as to lift one out and hold it in her hands. But she'd never unfolded the stationery.

She'd never read so much as one word of Mel's letters to Philip.

And if Melanie had offered to let Rosalyn place her own missives inside the box, which she had not, Rosalyn would've declined. She understood the letters were Mel's way of coping with the loss of her husband, and that even if the words proved mundane, they were very, very personal. It would be an unforgivable intrusion into Melanie's privacy—and Philip's—to read them. The intimate act of writing and leaving epistles at the grave seemed much more the purview of husbands and wives than siblings.

And although, secretly, Rosalyn resented Melanie for finding an outlet for her grief, when she had not, she understood that was a petty sentiment. In the end, simple human decency won out, preventing Rosalyn from reading the private messages from a widow to her lost husband.

*Until today.*

Now, waging the last vestiges of mental war with herself, Rosalyn placed her roses, stem by stem, into a matching marble gravesite vase she'd had installed just one week after discovering the tribute box. Ashton had noted that, to some degree, Ros's vase seemed like a competitive gesture, but she disagreed. It wasn't nearly as costly or elaborate as the marble box. She'd simply wanted something beautiful to hold flowers for Philip. She wasn't trying to win a *best-headstone-accessory* contest with Melanie.

And she was definitely not competing with her to prove who missed Philip the most.

But if she had been, today, by virtue of an unforced error on Melanie's part, Rosalyn would have won.

Because a few hours ago, Mel had called from Hawaii with the news that she and Blake had eloped—crushing Rosalyn's spirit.

It seemed Blake and Melanie had written their own vows and gotten married on a beach at sunset. A local minister had pronounced them husband and wife and then blown a conch shell—barely three months after Rosalyn had arranged a lunch date for the pair at a Tucson wine bar. And a mere two weeks after a very public proposal that, in Rosalyn's view, had put undue pressure on Mel.

Just last week, Mel had assured Rosalyn that she and Blake were planning a long engagement and a formal ceremony that included family. Now they were husband and wife.

Mel was no longer Philip's widow—she was Blake's bride.

How could Blake have persuaded her to marry so quickly?

*The answer's obvious. He took advantage of her loneliness.*

"Forgive me, Philip." Rosalyn knelt on the soggy grass and dialed his birth date into the lock, then opened the box. "I know I have no right to read these. I feel like I'm betraying you as much as Melanie. But I'm the one who set Mel and Blake up on their first date."

In so doing, she'd given Blake her stamp of approval—her blessing for him to court a vulnerable woman. "I have a bad feeling about this whole thing. I *thought* he was a good guy, but after seeing the way he manipulated her at The Ocean's Table, and how quickly he moved to seal the deal, I just don't know."

Had Blake *deliberately* chosen the very spot where Philip had taken Mel on their first date for his proposal? And what about Blake claiming to be awkward around Melanie? She ground her teeth, remembering the way he'd pleaded for Rosalyn and Ashton's help.

Rosalyn couldn't help thinking she and Ashton had both been played—tricked into serving up Mel on a platter. And *if* that were true, it meant she had helped Blake take advantage of the very woman she'd promised to protect. With tears stinging her eyes, she plucked a letter from the top of the pile.

*Don't.*

Her conscious prickled.

*These aren't meant for your eyes. Reading them won't change anything.*

"Maybe not. But if I can figure out what's going on in Mel's head, it might help me to help her."

*She didn't ask for your help.*

*Look what a mess you've already made by meddling.*

"I'm doing my best. I'm trying to watch over her for Philip," Rosalyn told the wind, and then unfolded the letter, minding not to smudge its creamy paper or rumple its corners.

*Dear Philip,*

*So many times, I try to conjure you in my mind's eye to no avail. But today is a good day. As I write this letter, I can picture your face. I sense you beside me. Your presence is so real I can feel the warmth of you, taste your breath, feel the beat of your heart.*

*And that is confirmation that I'm on the right path.*

*I have so much to tell you, but I won't bury the lead.*

*Blake has asked me to be his wife.*

*When I put those words on paper, I think it impossible that I could ever belong to any man except you. But then, I close my eyes and hear you imploring me. I feel you squeezing my hand until I wince.*

*Your words: You must go on living, really living, Mel. For me.*

*Even though I promised you, I never believed I would be able to keep that promise. I never wanted to believe I could. I only did what I had to in order to survive. I knew that wasn't the right way to honor you, but I simply had no desire for... anything. Nothing, no matter how big or small, could bring a smile to my face.*

*I didn't want to open my eyes in the morning.*

*Little things like brushing my teeth, combing my hair, seemed too, too much.*

*But now, thanks to Rosalyn, all that's changed.*

*Your sister has been my rock. We've grown even closer than when you were alive. But I can't lean on her forever.*

*When she encouraged me to give Blake a chance, it occurred to me that I must be something of a burden to her. She never complains, but then, she wouldn't. I have to read between the lines of her gentle urgings, her attempts to pull me into the sunlight. She does it for your sake, I'm certain of that, but she needs to guard her own happiness, instead of worrying about mine.*

*The realization that I've been dragging her into my despair snapped me to my senses.*

*I decided, for all of our sakes, to open my mind and my heart to Blake.*

*And after spending time with him, I see the care with which he treats others, and I know he is an honorable man.*

*I put my trust in him.*

*And once I did, my whole world opened up.*

*Thanks to Blake, I can move forward. I don't know if I can ever be truly happy without you, but for the first time, I want to try.*

*I know what you're thinking:* Blake! Really? Must you choose a man I find so distasteful?

*But you were wrong about him. Just like you were wrong about Ashton. You never thought he was good enough for Rosalyn, but let's face it, you didn't think anyone was good enough for your baby sister. And because Ashton fell out of favor with you, so, by extension, did his best friend.*

*Ashton's changed. If you could see how well he cares for Rosalyn these days, what a comfort he's been to her since your death, you would forgive any fault you found in him before.*

*Now, let me tell you more about Blake.*

*He's so like you!*

*His music collection is filled with Chopin. Hemingway is his favorite author. And, just as you were, he's quite the philanthrope.*

*He's the director of a nonprofit. I've asked him to vet a*

number of charities and earmark them for donations from me
—from us. I would have nothing if it weren't for you.

But not to worry. Even though I can't deny that a large
part of my attraction to Blake is in the ways he reminds me of
you, I do know he is not you. I assure you the man has merits
of his own. We've only been dating three months, but in that
time, I've gotten to know so much about him. I feel so much
more like myself whenever I'm around him.

I can be someone other than "Philip's Widow" now.

When Blake first proposed, I almost said "no", because no
one can ever take your place in my heart.

Then I remembered all his assurances that replacing you
isn't his aim.

He understands that you, my darling Philip, are the love of
my life, and you always will be.

He says what matters most to him is that I am the love of
his life.

What other man would be willing to accept the scraps of
my heart? I promised you that I would be as happy as I could,
and now, I've found a way to keep my word.

To carry on living.

I said yes.

Rosalyn folded the letter just so, lining up every crease, as
best she could, then snuggled it atop the pile, at the same angle
she'd found it. She closed the box and, with numb fingers,
scrambled the combination. Once she got to her feet, her knees
threatened to give way and she crumpled onto the wet grass, put
her face in her hands, then waited for an avalanche of tears that
never came.

The letter shredded her heart, but it seemed she could not
cry—maybe because her mind was racing, reeling from Mel's
revelations.

Philip hadn't approved of Rosalyn marrying Ashton, and

he'd told her so. But after they'd said their vows, he'd put his reservations aside and had given her his full support. It stung to find out he'd never really moved past all that. In a way, it was Rosalyn's fault. Since childhood, she'd made a habit of leaning on Philip—he was her big brother, after all—and she'd complained more than once about the abundance of time Ashton spent with Blake. But when Philip fell ill, she'd curtailed her complaints. She'd realized how fortunate she was to have a husband she loved, and who loved her—even if neither of them were perfect.

Now, it made her stomach clench to think Philip didn't approve of Ashton. But what truly gutted her was the part about Blake and Philip being so much alike. In all the years she'd known Blake, Rosalyn had never once caught him reading Hemingway or found him listening to Chopin. Blake liked rock music—Pink Floyd was usually blaring on his stereo. Apparently, despite his promises, he'd used the "Ashton Method" on Melanie and misled her into believing he was someone he was not.

Unless Ros was wrong and all those things were actually true?

Did she know Blake well enough to swear they weren't?

Bracing her hands on the ground, she stood up.

It was her responsibility to find out.

She'd pushed her brother's widow into the arms of a man she apparently didn't know as well as she thought she did. Shaking her head, she turned away from Philip's headstone, and then she heard crunching, crackling, like someone walking over twigs and leaves.

"Hello?" Rosalyn whirled in all directions. "Who's there?"

Had someone seen her open the box?

Or was her guilty conscience making her imagine things? She lifted a hand to her eyes to block the sun and tried again. "What do you want?"

A strong wind whirred through the trees and whipped her hair into her eyes. She batted it away, planted her arms akimbo and made herself as tall as she could. "Whatever game you're playing, it's not funny. If you have something to say, come out in the open and show yourself."

# NINE

## NOW

*Do not tell her what you've been up to.*

Lola Sampson's back stiffened, and her hands clenched in a painful, involuntary spasm. The battle raging inside her was manifesting itself physically, and there was no chance her psychiatrist would fail to notice.

Dr. Anita Gainey, Lola's therapist, kept the office lights soothingly low, the décor soft and homey with layered pastel colors and comforting rugs. Two wingback chairs, their high backs offering patients a sense of safety and security, faced one another—but not squarely. The off-center setup gave Lola the feeling she was seen, but not in an intrusive way. She could choose to meet Dr. Gainey's canny gray eyes or, just as easily dodge her gaze.

*Dodge.*

"You're doing 'the claw' again." Dr. Gainey slipped her glasses off and let them hang carelessly from a delicate, aged hand. "What are you thinking?"

Lola's therapist wasn't the first person to notice the way Lola's fingers seized up whenever a particularly upsetting thought occurred, but she had been the first to suggest it was a unique, neurological reaction akin to a fight-or-flight response. Instead of chiding her about it, like her mother had always done, Dr. Gainey suggested it might be a useful tool to help Lola recognize when it was time to hit pause and explore what was bothering her.

"Blake and Ashton have been on my mind a lot recently." The internal pressure she felt momentarily triumphed over her need for secrecy. "*They* are what I was thinking about."

*Be very careful.*

Dr. Gainey crossed her legs and slipped her glasses back on, situating the frames over each ear beneath neat wisps of short, dyed-black hair, then blinked rapidly, as if debating her response.

Lola waited for an admonishing look, but one never materialized.

"I'm glad you trusted me with that. It's important for you to be honest if we're going to make progress."

She should've realized Dr. Gainey wasn't going to frown at her and cluck her tongue. Dr. Gainey was not her mother. She was far too professional to intentionally make Lola feel small. Nonetheless, she felt herself shrinking into her chair. "You're disappointed in me. I know you are." *Even if you don't show it.* "But I can't stop myself."

"It would be presumptuous of me to feel either disappointed or pleased with you. That's not what I'm here for. My job is to help you in any way I can. I'm on your side, always, Lola."

*You wouldn't be if you knew the truth.*

"With that said, I disagree, wholeheartedly, that you can't help yourself. We've practiced ways to control your unhealthy thoughts and urges surrounding those two men, and they've been working quite well up until now. And though I'm not *disappointed*, I am concerned that those methods are no longer working for you. You have every reason, every right, to be angry with them, but if you're obsessing again, that keeps you stuck in the past. Please tell me you haven't tried to approach them again."

"They didn't see me, and besides, the restraining order expired a long time ago."

"They can always get another one."

"I suppose so. And, about three months ago, I did have a bit of a close call."

"Three months ago? And you're just now bringing it up?"

Lola looked up from her lap. "I was wandering around near Blake's house, with no real purpose at all." *Liar.* "Just scratching a very intense itch, I guess you could say. When Rosalyn came out onto the balcony above me, I had an irresistible urge to call her name."

"She's Ashton's wife, right?"

"Uh-huh."

"And *irresistible* meaning you did, in fact, call out to her? Why would you do that?"

"Because someone should tell her the truth about the man she married and his best friend. Maybe I was trying to protect her."

"Or maybe not? Which is it? Because if you have some reason to believe Rosalyn is in real danger you should go to the authorities. In fact, if you have any evidence of that, *I* will go to the authorities. I have something called 'a duty to warn'."

*Which is why I can't tell you the truth.*

*You'd have to warn everyone about* me.

"Be real with me, Lola. Do you know of *anyone* who is planning to harm Rosalyn, *or* Blake? Have *you* experienced any thoughts or impulses that could put them in danger?"

"You know what they did to me." *Walk it back while you still can.* "But no. Even though I can never forgive them, I won't hurt them. I swear I would tell you if I felt like I might. Just like I told you the truth about what was on my mind. I didn't have to. I could've said I was doing the 'the claw' because I was thinking about my mother. You would've believed that."

"And that would've been a waste of *your* time. Here's what's bothering me, Lola. You seem to have found a way to cope with the past. There will always be painful memories and issues that resurface at unexpected times, but you've kept far away from those men for years—ever since they took out a restraining order against you, and you decided to heed it and get on with your life. So, why do you think you got 'an itch' to check up on them, and why didn't you tell me at the time?"

*I couldn't tell you then, because I knew you'd try to stop me. I wish I hadn't told you now.* "It just didn't come up."

"I'm not sure I buy that, but let's get to the heart of the matter—there *has* to be a reason. Something had to trigger you. Otherwise, why risk going to Blake's house?"

"I don't expect you to remember."

"Remember... oh, my." Dr. Gainey pressed her fingers to her temple. Her expression didn't change, but Lola could hear the regret in her voice. "The ten-year anniversary was a few months back. I'm so sorry I overlooked that."

"You shouldn't feel badly about forgetting. I'd have brought it up if I felt like talking about it."

"The anniversary of a trauma is always important—and a milestone like ten years even more so. It makes sense this would all come bubbling up again. But for your own benefit, you must stay away from those two... and I do wonder why you called out to *Rosalyn*. You've so rarely mentioned her."

"I don't know what came over me. It would have been very bad if either Blake or Ashton had seen me. I agree it was a fool-ish, foolish thing to do. But, when Rosalyn came out on that balcony all alone, it seemed like fate. Like I said, it was an impulse. Not a plan." *Not then.*

"And how did Rosalyn react?"

"She didn't hear me. At first, I thought she did. She leaned over the balcony, but then Ashton came outside, and he grabbed her. She was more or less upside down, and he was holding her by the legs, and I thought, for a second, she was going to fall. Actually, I thought he was going to deliberately drop her off the balcony. My heart was pounding so hard I thought my chest would explode. And then, when he pulled her back and put her down, I got worried that he'd seen me. So, I ran away." Lola twisted a knot into her hair. "Looking back on it, I don't think he did see me, but at the time, I believed he knew someone was there, and that was the only reason he didn't drop her. He didn't want a witness to his crime. Rosalyn has always seemed so happy with Ashton. I assumed he and Blake would have no reason to hurt her as long as she didn't know what they'd done. That *not* knowing would keep her safe."

"I'm trying to figure out whether you feel protective toward Rosalyn, or if you're angry at her for being with Ashton. For loving a man who hurt you so badly."

"Can't both of those things be true? Which do you think puts Rosalyn in more danger, knowing or not knowing that those two are monsters?"

Dr. Gainey fixed her gaze on Lola. "I think it's important to dig deeper into your true intentions. Shall we set an extra session this week? I have your word you won't hurt anyone?"

"You have my word. When I saw Rosalyn out on the balcony alone, I realized how vulnerable she is, how exposed. Living in that house with Ashton. Hanging around with Blake." Vulnerable was an understatement. Rosalyn was low hanging fruit.

"Are you free on Thursday at two o'clock?"

"Sorry, I don't think I am." She couldn't tell her therapist the truth. Her close encounter with Rosalyn on Blake's balcony had given her a fresh idea for exacting revenge—one that had been percolating long enough—it was now or never. Time to act. And Dr. Gainey had a way of prying the truth out of her. It was simply too risky to continue their weekly sessions. "I need a break from therapy for a while."

Off came the glasses. "Lola, let's meet again and talk some more. If Thursday doesn't work for you, we can set a different day or wait for your regular appointment."

"I'll think about it," she lied.

She had other things to do.

# TEN

## NOW

As Rosalyn and Ashton approached Blake's house, arms swinging between them, Rosalyn cast a glance at their entwined fingers, and her nerves eased a bit. Ashton had paid his way through college by working construction on the side, and, back then, it had shown in the nicks and cuts around his close-cropped nails.

Now he was the owner of a successful online art company. And even though his blue-collar days were in the rearview mirror, he still enjoyed doing yard work and tinkering in the garage. His rough-hewn hands remained one of the things she loved best about him.

"You've got the key?" They'd reached Blake's front stoop.

"Think so." He dug in his pocket. "He gave it to me for emergencies, though. I'm not sure he'd want—"

"It'll be fine. Blake wouldn't have given you a key if he didn't feel comfortable with you going into his house. Anyway, this isn't for his benefit so much as Melanie's, and you know he'll approve of anything that makes her smile."

"You've got that right."

"An elopement to Hawaii is romantic. But Mel missed out

on a lot. She didn't get a bridal shower, or an engagement party, or any of the hoopla that goes along with a formal wedding. And she didn't have her family and friends with her. I think it's important to do something special for them. I want to show her that we're in her corner even if the elopement was a shock."

"I know you're not thrilled." Ashton opened the door and ushered her inside.

Blake's house was located in one of the ritzier neighborhoods in Tucson, and the vaulted ceilings and open floor plan lent it a luxury air. But it was smaller than Melanie's house, right across the street. In all probability, the newlyweds would choose to keep Melanie's place over Blake's. "Who says I'm not thrilled?"

"It's obvious. And I promise I didn't know they were eloping. I would've told you."

"I should hope so." But secretly, she wasn't so sure. After all, Blake had been pining over Mel for years, and Ashton had never so much as dropped her a hint.

"Do you think they're going to stay here or move into Mel's house? Her place is bigger and it actually has furniture in every room. It seems like we should be jazzing her house up instead," Ashton said.

If the purpose of the visit had *only* been a homecoming surprise, sure. But she wanted to get a good look around, and if she'd admitted that, Ashton would have never agreed to unlock the door to Blake's kingdom. "Who knows where they'll end up, but it's traditional to come back to the groom's place. Besides, I don't have a key to Mel's, so it's a moot point."

He sent her a quizzical look.

When Philip was alive, Rosalyn had always had an emergency key. "She'll get around to giving me one, I'm sure. It just hasn't come up."

"Maybe she wants a little privacy." Ashton sighed. "Let's get on with it."

Was that a dig at her for meddling? "Such enthusiasm. But don't worry. I'll handle it myself and show you my masterpiece when I'm finished. Isn't there golf on?" It seemed to Rosalyn there was *always* a tournament on television.

Ashton found the remote and headed for the couch without even bothering to respond.

*That was easy.*

Rosalyn found Blake's bedroom, shut the door and slipped off the backpack she'd brought with her. The night she'd heard someone calling her name from below the balcony, Blake had specifically said he didn't have indoor cameras—so at least she didn't have to worry about getting caught snooping. Still, if her heart were a horse, the way it was galloping it would win the race.

*First things first.*

It only took a minute to sprinkle rose petals on the counter in the en suite bath, but getting them into a giant heart-shape pattern on the bedspread took longer than she'd anticipated. After finally finishing, she propped up a box, wrapped in silver paper between the pillows, and set out some chocolates near the wedding gift—a scrapbook for the new memories she hoped the happy couple would make.

Then, suddenly, her eyes watered. It was impossible for Rosalyn not to think about Philip and all the life experiences he'd missed out on, especially the children he and Mel would never have. But Philip hadn't wanted Mel to die along with him, to miss out on the good things in life.

Rosalyn blinked away her tears. She'd promised Philip she'd look after Mel, and that's what she'd been trying to do when she set up that lunch date with Blake. Now, she wished, with all her heart, that this union would bring Mel happiness—but she wasn't going to settle for hoping. She was going to do what she should have done before pushing them together.

She needed to find out more about the man who'd been in such a rush to marry her brother's widow.

It wasn't in her nature to spy, but in this case, she felt duty-bound to open a few drawers, and power up the desktop computer in the corner of the bedroom. She didn't know what she was looking for. A journal seemed unlikely—Blake wasn't the type, but you never knew.

Credit card bills?

Calendars?

After twenty minutes of searching, she came up with a big goose egg. There was nothing remotely revealing in any of his drawers. His medicine cabinet was empty except for shaving supplies, and though she'd powered up his desktop, it was password protected and she'd failed, multiple times, to guess it correctly.

Deflated, she zipped up her empty backpack.

It was a *good* thing, really.

She hadn't found a shred of evidence of a double life or any other wild and crazy thing she'd been suspecting. If she knew what was good for her, she'd stop watching true crime shows and mind her own business from here on out.

Except a lot of Blake's claims—the ones she'd read about in Mel's graveside letter to Philip—seemed dubious.

*Dubious?*

It was more than that. She simply didn't believe he'd presented himself honestly to his new bride. And this rush to marry didn't feel right. But it was a fait accompli, and even if she spent the entire day trying, it was unlikely she'd be able to hack into Blake's computer. "Ashton! Come and see what I've done."

A moment later, he flung open the door and whistled.

"You think Mel will like it?"

"She'll love it. I know how hard this is on you, hon, and I think it's great you set aside your own feelings to make

Melanie happy. Philip would be proud of you." He turned her to him and planted a kiss on top of her head. "*I'm* proud of you."

"I just want Mel to be happy." *And safe.*

"Blake's a good man. Sure, it was sudden, but when you know you know."

"I get that. But do you think he's shown her his true colors?"

Ashton's shoulders stiffened. "What do you mean by that? 'True colors' sounds so nefarious."

"I should've said 'his true self'. Do you know if he reads Hemingway?"

He took a step back. "What's this about, Rosalyn?"

She met his gaze. "You may have known Blake a long time, but—"

"You've known him almost as long as I have."

"But not nearly as well. I've never spent much time alone with him."

He sat down on the bed, and her beautiful rose-petal heart collapsed.

"Ashton!"

"I'll put it back. Come over here."

She stared at his hands, those wonderful, loving hands of his, but stood her ground. "It's not that I don't trust Blake. It's that I don't trust his relationship with Mel. Has he told her he had a crush on her all those years ago?"

"I expect he has, hon. They're married now, and you're going to have to accept it, whether you like it or not. But, if it will make you feel better, I'll text Blake right now and ask him if he reads Hemingway."

"No!" Mel would see the text, too. Then she'd realize Rosalyn had broken into Philip's tribute box. "Can you just tell me more about Blake? Like, is he close to his family? What does he do for a living? All I know is he calls himself an entrepreneur."

"Not close with the fam. And you say 'entrepreneur' like it's a bad thing. In case you haven't noticed, you're married to one."

"Yes, but I understand your business. I know what you do. You sell fine art online. I don't have a clue what Blake actually does every day. Does he sell products? Is he a business consultant?"

"He dabbles in a lot of different things and does quite well. I haven't seen his tax returns, but he always has money for whatever he wants... and he heads up that nonprofit, Opportunity Knocks."

"It's good that he's charitable."

Ashton eyed the bedspread. "We can keep talking if you want, but if you're feeling better about Blake, we should get to work on that rose-petal heart. I'm sorry I made such a mess of it."

"In a minute. Being back here at Blake's house reminds me of... well, you know that night with the javelinas?"

"What makes you bring that up again after all these months?"

It would be such a weight off her shoulders to confess that she'd been to Philip's grave and broken into his tribute box, and that someone else might have seen her, might have been watching her, just like that night on the balcony. Only Ashton thought she spent too much time at the cemetery. Once, he'd even called her devotion to Philip's memory... and to Melanie... *borderline obsessive*.

For now, it wouldn't hurt to leave the part about being at Philip's grave out of it. "I went along with the javelina theory that night because I had no hard evidence. But I'm telling you, a person called my name from below that balcony."

"If you say so, I believe you. Maybe I was too dismissive that night, but you didn't sound nearly as certain at the time. How sure are you?"

"Ninety-five percent, give or take."

"Then we need to bring this up with Blake and Mel. We'll tell them tomorrow when we pick them up from the airport."

"Shouldn't we show them their bed of roses first?" She really did want to surprise Mel and see her smile.

"Right after that, then. If there *was* an intruder on the property, now that he has a wife, I'm betting Blake will want to beef up security."

She swallowed hard. "We should look into that, too. Maybe get an outdoor camera and motion sensors."

*Because I'm certain someone is following me.*

# ELEVEN

## NOW

Detective Julian Van heaved against the sill and the window groaned open—the smell of the cat box was too strong. "When was the last time Whiskers saw the vet?"

"The what? Oh, a veterinarian." Walter's surprised voice told the tale—Whiskers hadn't *ever* seen a vet.

That didn't mean Walter didn't look after him as best he could, but he likely had never thought of getting the animal a once-over, or even if he had thought about it, he undoubtedly would've had to prioritize other things—like food and electricity.

"No offense," Julian said, "but his urine's a little strong. When we're done here, we'll take Whiskers by Pet Paradise. I take my cat there, and they let me walk in whenever I want. Perks of being a cop. Plus, Dr. Ginger has the hots for me."

Walter seemed impressed. "You got a cat?"

But apparently not for the reason Julian had assumed. "Yeah."

"You think Whiskers is sick? I thought that was just how cats smelled."

Walter was probably worried about how he'd pay. "I could

be wrong, but we should find out. I'll sweet-talk Dr. Ginger into giving him a check-up for free." Julian planned to pay for the exam and any medicine Whiskers might need, but Walter didn't need to know that.

"You really think she's sweet on you?"

"Don't doubt me, Walter. I tell you I'm the man of her dreams." *If only.*

"Then it's worth a try. The rest of Zoe's haul from the flea market is over there." Walter nudged Whiskers out of the way and pointed to a beat-up cardboard wardrobe. "That's the last of it. The only stuff you haven't been through will be in that box."

Julian had been coming by once a month, searching Zoe's junk pile little by little. She'd accumulated a massive amount of "treasure"—and Walter had thrown nothing out. But Julian was taking far more time than needed, helping Walter straighten and organize as they went, because he liked having an excuse to stop back and check on him.

*The final box.*

Julian rubbed the back of his neck. He could invent other excuses to visit, but this would probably be his last shot at finding a new lead in the Zoe Wessex case.

*Best get on with it.*

He pried open the top of the wardrobe box and took a step back. The odor of used clothing, that had been packed away for a decade, was almost as bad as the aroma wafting off of Whiskers. He pulled a mint out of his pocket, popped it in his mouth and passed one to Walter. Then he approached the wardrobe box and peered down, dismayed, but not surprised, to find the tall container stuffed to the brim and not a single article of clothing hung up on the top metal bar. He pulled on latex gloves and passed another pair to Walter. Then he removed a pair of ladies' slacks from the wardrobe, checked the pockets, folded it and put it on the bed.

Walter chortled and kicked the box over. "Better dump it all out on the floor. It'll take years the way you're going at it."

That was the point—but they'd come to the end of the line, so he might as well cut the cord. He lifted the upended box, and its contents spilled onto the floor—a giant mound of discarded dreams disguised as women's clothing.

Julian picked up a blue silk dress.

No pockets.

He shook it and a broach clattered to the floor.

"We'll put this in the *closer-look* pile." He handed the broach to Walter who placed it on the dresser. By now, they'd developed a routine.

Julian quickly rifled through the pockets of various jeans and slacks, pulling out occasional slips of paper or other treasure—like chewing gum wrappers and cigarette lighters. Anything with writing or monograms, or other interesting features, he gave to Walter to set aside. He'd gotten through about half the pile when he got bored and decided to switch to the more promising items: The bunch of purses with tarnished, tangled, fake gold chains.

He opened a pink clutch with a dirty white lining. First, he scanned it, and then after verifying there were no surprises like razor blades or scorpions inside, he patted the lining for hidden contraband.

Nothing.

"Next." He held out his gloved hand to Walter, who slapped a second clutch into it.

The process repeated, and repeated, and repeated.

Julian rocked back on his heels and wiped an arm across his sweaty forehead, he couldn't help feeling disappointed. "That's the last of the purses."

Walter leaned over the edge of the bed. "I see another one. Looks like it got kicked over here—under the bed."

Sure enough, a chain looped out from beneath a blouse near

the edge of the bed. One of Julian's legs had gone numb from sitting on it too long. He stood up and rubbed his thigh, then retrieved what turned out to be a brown leather handbag with a gold shoulder strap and sat down next to Walter.

Julian snapped open the latch and smiled.

"What?"

"I found something." He pulled out a folded piece of paper and an old photograph. "Not sure it's anything important but we'll add..."

*Wait a minute.*

"Walter, is that Zoe in the photo?"

"Yes. I haven't seen that one before, but she looks about sixteen."

"I didn't know she... who's the other girl in the picture?" There was absolutely no way the Wessexes would have kept this from him. "Did Zoe have a sister?"

Walter shook his head. "You think we wouldn't have told you? That's a girl who used to live down the way. She was a year or two older. Zoe looked at her like a big sister, though. Then she married some guy in the army and moved to Germany. Zoe was heart-broke when she left."

Julian cleared his throat, sheepish that he'd doubted Walter. He unfolded the yellowed sheet of lined notebook paper. On it were several pencil sketches. He smoothed out the wrinkles and scooted closer so Walter could exam the drawings along with him.

As they studied some emblems Julian couldn't quite figure out, Walter sighed.

"What are these? Any idea?" Julian squinted and read the words at the bottom of the page, written in calligraphy, "Zoe's Closet."

Walter's eyes were moist, his face pale. "If I tell you, you have to promise not to stop looking for Zoe."

Julian squared his shoulders and faced the old man. "I told you I will not stop looking. Not until we find her."

"Not even if you think she might have run off."

"I've always thought she might have run away... or that she might not have. But no matter what, I stand a much better chance of finding her if you tell me the complete truth."

Walter looked away and back. "All right."

"All right what?"

"This is it, the end of it? You've got nothing after all these years, and you've tried your best. This isn't just the last box—it's my last chance. If I don't give you something to go on right this minute you'll stop looking for Zoe. But if I tell you, you'll stop looking."

"I won't. What the hell is it you haven't told me?"

Walter groaned. "The day before Zoe vanished, Hannah and I went to the bank and withdrew ten thousand dollars in cash."

Julian smoothed out his forehead with his palm.

"You're surprised we had ten grand—it was our life savings."

"And Zoe stole it." Hannah and Walter had kept that important detail a secret because the police would have rightly assumed Zoe had, of her own volition, fled with every dime her grandparents had managed to scrimp and save over the course of their lifetime. Hannah and Walter refused to believe she would do that to them—and Julian had been a schmuck for not seeing it all along. He'd let his empathy for Hannah and Walter lead him down the garden path. No wonder the guys at the station nicknamed him "Detective Lost Cause".

He deserved it.

Walter scrambled to his feet, eyes bulging, spittle forming at the corners of his lips. He pointed a bony finger at Julian. "You see! That's why I never told you. Zoe did *not* steal our life savings. We *gave* it to her!"

"Calm down, Walter." The flush on Walter's face and neck,

the way his frail frame trembled, alarmed Julian. He needed to diffuse the situation before Walter gave himself a heart attack. "I'm sorry I jumped to conclusions. You told me once that Zoe had an 'investor' but you didn't know his name. Was it you and Hannah? The two of you invested in Zoe's Closet?"

"Yes. She had such big dreams, but there was no way any bank would loan her money."

Julian scanned the paper in front of him. "And all these drawings are..."

"She was designing a logo."

Julian could see how Hannah and Walter had been seduced by the prospect of helping their granddaughter to succeed in the world. "You understand that she was scamming you."

"I do not." Walter folded his arms across his chest.

"You handed Zoe ten thousand dollars in cash, and she vanished the next day."

"She didn't leave on her own. Don't you see the way she was doodling and daydreaming about Zoe's Closet? And her dream was about to come true." Walter jabbed Julian's chest with his finger. "You gave me your word. You gave Hannah your word."

"I'm not going to stop looking for her." He gently pushed Walter's finger away. He didn't know whether Zoe Wessex had been an innocent dreamer or a conniving schemer. But he did know that walking around with ten thousand dollars would have painted a giant target on her back.

# TWELVE

## NOW

This spot was perfect for lunch. Rosalyn settled herself onto the log bench at the Bug Springs Trail overlook and broke into her backpack. By the time Mel, who'd been hiking a few paces back, reached her, she had two peanut butter and jelly sandwiches, two apples, and two chunks of cheese laid out on a napkin.

Mel lowered herself onto the bench, swigged from her water bottle and grabbed a sandwich. "A feast for the soul."

"I agree. I'd rather be eating PB and J with you, looking out over this beautiful canyon, than dining at a king's table." Rosalyn crunched into an unpeeled green apple and held back the rest of her thoughts, the ones about how she wished Philip were with them. The last thing she wanted to do was rain on Melanie's newly married parade by reminding her of what she'd lost.

"I'm glad we're finally getting some girls' time." Mel looked away. "We haven't really had a chance to hang out since the elopement. I mean, just the two of us, without the men. When Philip died, I was lonely, but after a while I got used to the solitude. And I have to admit I enjoyed being the captain of my ship. I went wherever I wanted, whenever I wanted. But now, it seems I'm never alone."

Rosalyn wrinkled her brow.

"Don't get me wrong. I love the way Blake showers me with attention... most of the time."

Were those tears in Mel's eyes, or just the wind? "Most of the time?"

Mel seemed to be looking everywhere but at Rosalyn.

"Whatever is on your mind, I'd be glad to listen. You can tell me anything."

"I wish I could talk about it, but I don't think Blake would want anyone judging our marriage."

"I promise, no judgment." She raised her right hand, her fingers sticky with jam. "And I swear I won't say anything to Ashton—even if he tries to invoke spousal privilege." Considering how long he'd kept Blake's secret crush on Melanie from her, Ros was entitled to a little leeway of her own. "What happens on Mt. Lemmon stays on Mt. Lemmon."

"Ashton and Blake are thick as thieves. What if you let something slip?" Mel licked her fingers and then wiped them with a napkin. "I'm sorry, but I can't take the chance. I don't want anything I say getting back to Blake—he's so sensitive—I'm afraid it would hurt him."

"But I never slip. I'm a rock star at keeping secrets."

Mel arched a brow. "Is that so? Then, first tell me a secret you've kept faithfully from me."

"I'm not falling into that trap—if I do it would prove me untrustworthy."

Mel shrugged, and they gobbled the rest of the meal without talking. Mel had come so close to confiding in her, Rosalyn hated to let the moment pass. Mel needed someone to talk to. A living, breathing person. Letters to Philip were all well and good but he couldn't give her a hug or a bit of sage advice when called for. "What's so terrible you're worried about it getting back to Blake?"

"Oh, gosh." Mel jumped up and brushed crumbs off her jeans. "Nothing. I only meant that with us being newlyweds, I don't want to spoil the glow."

"Don't take this the wrong way, but you're not glowing. You're sweating."

That drew a smile from Mel, and Rosalyn breathed a sigh of relief. Thank goodness her attempt at humor had been well-received. Her sister-in-law was such a private person it hadn't been easy to build camaraderie. They were still working on it.

"Do you *promise* you won't tell anyone?"

"I do."

Mel sat back down and stretched her legs in front of her, tapped a finger on her chin. "Does *anyone* include Ashton?"

"It does."

"Okay. It's not a big deal. But things moved so quickly between Blake and me, we didn't really have a chance to learn about all of each other's quirks. And, if I'm being honest, there are some things about him that make me a little uncomfortable."

Rosalyn longed to jump in with questions but she didn't want to break the flow.

"From the beginning, he was clingy—but I felt needy, too. He shadowed me everywhere I went. I figured once we got married, he'd feel more secure, and so would I. And I do, but Blake seems *more* insecure now, and about things that don't even make sense —for example, the bed of roses you and Ashton made us."

"I thought you liked it."

"I *loved* it. And that was the problem. Blake felt that he'd let me down because he didn't think of it himself. And he mentioned not liking that the surprise came from Philip's sister, and therefore, indirectly from Philip himself. He said it was like Philip had prepared our bed and then climbed in with us."

"He said that?"

Mel nodded. "He's incredibly sensitive about Philip. If I bring up his name, or if he catches me looking at an old photograph, he'll storm out of the room. It's really taken me aback, because before Blake proposed, he told me he would never try to take Philip's place in my heart."

Rosalyn's stomach churned with guilt. She already knew about Blake's promise because she'd read Mel's letter. With every fiber of her being, she wanted to confess, but Melanie might never trust her again if she did.

"I realize now how unfair of me that was—to expect him to accept only part of my heart." Mel reached for Rosalyn's hand. "I loved your brother with *all* of my heart. And as strange as it sounds, I married Blake, partly, to please Philip. He made me promise to remarry."

It didn't sound strange to Rosalyn. She'd facilitated things between Blake and Melanie for the same reason. And now, she was *almost* certain she'd made a big mistake. "Do you wish you hadn't eloped? Because, please forgive me if I'm overstepping, but it's not too late to—"

"Oh, but it is. I've taken a sacred vow to love to honor and to cherish. I would no more break my vows to Blake than I would to Philip." Mel was on her feet again. "The person who has to change in our marriage is not Blake. It's me. I have to learn to give more."

She squared her gaze with Mel's. "I'm going to support you, no matter what you decide about your marriage, but I feel like there's something you should know."

Melanie took a step toward her. "I'm listening."

"I think part of the reason Blake is insecure is that he's admired you for a lot longer than you know. Back in college, he had a major crush on you. And it was awkward and difficult for him when you turned up married to Ashton's brother-in-law."

"Is *that* the secret you've been keeping from me?"

*One of them.* "Yes."

"Then not to worry. Blake told me all about how he used to come into the bakery where I worked in college, and how he was too shy to even ask my name. I find that quite endearing. It's one of the things that deepened our relationship. Made it move along so quickly—him being so vulnerable, so real with me. There are other things, too, of course. In a lot of ways, Blake reminds me of Philip."

"Oh?" Rosalyn feigned surprise.

"Yes. Especially his philanthropic nature. He spends most of his time on the nonprofit he heads up."

"What's the name of it, again?"

"It's called Opportunity Knocks. They help deserving individuals find funding for their dreams. Like a mom-and-pop shop that needs money to expand, or a person with bad credit who can't get a traditional business loan."

Opportunity Knocks was definitely a mark in Blake's plus column.

Melanie checked her watch, and Ros got the feeling she wanted to leave, either because she'd revealed too much, or Ros had butted in too far. "I didn't mention to Blake that we were hiking, and I'd like to get home before he does. We should head back."

"It's mostly downhill, so it won't take long. Don't worry." Rosalyn was still stuck on the part about Blake being upset because *Philip's sister* had planned a homecoming surprise. Was that who she was to him now? Not Rosalyn. Not even Ashton's wife, but *Philip's sister*. If Blake resented her now, imagine how he'd feel if he knew she'd gone through his things and tried to hack into his computer.

On the way down, nothing more was said about the state of Melanie's new marriage. Instead, they stuck to safe subjects like bluebirds and wild strawberries and worn hiking boots. In the parking lot, the hug Melanie gave her before she climbed into her car felt more like a token gesture than a warm embrace.

For all her good intentions, it seemed she'd made Mel *more* uncomfortable. And now that she thought about it, her suggestion that it wasn't too late for Mel to undo her marriage to Blake —even though she hadn't actually finished the sentence, her meaning had been clear enough—was probably a bridge too far.

Rosalyn watched Mel peel out of the lot, and then sagged against her Jeep Cherokee. With a sigh, she opened her trunk and dumped her gear inside. When she turned back around, she saw someone, out of the corner of her eye. For a moment, she thought Melanie had returned, but she hadn't heard a car, only the slap of athletic shoes on concrete.

A tall woman with a big-brimmed hat marched up to her.

"Rosalyn?" she said. "My name is Sherry Anne. You don't know me, but I've seen you out here on the trail before—with your brother. And again, at his funeral."

"You knew Philip?"

The woman sent her a soft smile. "I hope you don't mind me introducing myself. But Philip was a wonderful man, and I just wanted to tell you that."

# THIRTEEN

## NOW

Lola balanced on the edge of a white fabric-covered sofa, fiddling with the brim of her sunhat, inspecting it for dust and grime. She'd be mortified if she placed the hat beside her and it left a smudge on the pristine cloth. She could imagine the conversation, later, between Rosalyn and Ashton.

*"What happened to the couch?"*

*"Oh, I met this woman on my hike. Well, after my hike. And I invited her over for tea. I guess she was dusty from the trail. We both were. It'll come out. I know a trick."*

*"A stranger? We've talked about this. You're too friendly by a mile and someday it's going to get you into trouble. What were you thinking?"*

*"Darling, she knew Philip."*

*"What's her name?"*

*"Sherry Anne something."*

*"Don't recall him mentioning a Sherry Anne. What does she look like?"*

*"Wavy, platinum blonde hair. And tall. So very tall."*

Lola clutched her hat to her chest, crushing the floppy brim in her fist. She'd spent two days and a small fortune at the salon for a digital perm and extreme blonding, but there was little she could do to disguise her height—five foot eleven and a half, shoeless. Would the new hair be enough to throw Blake and Ashton off the scent? Or would they know, as soon as Rosalyn told them about the tall woman, that she was back?

Approaching Rosalyn was long overdue. The night she'd appeared on the balcony, Lola had realized how vulnerable she was and the seeds of her revenge plan had taken root. But she had to steel her nerves and harden her heart first. And, so, she'd watched Rosalyn for months before deciding it was finally time to go for it.

The other day, at Philip's grave, she'd intended to introduce herself, but then had lost her nerve.

*That's okay. Practice makes perfect.*

Her plan wasn't yet fully fleshed out, but gaining Rosalyn's trust was step one.

Coming to her house was risky. But the chance to further her mission—seek out and destroy Blake Tyler and Ashton Hightower—compelled her. There were so many reasons to keep away from them: common sense, her mental health, her safety and her personal freedom, to name a few.

But none of those reasons outweighed her need for revenge.

No, not revenge.

*Justice.*

Besides, she was sick to death of hiding in the shadows like a little mouse.

Part of her almost wished Ashton would come home and discover her chatting over tea and cookies with his sweet, inno-cent wife, Rosalyn.

*Fine with me if he catches me.*

Blake and Ashton were the ones who should be afraid. She'd already landed one blow to Ashton, practically destroying his online company with that forged painting—and she was just getting started.

Lola tossed her hat to the side and straightened her back, flipping her fantastic, wavy hair over her shoulders.

Rosalyn returned bearing a flower-stenciled wooden tray, then set it on the coffee table between them, and took a seat opposite her.

Lola's eyes landed on Rosalyn's plain gold wedding band and tiny diamond solitaire. By now, Ashton could surely afford better, and with the money Philip had left her, Rosalyn absolutely could. It was sweet she hadn't traded her original wedding set for a grand diamond—and what was up with that old Timex on her wrist that she kept touching?

Lola straightened her back. She couldn't think about how nice Rosalyn seemed. "Are you sure I'm not interfering with your day?"

"Not to worry! My husband's golfing with his best friend. They won't be back for hours. I was planning to kick back and take it easy for the rest of the afternoon. I'm beat after that hike."

"You're tired. I should go."

"What? No. I've just made tea. And you haven't told me, yet, how you know—how you knew—Philip."

"Your brother was a wonderful man." She'd said that already. She'd had a good twenty minutes in the car to come up with a story about how she'd met Rosalyn's brother. But on the way here, she'd been too nervous about the possibility of bumping into Blake or Ashton to concentrate on fabricating another lie.

"Thank you for saying so. I'm eager to hear more about your relationship. Discovering a friend of Philip's, that I never knew about, feels like I've been rummaging around in my closet and stumbled upon a Christmas gift I'd forgotten to unwrap. I can't wait to find out what's inside." A sheen of tears made Rosalyn's brown eyes glow, and her chin quivered, ever so slightly, as she smoothed a hank of her silky auburn hair behind an ear.

Obviously, Rosalyn loved her brother and was still grieving for him. Lola wished she could tell her the truth: *I never met your brother—it's Blake and Ashton I know. They are the reason I'm here.*

She hated using Rosalyn's dead brother like this, but a fake friendship with Philip was her entrée into Rosalyn's world, and Rosalyn was her easiest path to revenge.

"Sherry Anne?" Rosalyn was looking at her expectantly.

*Just wing it.* "I met Philip about ten years ago at a... coffee shop."

A big grin spread across Rosalyn's face. "Back in his single days."

"It wasn't like that. The place was crowded, and he asked if he could share my table. There was only a *little* flirting."

"Do tell." Rosalyn's eyes brightened.

*She's eating this up.* "I won't deny there was banter, but then we started talking about... our favorite books. I said mine was *Pride and Prejudice* and his was..." She paused, took a sip of tea, hoping that Rosalyn would drop her a hint as to her brother's tastes in literature.

After a moment, Rosalyn supplied, "*The Sun Also—*"

"*The Sun Also Rises*," Lola quickly put in, talking over Rosalyn as if she'd been just about to say so. "Such a Hemingway fan."

"Were you, too?"

"Not then, I wasn't. But Philip talked me into giving the book a try, and he promised to read *Pride and Prejudice.* Anyway, the next week, I went back to the coffee shop, not really expecting to see him. But he turned up, book in hand, and the rest is history."

"A history I'd like to hear more about."

"That's pretty much it. Philip and I started our own book club. Two strangers who got together most Tuesdays to talk about what we were reading. But when I say he was wonderful, I mean it. I've had some rough times in my life." That was true enough. "And he always listened, supported me, shared his advice but didn't judge me if I didn't follow it. This went on for a few years, I'd say, and then one day he just stopped coming. I was so disappointed, and I never understood what had happened. Then I read in the papers that the man who'd invented The Chuckle had died. I went to the funeral, and that's where I first saw you. It's how I recognized you, today, at the trailhead. So, I thought I'd just work up my courage and say hello."

*Not a bad story.* She half believed it herself.

Rosalyn touched her wristwatch—a habit it seemed. "I'm so very glad you did. I wonder if the reason Philip stopped meeting you for book club was because of Melanie."

"His wife?"

"Yes. He might have thought it was inappropriate to be meeting a woman at a coffee shop every week."

"I can certainly see that. Is she the jealous type?"

"Mel? Oh, no. But Philip was a good husband and he would never have done anything to hurt her."

"Beyond reproach. That's the kind of man he was."

"I agree... Sherry Anne, if you don't mind my asking, what are you reading now?"

Okay. This was working out better than she'd hoped. "Something *fabulous. Juror Number Three.*"

"By Patterson?"

"Yes, with a co-author, Nancy Allen. What about you?"

"*Black Widow*—it's a crime thriller by a terrific indie author I just discovered, Belcamino, I think is her name." Rosalyn clanked her spoon on the side of her cup. "I wonder... would it be presumptuous of me to suggest..."

"Please! I'd love to pick up with you where Philip and I left off."

"We could even meet at the same coffee shop. What's the name of it?"

Lola gulped her tea too fast, burning her throat. "It went out of business a while back, I'm afraid. But we could meet wherever. I'm open."

"Just up the street there's a—"

"Oh, I don't love the big chain shops. I know a spot run by locals near the university." There must be one, and it might not be safe to meet so close to Rosalyn's home. Too much risk of running into certain people. Now that she was in the inner circle, she didn't want to blow it. From now on, she'd be more careful. "I forget the name, but I'll text you." Her hand shook, just a little, when they exchanged phones. Dr. Gainey wouldn't approve, but Dr. Gainey was out of the loop, now. "Put your number in."

"There." Rosalyn beamed as she took back her cell. "This is going to be great. I wonder if we should invite Melanie?"

"Oh, I uh..."

Rosalyn put a finger to her lips. "Say no more. I can see how that might be awkward. Even if you and Philip weren't actually an item."

"Thanks for understanding. I'd love it to be just us."

"Me too. It will be more special that way." She sighed. "This is one of the best things that's happened to me since Philip died. Making a new friend. It feels like a way to keep him close. I'll try not to bend your ear too much about family, though. We can stick to the books."

"Not at all. I'd love to hear *all* about your family. Philip and I never stuck to the assigned topic. That's how we became such good friends. And I have to confess something—he talked about you all the time. I think he would've wanted me to look out for you."

"I don't need looking after, but that's very kind of you."

"It must be hard, losing your brother at such a young age. Are you okay? Is your husband... what was his name again?"

"Ashton."

"Is Ashton supportive?"

"He's great... whenever he's home." Rosalyn's ears turned pink, as if she'd said more than she'd wanted to.

"Does he travel for work?"

"No. He has an online company, but he does have an office and a staff. Aside from the occasional out-of-town conference, he conducts his business from Tucson."

"Then what keeps him away from home? Are you a golf widow?"

"You nailed it. It's really nothing worth complaining about. He's a very loyal person, which is such an admirable trait, but his best friend has been single up until quite recently. Ashton spent a lot of time with him—they'd take trips together, go out on the town."

"And that's all changed now that this friend has found his match? Are you happily married?"

Rosalyn drew back, seemingly startled.

Lola realized she'd been peppering her with questions. "I hope I haven't crossed a line. I don't mean to be so personal." *Yes, I do.* "We've only just met."

"You surprised me, that's all. But yes, I'm very happy with Ashton. There's no such thing as the perfect husband."

"No." Lola took a sip of tea. "I suppose there's not."

# FOURTEEN

## THEN

I open the ledger. $11,933 minus $2,106 in expenses.

I tap my pen against my teeth. "Shut it down."

From the bed, he groans. "Come back to bed, Zoe. Just give me a little more time, and I promise I'll make it pay off."

"We're bleeding money—my money."

"You mean Walter and Hannah's money."

"They gave it to me, so it's mine."

"I've brought in a buck or two for our ventures along the way—we agreed to split everything equally. It's *our* money," he says calmly.

"And yet, you're the only one enjoying it." My voice is unnaturally shrill. I sound jealous, but I'm not. Not of *Her.*

He throws one leg over the covers, revealing his naked body. "I'm not enjoying it, babe. I'm doing this for us. You seem to have forgotten you're the one who chose her as my mark."

"I didn't tell you to take her to Laguna Beach."

"Not specifically, but you instructed me to romance her. It was a weekend getaway, and you didn't have to double the cost by booking a room at the same hotel, just so you could spy on us."

"You were slobbering all over her morning, noon and night. Someone's got to keep you on track."

"It's business, Zoe... baby doll." He lifts his hands over his head and his triceps ripple.

I hate how much I yearn for him. Thinking about him all the time is getting to be a problem for me. "Admit that she's beautiful. Admit that you like her."

"She's a nice person. I *do* like her."

*And unlike me, she's rich enough to give you everything you want.*

I close my eyes, suddenly lost.

Is he going to leave me?

Maybe I shouldn't have kept him out of my bed all those years. When I tricked that shopkeeper so he wouldn't call the cops on him, he was only a kid—we both were. And I was grateful to be around a guy who didn't try to force himself on me. So, we just carried on in our weird undefined partnership: we stole together, lived together, *grew up* together, but until last night, we never slept together. And we certainly never talked about our *feelings*. What we mean to each other.

It's understood we'll part ways once we've saved enough money—that's the bargain we made. But we keep moving the goal post, so it's never seemed imminent before.

First, we said we'd go our separate ways when we had one thousand dollars each.

Then five thousand.

And now it's ten thousand apiece.

After Walter and Hannah "invested" their life savings in my fictional second-hand clothing shop, I realized we might actually get there. But it still seemed a long way off.

He wants to go to college. He can get grants and financial aid, but he needs money for expenses.

I don't give a crap about formal education. I'm self-made. I want excitement and a ticket to the finer things in life. College is fine for him, but my dreams are bigger.

*Separate ways is the only answer.*

If I stick with him forever, I'll never get the life I want.

He wants to go "legit".

He wants to get married and have a bunch of kids and live in the suburbs.

The thought of that turns my stomach.

I cross the room and sit down on the bed beside him. "I said shut it down."

He grabs my hand. "Zoe Wessex, are you jealous?"

Even though we agreed it was time he made use of his good looks, I don't like it. The thought of him touching *Her*, kissing *Her*, makes me want to throw up. I'm losing my edge, and it's my edge that keeps me alive. "Don't be stupid."

"Admit you're jealous, and I'll call things off with her right now."

"I'm not. It's just that the five thousand dollars you've scored so far isn't enough. Not when you had to spend twenty-five hundred to squeeze it out of her. You need to find a mark with more expendable cash."

"No way. She's loaded. Her car could bring twenty-five thousand on Craig's list, easy. I'm sure I can convince her to sign it over to me. We'll do an official bill of sale for, say, five hundred dollars. And then she can't change her mind and take it back after we break up."

"Are you sure you're up for this?"

He's come a long way since the day he got busted stealing a shirt and socks. But his contributions to our ventures have always come from shoplifting and fencing goods.

I'm the one who scams *people* for money.

This is his first foray into human targets, and I'm not sure he's built for it.

"It's okay if you're jealous, baby. Maybe we should talk about this—about us."

*That's it, then. Separate ways.* "There is no us."

"We've been together longer than a lot of married people."

"Because we keep it professional."

He lays a warm hand on my chilled shoulder. "Not last night we didn't."

"Last night was a mistake. It can't happen again. Considering how soft-hearted you are, and how much you 'like' her, do you think you can go through with it? Finish the job and get the title to her car."

"I can, and I will."

"How much longer? And how much is it going to cost?"

"I'm meeting her tomorrow—and after she signs over the title, I'll take her to dinner to celebrate, so I'd say seven hundred dollars ought to be enough. Five hundred for the car and the rest for—"

"No celebrating. Once you've got the title, you don't need to keep playing your role."

"There's no reason to be cruel. I want to take her to dinner. Break up with her face-to-face. Tell her it's me and not her."

"You want to take her home and screw her one last time."

"So what? You're not jealous, right? You said last night was a mistake, so what's it to you?"

"Two hundred dollars extra is too much."

"That's it? It doesn't bother you that she's falling for me?"

"I want to be sure *you* don't fall for her. And not for the reason you're implying. If you get too involved, even if you manage to go through with it, then what you did to her is going to haunt you. You don't understand that life has dealt us a crap hand, and we have every *right* to stack the deck in our favor."

"Oh, I see. *You* feel bad about taking Walter and Hannah's life savings. That's why you're talking about *me* getting haunted by my conscience."

I shake my head.

"Zoe, don't say anything until I'm done talking. Just listen and let me say my piece. You'll pay them back. After I fence that necklace I stole last month, and I get the title to her car, you can pay Walter and Hannah their ten thousand and we'll still have enough for me to register for school and you to do... whatever you want."

"Hannah and Walter think I'm dead."

"The cops explained to them you probably ran off, which you did."

"I can't go back. I can't face them."

"You think it will hurt them more to know you're a thief or to let them think you're dead?"

"I don't want to go home. I don't have a home." *Except you. You are my home—but I can't let myself be caught in a trap.*

Like my mother before me, I'm a free spirit. I can't handle all the rules at Hannah and Walter's house. And I can't play house with *him* anymore, either. "It's not like they're my real parents."

"But they're your real grandparents, and they love you."

"If Walter and Hannah are so freakin' wonderful, how come their only daughter wound up like she did? I hold them responsible for my mom's death."

"That's not fair."

"We're *not* paying them back."

"Up to you. But in that case, we have plenty of money for me to take her to dinner."

*And get laid after.*

We have to go our separate ways, soon, but I'll be damned if he'll be the one to leave *me*. "Knock yourself out. I'll give you *eight* hundred so you can treat her to vintage champagne. Just be sure you get that car."

# FIFTEEN

## NOW

Rosalyn shaped a hank of hair into a face-framing side-swoop and secured it with bobby pins. Then she leaned closer to the mirror to apply a natural shade of lipstick. It was important to look nice for her new friend.

Sherry Anne, even dusty and sweaty from her hike the other day, had been the picture of elegance with her movie star hair and her big, intense eyes, but mostly because of her height. The woman was positively statuesque. Rosalyn wouldn't be a bit surprised if she turned out to be a model or an actress.

That wasn't the only reason she was taking extra care with her appearance this morning, though, or why her hands trembled as she buttoned her peach blouse and shimmied into a pair of white capri pants. Irrational as it might be, she felt as if she was getting ready for a coffee date with Philip. By re-enacting the book club he'd created with Sherry Anne, she thought he'd be with them in a way. Not that she believed in ghosts—she didn't—but there were times when she felt her brother's presence.

Meeting his old friend, Sherry Anne, had been one of those times.

She touched her Timex, trying to recapture that feeling.

Besides, she was intrigued by this woman. There was something awfully mysterious about her. The name Sherry Anne didn't suit her one bit. She deserved an exotic moniker like Tristesse or... she glanced at her watch... she better get a move on. The Gourmet Grind was a good half hour away, even with light traffic.

Hurrying into the living room, she called ahead of herself, "Honey, have you seen my purse?"

"On the coffee table." Ashton lounged wide-legged at the edge of the couch.

"Thanks." She scooped it up and pecked him on the lips.

Blake whistled and got to his feet. "Where're you off to looking so smart?"

"To meet a new friend, and I want to make a good impression." She did a little curtsy, tugging out the fabric of her capris. "Will I do?"

"You look beautiful. Peach is your color."

"I swear, Blake, you never needed any help from Ashton or me. You know just the right thing to say to make a woman feel good." There, she'd said it. Would he read the subtext and acknowledge the truth—that he'd misrepresented his skills with the opposite sex?

"You gave me the confidence to be myself." He came over and gave her a side hug and then returned to *his* chair. Blake spent so much time at their house, he'd basically claimed that spot as his own.

For the men, Saturdays were usually golf days in one form or another. It appeared, from the bowls of chips spread out at 10:30 in the morning, this was going to be a Golf-TV marathon. Good thing she had something of her own on the docket. It took the sting out of being a sports widow. "I'll be back in a couple of hours. If you need me to pick anything up on the way home, just text."

"Is Mel going with you to see your new friend?" Ashton asked.

There was no reason to feel awkward—she could hardly be accused of neglecting Melanie.

She fanned heat from her face. "I just met this woman the other day, and she was the one who invited me." Was that right? She couldn't recall whose suggestion the book club had been.

Blake lifted one shoulder. "You don't have to explain. Don't put her on the spot, Ashton. Your wife and my wife are both allowed to have other friends."

"I don't mind explaining. It's a book club. Sherry Anne—that's her name—was a friend of Philip's before he met Melanie. I think she might have had a crush on him or maybe not but anyway we've only just met so we're getting to know each other. Maybe we'll expand the 'book club' later on."

Ashton leaned forward, clasping his hands between his knees. "This is the first I've heard of you meeting a friend of Philip's. Why didn't you say anything before?"

"I don't know." She'd had an inexplicable urge to keep Sherry Anne a secret for as long as possible. "I-I guess because she was Philip's friend it felt extra special to me. I thought if I talked about how excited I was to have found her, I might jinx it."

"That's super sweet," Blake said. "How exactly *did* you find her?"

"She found me. She came up to me in the parking lot for the Bug Springs trailhead and introduced herself. She said she recognized me from Philip's funeral. And then we came back here for tea and a chat and she told me about how she and Philip had bonded over books and..." She paused for air. "I'll stop rambling now."

"You invited a total stranger into our house?" Ashton asked in a tone he usually reserved for people who cut him off in traffic or mistreated someone he cared about.

"I invited my brother's friend to our home. I wasn't aware I had to ask permission to have a guest." Why was she being so defensive? If he'd spoken sharply to her, she'd been even sharper with him.

"You're twisting this to make me sound unreasonable."

"No. You're actually being unreasonable." Ashton was over-reacting, but so was she. Naturally, he was surprised that she hadn't mentioned any of this to him until now.

"Ashton's concerned, that's all. And that's a husband's job, isn't it? To look out for his wife?"

Of course, Blake would side with Ashton. It got under her skin for him to insert himself into a personal disagreement. She wanted to tell him to butt out but settled for being the mature one in the room. "I'm going to be late. Ashton, I'm sorry it made you uncomfortable for me to have a friend over."

He climbed to his feet. "Please don't take this the wrong way. I trust your judgment—but I'd rather you not go meet this person until I can find out more about her."

A stabbing pain attacked near her temple. She took a slow breath, held it and released it. She needed to take things down a notch. This wasn't Ashton's style. He was usually so laid-back. But she'd nearly been bitten by a snake in her car, and then there was the balcony incident—they'd been talking about getting a home security system but they hadn't installed one yet. She could see why he might be more worried than usual. "Okay. What do you want to know?"

"What does she look like?"

"Stunning. She's really beautiful, with long, wavy blonde hair and she's tall. *Very* tall." She'd volunteer more information about Sherry Anne, but she realized she didn't actually know anything more.

Rosalyn looked at her wrist.

"It's sixty seconds later than the last time you checked your watch. Why don't you text this woman and tell her you can't make it?" Ashton asked.

"I'll text her that I'm going to be a few minutes late. But I *am* going to meet her. You can track me on my phone if you like. We'll be at Gourmet Grinds on University Drive. I'm sure I'll find out more about her—that's kind of the point, for us to get to know each other better." She pressed her fingers against her throbbing temple. "I think you're making too much of this. Am I missing something?" She dropped onto the couch, pulled out her phone and texted Sherry Anne:

*Ten to fifteen minutes late. Hope that's okay*

*No problem! I'll grab a table*

Ashton picked up her hand. "I'm not trying to dictate what you can and can't do, or who you can and can't be friends with. I'm simply asking you to be careful. You're the one who keeps insisting someone was hiding under Blake's balcony, calling your name. You even suggested we get a security system."

"I do want one. In fact, I wish you weren't taking so long with the comparison shopping. But Sherry Anne is *not* Blake's trespasser. She's not like that."

"She approached you at a trailhead. How do we know she didn't follow you?"

"Sherry Anne wouldn't do that."

"How do you know?"

"I just do. I can tell she's a good person. I feel it in my gut, and I've got good instincts about people. But it's also based on what she told me about Philip. She knew that his favorite book was *The Sun Also Rises*. How would she if she wasn't telling the truth?"

"Anyone could find out something like that by checking his social media pages," Blake put in.

Blake would know, since he'd claimed to be a Hemingway fan in order to win Melanie's heart. "To what end? What possible reason would Sherry Anne have for pretending to be my brother's friend?"

"To what end would someone hide in the shadows and call out your name? If you text her and ask her to come *here* for coffee, then Blake and I can meet her and ask a few questions," Ashton said.

The stabbing pain was getting worse, and her mind was made up. "No."

"Why not?"

"Because you're making a huge deal out of nothing, and I'm not sure why. You were hardly even worried about the balcony incident, but now you suddenly think Sherry Anne is some kind of criminal or spy or heaven knows what."

"Maybe her name's not really Sherry Anne," Ashton said. "You could ask to see her driver's license. It's not an unreasonable request since she approached you out of the blue."

"Take a selfie with her," Blake suggested.

She had hoped to get a selfie, but now there was no way she would do that. She didn't want the men uploading the picture into a facial recognition software program. These two were acting paranoid, and she wasn't going to allow them to invade Sherry Anne's privacy or ruin their fun.

Rosalyn pushed off the couch. "Thank you for loving me and watching out for me. I've got location services on my phone turned on. I'll text you when I get to the coffee shop and again before I leave. But let's get this straight, I'm not going to grill Sherry Anne and report back to you. I won't do that to Philip's friend."

\* \* \*

Blake grabbed a beer and sprawled on the couch in Ashton's family room, waiting for the sound of Rosalyn's car pulling out of the drive. He didn't want her coming back inside for forgotten keys and busting in on their conversation.

Ashton stood, arms folded across his chest, staring past him.

Blake had started the day looking forward to spending it in front of the tube, but that had changed now. Golf was officially the last thing on his mind.

He heard the car door slam. An engine whirring.

"She's gone," Ashton said.

"You need to take it down a notch." Blake sipped his beer. "What the hell was that about?"

"Protecting my wife."

"From what?"

"Don't you see? Someone was skulking around under your balcony. Rosalyn is sure of it, and if she's sure, then I'm sure, too. Then, a total stranger approaches her in a parking lot claiming to be a friend of Philip's—a *very tall* friend of Philip's."

Blake had wondered, after the balcony incident, if Lola might be back. He'd kept his concern to himself, hoping Ashton wouldn't go there in his head. But the minute Rosalyn mentioned her new friend's height, he'd suspected Sherry Anne was really Lola, and Ashton had obviously reached the same conclusion. "I'm not saying it hasn't crossed my mind that Lola could be up to her old tricks, but we don't know that for sure."

"This is all highly suspect," Ashton said.

"I agree. But before we run amok, we need to find out if Sherry Anne is or is not Lola."

"How are we going to do that? Ros refused to invite her here, and she won't take a selfie."

"She's meeting her at Gourmet Grinds. Let's go hang outside the coffee shop, discreetly of course, and wait for Rosalyn and 'Sherry Anne' to come out. Then we'll know whether she's really an old friend of Philip's or an old friend of *ours*. You came on way too strong in there, buddy. Keep it up and Rosalyn will figure out you're hiding something."

# SIXTEEN

## THEN

Last month, I deposited a cashier's check for twenty-five thousand dollars into our bank account.

He made good on his promise.

He got the car from Lola and sold it the very next day on Craig's list.

We split the money like we agreed, and then we wished each other well. He enrolled as a freshman at the university, applied for a bunch of financial aid and moved into the dorm. He's an undeclared major but he's leaning toward a business degree. I'm not sure where I'll go or what my future holds. I'm not going to waste my time sitting in a classroom listening to some high and mighty professor who hasn't lived through anything and thinks he knows everything.

The *world* is my classroom.

I am going to miss him, though.

I don't like to think about waking up in the mornings and him not being there.

It's hard to explain what he means to me. I don't *need* him to get by. I'm the one who showed him the ropes, not the other way around.

And I don't *love* him.

At least I don't think I do. I researched the term "love", because I want to understand what everyone else is always talking about. From what I can tell, other people seem to crave love the way I crave money. I read that if you love someone, you care more about them than yourself, and I just can't wrap my head around that.

I crave money because it means security for *me*—Zoe.

It means I'll always have a place to live and enough to eat, and if, heaven forbid, I ever have a kid, she won't wake up next to Mommy's corpse because I can't handle the cards life dealt me.

I know how to stack the deck.

I control my own destiny.

I don't feel guilty for what I've done, or for what I will do in the future to survive, and that makes me powerful—Zoe Wessex takes from others... she does not allow others to take from her.

*Lola* has made a big mistake trying to take him away from me.

Even after he dumped her, even after he scammed her out of her car, she keeps chasing him. Lola says she's "in love" with him, and that makes her stupid.

It also makes her my enemy.

I'm leaving him of my own free will, but I will not allow anyone else to claim him.

He is *mine.*

I can hardly believe he wants to keep Lola.

"Why not?" he said. "If she's willing to forgive me? I told her I sold the car and spent the money on tuition and she wasn't exactly cool with it but she said she understood why I did what I did and she forgave me. I'm going legit, and unless you're going to stick around, Zoe, I don't see the problem."

*The problem is you belong to me.*

*Stupid boy.*

*Stupid Lola.*

She's on her way to meet him now.

I bet she thinks she can cast a spell on him like she's probably done to plenty of other unsuspecting men.

He thinks she's a *victim*. He feels sorry for her. He "likes" her.

But she can't fool me.

I see right through her.

Lola is not the victim in this scenario, and she's far from innocent.

# SEVENTEEN

## NOW

With a mocha mint Frappuccino freezing the palm of one hand, and a cell phone warming the other, Rosalyn stood, back against the wall, in the coffee shop. Her gaze boomeranged between the doorway and the tables and then back to the doorway. Knowing how crowded coffee joints, or any kind of eatery near the university got, she'd planned to arrive early, but Ashton and Blake had thrown a monkey wrench into that plan with all their questions.

Since she'd been late, she'd fully expected Sherry Anne to beat her here, but she didn't see her anywhere.

Every table was occupied. Some by placeholders—books, sweaters, backpacks—and others by actual humans—spiky-haired tattooed students, preppy blondes with Brazilian blow-outs and designer bags, and one violet-haired senior citizen clacking her bright-red fingernails against a faux-marble table-top. All of them had one thing in common: they were not Sherry Anne.

*She stood me up.*

Or maybe she'd decided not to wait. Since their initial encounter at the trailhead, they'd texted several times and had eventually set the inaugural meeting of their informal book club for this morning at 10 a.m. It was now pushing eleven, and Rosalyn still hadn't managed to secure seating.

At first, she'd deferred to others because Sherry Anne had yet to arrive, and it felt wrong to occupy a spot meant for two for very long. Then, she'd tried to settle her nerves by browsing the magazine rack, and finally, once she'd deemed it time to make a real bid for a seat, she'd been bested by more aggressive table watchers.

Her head was beginning to ache from the constant din of clanking utensils and buzzing voices. She inhaled deeply, taking in the shop's rich aroma.

*Five more minutes and then try texting her again.*

By now, some people might have sent a *where-are-you* inquiry, but the last thing Rosalyn wanted to do was scare off Sherry Anne. Especially since they'd already confirmed that it was okay for *Rosalyn* to be late. Either she was coming or she wasn't. If she didn't show, Ros would extend a no-pressure offer of a rain check.

Her phone buzzed in her hand, and she popped open her eyes.

Sherry Anne: *I'm outside*

Rosalyn: *Hooray! I don't know how I missed you*

Sherry Anne: *Grabbed us a table already*

*Outside?* Rosalyn hadn't thought to check the outdoor patio —it might be only mid-morning, but it was already over 90 degrees.

Sherry Anne: *Suck it up*

And then:

*Underneath spray misters*

"Pardon me. Pardon me." Rosalyn made it through the crowd and out the side entrance. She stepped onto the patio, squinting against the bright sunlight, and grinned.

A woman in a big-brimmed straw hat was waving like mad.

Rosalyn strolled casually over, but, truly, she felt like running. "How long have you been here?"

"I was late, too. I've been here about half an hour."

"We must've just missed crossing paths. How can you stand it out here?"

Sherry Anne pulled off her hat. "Sit. The misters and the fan are blowing right on us. I'm practically shivering."

"Really?"

"No! But I promise the heat is manageable, and it's way too noisy inside. I want to be able to hear you."

For the first time, Rosalyn noticed a delicate wire curling behind Sherry Anne's ear. She was wearing a hearing aid. Ros was naturally curious about that, but no way would she interrogate Sherry Anne. She took a seat across the table. "*And* there's an awning. I shouldn't have complained."

"Complain away. I'd prefer the indoor air conditioning, too, but there's nobody else around out here, and I'm hard of hearing."

"Oh?" Rosalyn sipped her Frappuccino, noticing an empty cup in front of Sherry Anne, along with the book they were meant to discuss opened face-down on the table.

"I lost my hearing in my right ear when I was eighteen."

She took another sip, and smiled. Should she ask more? She didn't want to appear nosy, but she also didn't want to seem disinterested, and Sherry Anne had brought the subject up.

"Was it an illness?" She'd heard meningitis could cause deafness.

"Someone beat me up," Sherry Anne said.

Rosalyn swallowed a giant freezing gulp of Frappuccino, sending her throat into spasms and forestalling her ability to express her shock and sympathy.

"I almost died, but, as you can see, I'm fine now—except for my hearing, and I lost some teeth, but you can't even tell thanks to my dental implants. My nose is crooked, but only a little, and I think that gives my face character. The real problem was heat stroke. The dude left me in the desert to die, but I got lucky and lived."

Sherry Anne's lack of inflection surprised Rosalyn, whose throat was clenching so tightly she could barely breathe. But the trauma had happened in the distant past, and she supposed Sherry Anne would have found a way of coping by now.

"If it hadn't been for a shaman wandering around looking to connect with the spirits, I'd have died out there. But he found me and called for help. A shaman with a cell phone, imagine that—*and* he had reception. He said it was mother earth watching over me. I know it was really good cell towers, but I didn't argue with him."

"I'm so, so sorry," she finally managed to get the words out. "I appreciate you sharing that with me. I don't mean to pry, but I want you to know I care, and I'm listening if you want to talk more about this. If you don't mind my asking, what happened to the man who did this to you?"

Sherry Anne's eyes went hard. "Not a damn thing."

"I don't understand."

"Just the way it goes. I couldn't identify him, because I didn't see him. He came up behind me and, we think, chloroformed me in a parking lot. One minute I'm headed to meet my boyfriend, and the next, I'm on my back, gasping for air with some guy standing over me chanting prayers. Broken nose, broken jaw, broken ribs. I *know* who did this to me, but he has an alibi, and I have no evidence. I could never prove it. And even if I could, it's too late now."

"Are you sure? I don't mean to be gauche, but Philip left me quite a bit of money in a trust. You were his friend, and I know he'd want to help. I can't promise anything, but I'm willing to ask the trustee at the bank if I could pay for your attorney." As soon as the words were out, she regretted them. She had absolutely no idea of Sherry Anne's financial situation. Sherry Anne might have more money than her. "Sorry if that's presumptuous. I just want to be helpful."

"It's incredibly kind of you to offer. But I'm afraid hiring a lawyer wouldn't do any good. The statute of limitations has run out."

Learning that the man who did this to Sherry Anne had gotten away with it was almost as devastating as hearing about the act itself. Ros couldn't wrap her head around any of it. "There must be something you can do."

"There's not. Not unless I go vigilante on him." Sherry Anne leaned forward. "Believe me, I dream about kidnapping him and leaving him to die. But I didn't survive all that just to wind up going to prison for murdering the guy." She wrapped a hand around her empty coffee cup and crushed it. "I would only kill him if I knew I could get away with it."

Rosalyn shivered—in the 90 degree heat. "You don't mean that."

"If you say so."

"I don't know *what* to say, except, again, I'm so, so sorry."

"Let's not talk about it anymore. I didn't mean to freak you out. But I thought if we're going to be friends, it was something you needed to know about me. Friends should be able to share secrets."

"I'd like that, very much—us becoming real friends."

"That's my plan, if it's okay with you. But friendship is a

two-way street. I told you my secrets, and now I want to hear yours."

The door creaked and a couple wandered through, checked out the patio, shook their heads and headed back inside.

"I don't have any secrets. And, luckily, I've never experienced any violence, though I've had plenty of heartbreak." Sherry Anne was listening intently, and the intimate details she'd just told Rosalyn made her feel the need to share something personal, too. "My dad died from a heart attack when he was only forty. My mom was killed in a car accident about five years later, and then, of course, you know about Philip dying so young from cancer. We really thought he might beat it, but it wasn't in the stars. I won't lie to you, since you haven't lied to me. I've been really lonely since he died."

"But you have Ashton."

"I do. And he's a wonderful man."

"But?"

"He spends a lot of time away from home."

Sherry Anne grimaced. "I remember you saying so before. It must really bother you."

"It does, but he's getting better about that. And I don't want to be one of those people who can't stand on their own two feet. When Ashton's online business took off, he encouraged me to quit my retail job to pursue my dream of becoming a freelance journalist. I love the work, and I'm doing fairly well—I've sold a number of magazine articles. But since Philip died, I don't see much of my old friends. I've been spending a lot of time with my sister-in-law... my former sister-in-law. Philip's widow has remarried."

"Oh?"

"Recently. Anyway, it'll be good for me to have a new friend of my own. I'm afraid when Philip got sick, I started spending less and less time with people outside the immediate family, and since he died, I've been so busy with Melanie, I never reconnected."

"Having a new friend will be good for *both* of us. I'd love to hear how you and Ashton met. I adore a cute meet story."

"Oh, it wasn't cute. In fact, when you said you were abandoned in the desert, I didn't want to say 'I know how you feel', because I don't, but I did have a frightening experience of my own. As I said, it doesn't compare to yours, but it's how I met my husband."

"Really?"

"My car broke down on a desert highway near Wikieup."

"The desert is a force of its own, isn't it?"

"It is."

"So, what happened?"

"Ashton rescued me. He was traveling back from a gambling trip. It was his twenty-first birthday so—"

"He celebrated in Vegas."

"Cliché, I know. But lucky for me. I was stuck on the side of the road with no cell service, and I was terrified. I didn't want to rely on a stranger, and Ashton was driving an old clunker. I wasn't sure whether to get in the car with him or not. But he sensed my anxiety and offered to leave me a bunch of water bottles and go for help. I stayed in my car with my doors locked, and an hour later he came back with the highway patrol. He showed them exactly where I was—he wanted to make sure they found me before he headed back to Tucson."

"And then Ashton asked for your number?"

"I asked for his. I wanted to meet up with him later to thank him. So, I did. Philip was uncomfortable with me meeting him alone, so he hosted a dinner at his house for me and my hero. Ashton and I didn't have an instant connection, but over time, it grew into what we have today."

Sherry Anne tilted her head. "And what is that you two have today?"

"Our marriage, of course. Our unconditional love for one another."

"You believe in loving unconditionally? No requirements, like say, being reliable, being around when you need him."

"Ashton is there for me when it counts. I mean that's how we met—he helped me when my car broke down, and he'd do that for anyone. He's very responsible, and he has a generous heart. I didn't mean to give you the wrong impression about him."

"You were being honest. Anyway, I can't have an opinion of Ashton since I don't know him. But I like the idea of you expanding your world. I bet Philip would approve of us becoming friends."

"I know he would. I feel it in my bones. Are we going to do this again? Can we make our book club official? Say, twice a month?"

"How about once a week?"

"That's great by me."

"And I'm sorry about missing you earlier. I should have come inside to look for you."

"I should have come outside to look for *you*." Rosalyn lifted one shoulder. "I feel bad. I thought you'd stood me up, and the whole time you were melting in the heat, waiting for me."

"We were both foolish. But... I just want to say one more thing before we get into book talk: you can't tell anyone what I just shared with you. Not many people know about what happened to me when I was younger—I can't stand to be pitied. I only told you because I'm hoping we can confide in each other. I tell you my secrets. You tell me yours. That's how great friendships develop, and someone had to go first."

"Like I said, I don't really have any secrets to share. But I give you my word I won't tell anyone yours."

"Not even your husband." Sherry Anne arched an eyebrow.

"I promise." She almost crossed her heart, she felt so privileged that Sherry Anne had confided in her. "That was a terrible trauma, and I completely understand how personal it is."

"Thank you." Sherry Anne's hunched shoulders relaxed. "I want to be clear on one other point: I will never leave you hanging, Rosalyn. If I can't make it to book club, I'll text you. I won't leave you waiting and wondering what happened to me. I give you my word on that."

# EIGHTEEN

## THEN

As she hurries through the parking lot, her long hair bounces from side to side, shimmering in the morning sun. Following ten paces behind her, I notice the seductive swing of her hips, the tan lines popping in and out of view as her shirt slides off her shoulder, and she tugs it back into place. A woman doesn't walk like *that*, she doesn't put on a strapless bra, unless she's looking for a certain something. These small details reveal everything I need to know about her, but I'm not relying solely on them. Before making a final decision, I did my homework.

For months, I've watched her in action.

The way she tosses her hair when she laughs.

The way she crosses and uncrosses her legs, inviting hungry eyes.

This morning, her chosen skirt is short, made from soft, stretchy red fabric that shows off the perfect curve of her backside.

She's putting on quite a show. "Look at me. Look at me. I'm yours for the taking."

I move in close, sniff the cloying scent of her perfume, then tug on my gloves.

*Be careful what you wish for.*

# NINETEEN

## NOW

Melanie's eyes popped open, mid-slumber. She lay alone in the bed that had once been hers and Philip's. Now it was Blake who slept beside her. How she wished they'd gotten a bed of their own. Some nights when Blake held her, kissed her, touched her intimately, he'd whisper questions in her ear: *Did Philip touch you like this? Do you wish it was him in this bed with you instead of me? Are you sorry you married me?*

She bolted upright and reached for the bedside lamp. Its soft, yellow light, sweeping across her satin comforter, turned its pale blue to grass green and, for an instant, she imagined she was in a spring meadow. That was her sleep-fogged brain, still reaching for a dream. She stretched her arms overhead, then lowered them and hugged her body.

*Did* she regret marrying Blake?

She shook her head. That was a question better left uncontemplated. Perhaps, remarrying so soon after Philip died had been a mistake. It seemed to have upset Rosalyn, despite her protests to the contrary. But Blake was her husband, and Rosalyn should accept it, because Philip had wanted her to be happy. It bothered her that, on their hike, Rosalyn had implied she could still undo her marriage to Blake.

It wasn't Rosalyn's place.

She threw her legs over the side of her bed, and then padded across the soft, shaggy rug to the small antique writing desk carved from walnut. She grasped the golden handle and pulled out the drawer that contained her pens and the monogrammed stationery Philip had given her one Christmas. With her index finger, she traced her initials embossed at the top.

*MM* for Melanie Monroe.

*You're Melanie Tyler now.*

With pen poised above the paper, she hesitated. She mustn't let Blake discover her writing letters to her dead husband.

*Where is Blake?*

She touched the tip of the pen to paper and drew a little squiggle to get the ink flowing. Then, she crumpled the paper and tossed it into the small gilded waste basket beside the desk, started again with a fresh, perfect sheet, unmarred by the scratching of a dull pen.

*My darling Philip,*

*Tonight, I am physically alone, and yet I feel your spirit with me. I lean on you, too much, I think, but in life, your strong shoulders always buoyed me, your gentle embrace comforted me in times of sorrow.*

*I know Blake and I can never have the kind of love you and I shared. That's once in a lifetime, and no matter how my heart aches from losing you, I can never regret what we had.*

*But I confess I'm a selfish woman. I want to laugh and smile, and yes, to forget for a while that I can never jump up to hug you when you walk through a door. That I can never kiss* your hand when it reaches for mine. That we will never have children...

I must stop these thoughts or they will drive me mad. I've made my bed, and now I must make things work. I love him, darling Philip. I do. Not in the same way I loved you but still, it is a real love, and we have so many obstacles in our path. Not the least of which is my comparing him in my mind to you.

He's not perfect. But I remind myself, neither am I. What must it be like for Blake, knowing he will never live up to my first husband? If he's jealous at times, he has good reason. I wouldn't want to live in the shadow of his first, true love.

In fact, I know I could not.

But my love for you is not our only problem. Rosalyn is as devoted to you in death as she was in life, and she has taken, quite seriously, the promise you exacted from her before your death, to watch over me.

She sees Blake's imperfections, as he hides nothing from anyone, and she worries for me. I don't know how to make her understand that the little digs she makes about Blake only make things worse for me.

Imagine if I enumerated Ashton's flaws to her?

I love your sister with all my heart, not least because every time I look at her face, I am reminded of you. But recently, I find myself walking on eggshells around her. Part of me wants to shake her. To tell her to mind her own marriage and stay out of mine, but I know that would only drive her away.

What shall I do?

If you were here, I would sit with you and you would advise me.

You'd say, "Leave it to me, I'll talk to her."

And she would listen. You'd tell her to breathe. To soak up the sunshine. To stop worrying about Blake Tyler. But if I say such things, will she hear me?

*I fear not.*

*I fear it would only widen the growing gulf between us, and I simply cannot bear to lose Rosalyn, too.*

*I hear a car in the drive. I don't dare let Blake catch me at this.*

*Philip, Philip, how I love you!*

Melanie quickly folded the stationery and slipped it inside an envelope. Then she sealed it with a kiss, and the moisturizer she wore on her lips left a faint outline on the envelope. She had just enough time to slide it back into the drawer, crawl back into bed and turn off the light before Blake staggered into the bedroom.

A click sounded as he switched on the overhead light.

Looming at the threshold, he frowned. "What were you up to in here?"

"Sleeping, darling."

"Then why was the light on?"

He'd been drinking. She could smell the booze on his breath when he climbed into bed beside her and reached for her hand. "All right, you've caught me. I couldn't sleep because I was worried about you. It's almost three o'clock. Where have you been?"

"At a bar."

At least he wasn't hiding it from her. "With Ashton? Hasn't he caught on that you're a married man, now?"

He tugged her closer. "Don't doubt my love for you."

"I never will."

He smelled like a tequila factory, but his speech was crisp. She narrowed her eyes at him, trying to discern how drunk, if at all, he really was. "Did you go somewhere else? After the bar? Was it only you and Ashton or—"

He touched his index finger to her lips. "Shh."

His pupils were dark and so large only a faint ring of blue

showed around them. His breathing was ragged as he pressed the length of his body against her. "Too many questions, my love. Sometimes I wonder if you trust me at all."

"I trust you. I wouldn't have married you if I didn't."

"Not the most romantic declaration I've ever heard, but I'll take it."

She sighed. If eloping with Blake hadn't reassured him, she didn't know what would. He'd always been insecure about her relationship with Philip—and now that she was *his* wife, somehow, he'd become more possessive and jealous than ever, and it was threatening to ruin everything. That electric frisson of sexual energy between them, the thing that so captivated her, and made her forget her problems whenever she was with him, was still there. In this moment, this quickly, her body was ready for him, aching for him to claim her. But in her head...

"I want to leave the lights on so I can see your face." He kissed his way down the side of her neck, and tugged the lace of her nightgown down to reveal her breasts. "Don't think about Philip."

"I promise," she managed to whisper, as her body arched into his caress.

"Was he a better lover than I am?" He pinned her arms over her head, and the look in his eyes was like none she'd ever seen before.

# TWENTY

## NOW

The instant Rosalyn dropped her overnight bag in the foyer of Blake and Melanie's home, Melanie dashed into her open arms.

Ashton and Blake had gone golfing in Casa Grande, and rather than make the 45-mile drive home and then back again the next day, they'd booked a hotel near the course. It made sense, given the early tee times, but if Rosalyn had been disappointed with the situation before, she was doubly so now.

To her way of thinking, Blake should be home with his new bride.

Mel had only recently regained her emotional footing, and you'd think Blake wouldn't want to leave her on her own. If she'd had any doubt about how vulnerable Melanie still was, the phone call she'd gotten from her, half an hour ago, erased it.

During that call Mel had cried and rambled, almost incoherently, about hearing strange noises. She'd seemed terribly frightened and had begged Rosalyn to come over.

"Shh." Rosalyn wrapped Melanie's clinging body tightly. "I'm here. You're okay. Everything's going to be fine."

"Oh, Ros." Melanie sniffled. "I'm so sorry for dragging you over here this late at night."

"Don't be. It's barely ten o'clock." Rosalyn patted her on the back and then eased out of her grasp. "We're family, and that means you can call me anytime."

"I worried you'd be angry with me."

"Why? I'm looking forward to our little slumber party—with Ashton and Blake away again, I'm feeling a bit forlorn myself."

Melanie's lip quivered. "I shouldn't be such a baby, but that's not what I mean."

"Then what?"

"Never mind. I really shouldn't say anything more."

"Stop worrying about me. I'm not sure what you're talking about, but you don't owe me any apologies."

Mel cupped her hand around her mouth and whispered, "I'm saying I'm sorry I eloped with Blake. We should have had a long engagement like we planned. I feel terrible that I didn't tell you ahead of time. I'm sorry, sorry, sorry. We should never have married so soon."

With her mouth covered, Mel's words were hard to understand. Ros wasn't sure she'd heard her right. "You're sorry you married Blake?"

Melanie smiled a forced wooden smile. Then she answered, rather loudly, "Oh, no. You've misunderstood! I'm sorry you couldn't be at the wedding. Blake and I both wish you and Ashton had been there. It was such a beautiful ceremony!"

Ros frowned. Something was off, and now that she'd had a moment to process, she realized what was going on. Mel probably felt guilty for moving on with her life, and she was worried Ros was angry with her for remarrying so soon after Philip died. "Philip's been gone more than a year. And we've talked about this. He *wanted* you to find someone. I wanted that for you, too. To be crystal clear, I'm not mad. I want you to be happy." She reached for her shoulders and gave her a mock shake. "Swear you believe me."

Melanie wiped her eyes on her sleeve. Such a pretty blouse —bright white, stamped with violets and vines, and at the cuffs, a hint of lace. "I do."

"Good. Now, do you want me to die of curiosity or are you going to tell me about these noises that've got you so spooked? Maybe offer me a glass of wine to go with the charcuterie tray I brought."

Mel's soggy face opened up into a genuine smile. "You've got a charcuterie tray in your overnight bag?"

"Half-eaten. Ashton planned a romantic tête-à-tête—a picnic on the kitchen floor last night. I think he feels guilty about another boys' trip. Frankly, I'm surprised Blake would leave you so soon after the wedding."

Mel glanced away. "Let's uncork that wine. I can't have you dying of curiosity."

Rosalyn retrieved the tray from her bag, and then followed Mel into the kitchen, and set it on the table. She'd imprisoned it in many, many layers of Saran Wrap to keep it from spilling onto her pajamas on the way over. "Got a buzz saw handy?"

"Leave it to me." Using a paring knife, Melanie expertly sliced into the layers of plastic and laid them open to reveal a smashed but delicious-looking mess of cheeses, olives, and meats. Then she poured the wine and set the kitchen table with napkins, utensils and two salad plates. "We can have our own picnic without the men, but I'm not sitting on the floor—especially not now."

"Any excuse not to sit on the floor works for me, but I don't get the connection. Why *not now*?"

"I told you on the phone, I heard noises."

Melanie hadn't made a lot of sense on the phone, she'd been frightened, and her words garbled. Now she was finally calm. Rosalyn took a breath, waiting for her to fully explain.

"I heard a noise in the bathroom, and it sounded like it was coming from *under the floorboards*."

"Ah ha. You think there's a troll living in the basement—but you haven't got a basement, have you? On the phone, I thought you were referring to noises outside the house."

"I wish it had been outdoors. We had security cameras installed on every corner of the roof right after Blake moved in with me."

Blake had a change of heart after Rosalyn and Ashton revisited the balcony incident with him and made it clear Rosalyn was certain someone had been hiding in the shadows. Whether it was because she'd convinced him, or because he wanted Melanie to feel safe, she wasn't sure. And it didn't matter. The important thing was Blake and Melanie had a robust security system at their marital home—Rosalyn and Ashton would have one, soon, too, but it had yet to be installed. Anyway, it seemed unlikely someone could get through Blake and Melanie's defenses as long as... "Did you set the alarm?"

"No." Mel flushed and picked up her phone, swiped and typed and then looked up. "There. The alarm's on, now, so don't open any outside doors."

"No problem. I'm in for the duration." It seemed pretty quiet. "When was the last time you heard that noise?"

Melanie puckered her lips and talked around a mouthful of cracker. "I haven't been back in my bedroom since. I was too scared. I heard knocking in the walls too. And buzzing."

"House noises?"

"I know, in my head, that I'm being ridiculous. I'm a cartoon character, a skittish woman, but my heart was pounding so hard, and I had this awful feeling like I was about to die. My hands were shaking. I could barely breathe."

"That sounds like a panic attack. Is this the first time something like this has happened?"

"I had a couple of panic attacks right after Philip died, but none since. I still have some tranquilizers from back then, but they're expired."

"You should throw those out."

"I should have. But I didn't."

"You took one?"

Mel nodded. "I shouldn't be drinking on top of that—but just one chardonnay can't hurt."

Rosalyn frowned at Melanie's glass, already emptied. At least she'd had some food with it. "Let's do a walk-through. We can clear the house like cops do, and then we can sit around and chat or watch TV, whatever you want until you feel relaxed enough to sleep."

"I'm suddenly feeling very brave. Let's start with the downstairs bathroom."

After a thorough search of the house, Rosalyn settled down on the couch with Mel. "Chat or binge watch?"

"Oh, I don't feel like binging my crime shows at the moment."

"We could find a romantic comedy."

"No, thanks." She yawned. "I can't thank you enough for dropping everything and rushing to my rescue tonight."

"I dropped nothing. I was moping around, wishing Ashton would call." In truth, she'd just picked up a book. It was one she'd promised to read before her next book club with Sherry Anne, but she wasn't going to have Mel thinking she'd imposed. She could tell by the look on her face she was still embarrassed to have let house noises throw her into a panic.

"I'm expecting a call from Blake any minute." Mel's eyes darted around the room, as if someone might overhear their conversation.

Rosalyn cocked her head. "Mel, you and Blake didn't install *indoor* cameras, did you?"

"Blake's hidden a few around."

"Hidden them from *you*?"

"Of course not. From *the public*. He says they're not much use if the people you're observing know they're being watched."

"But *you* know where they are."

"I think so." Mel straightened her back. "Ros... I didn't want to mention this when you first got here, but I don't need you to stay the night. I assume, since you brought that bag with you, you misinterpreted my request on the phone."

The conversation had suddenly turned formal.

Rosalyn reached for Mel's hand. "Are you okay? You sound nervous."

"But I'm not a bit nervous. Not anymore."

"Your voice is all wobbly."

"I'm tired, and I'd like to go to sleep. The pill and the wine, you know."

"Sleep sounds like a good idea." Mel had been so anxious for her to come over, she'd assumed she wanted her to stay the night, but maybe Mel now worried she was asking too much of Ros. "I wasn't kidding when I said I was looking forward to our slumber party. With Ashton gone, it's lonely at my place."

"You're just being polite." Mel shook her head, and the look in her eyes seemed even more skittish than when Rosalyn had first arrived. "I-I can't ask you to stay."

"Why not?"

"Because..." she lowered her voice and looked down at her wringing hands, "Blake wouldn't like it. He's a very private person, and I don't think he'd want me to have a guest when he wasn't around."

"I'm not a guest. I'm family."

"I-I don't want to hurt your feelings or seem ungrateful. But you should know that Blake decided to put up all these cameras at our house, outside and indoors, too, on the day we got back from our honeymoon."

"Because we told him we thought someone was sneaking around his house. Why are we whispering?"

"That's not the only reason. Blake was furious that Ashton let you into his house to make that surprise bed of roses for us.

He said he gave Ashton the key for emergencies, and he didn't want anyone invading his privacy. He had the locks changed on the doors, here, at this house, even though I told him I'd never even given you a key." Mel's hands were shaking.

"I understand completely." *That your husband's an ass.* "What if you pack a bag and we'll move this party to my house?"

"I can't. Blake wouldn't like it."

"We don't have to tell him. In fact, we don't have to mention I was here tonight at all. You can just delete the camera footage."

Mel shook her head. "Too late."

*What?*

She raised the volume of her voice. "I'd offer you another glass of wine, but since you're driving home soon, how about a water instead?" Mel pasted a horrible, fake smile on her face and set her phone down on the couch between them, inclining her head as if she wanted Rosalyn to see the text message from Blake that was flashing on the screen.

*Darling, you look so pretty in white*

# TWENTY-ONE

## NOW

After disarming the security system, Melanie slammed the front door, leaving Rosalyn standing on the porch with an overnight bag in hand and too much left unsaid. From Blake's creepy text, it was apparent to Ros that he'd been live-streaming them. She was shifting from one foot to another, debating whether or not to ring the doorbell and insist that Melanie let her back inside to talk, when a sudden wind whipped across her bare arms. An instant later, torrents of hot rain drenched her hair and her clothes.

*Dammit.*

She wheeled around and hurried down the steps, then trotted for the safety of her Jeep Cherokee. Mother Nature had sent her a clear signal:

*Time to start minding your own business.*

*You shouldn't have interfered in Melanie's life.*

*You shouldn't have set her up with Blake.*

But, didn't that make her even more responsible?

Despite the heat, the wind chilled her wet skin. She dove into her car and locked the doors.

"Hey, Siri, call Ashton."

As she fired on the ignition and pulled away from the curb, her phone automatically switched to Bluetooth.

"Calling Ashton."

Gripping the wheel with both hands, she peered through the rapidly swishing windshield wipers.

"Hey there, beautiful."

*Thank goodness.* "You picked up."

"I always do. Everything okay?"

"Yes. No. Maybe. I'm on the road. It's pouring buckets, and the visibility is poor, but there's no traffic, so I should be fine."

"What are you doing out in the weather at night? Be careful driving—I can call you back later so you can focus on the road."

"No, please. I need to hear your voice. Like I said, traffic's light. I'm just heading home from Mel's. I was planning to stay the night but she got weird on me and basically kicked me out."

Silence.

*Oh damn.* "Is Blake with you?"

"Yeah. We're playing poker in his hotel room with two guys we met on the greens. But I can step outside."

"Don't bother. I'll call you in the morning." She couldn't speak freely with Blake standing right there. And if Ashton left the room, Blake would want to know, later, about the conversation.

"Is something the matter with Melanie?" Blake's voice boomed out.

*That's just great.* She'd been on speakerphone this whole time.

"She's fine." Blake had been watching them on the security cameras, and eavesdropping on her conversation with Ashton, so there was no point in denying she'd been visiting Mel. But the less said the better. "I got lonely without Ashton, so I thought I'd stop by. And we heard some funky noises, but they turned out to be nothing. Just the usual house creakings and groanings."

"What did you mean when you said that Melanie *got weird* on you?" Blake asked.

"No, no. I said she got *tired*. Me too, actually. The weather's pretty rough so I'm going to hang up."

"Text when you get home, so I know you're safe," Ashton said. "Love you."

"Will do. Love you more."

Once home, she texted Ashton, and then stripped out of her wet clothes in the garage. The night was warm, and they'd recently updated the house with wood flooring—she didn't want to drip all over it, so she wrapped her clothing into a bundle and laid it on top of Ashton's tool chest. Tomorrow would be soon enough to deal with the laundry.

Inside, she turned the air to a comfy seventy-four degrees, rubbed her bare arms, and headed for the kitchen. It had been a long time since she'd walked around naked in the house. In fact, she didn't remember ever doing so. She eyed an open bottle of chardonnay on the counter and shrugged.

*Why the hell not?*

She poured a glass, then scrunched a clean dish towel through her damp hair.

Wishing she hadn't left her charcuterie board with Mel, she opened the fridge, and settled for a vanilla yogurt. After peeling the lid off, she licked the top, tossed it into the trash, and sighed.

The feeling of doom that had descended upon her was lifting. It might be her lack of clothing or being completely alone in her own home with no one there to judge her, but regardless of the reason, she felt suddenly free, and in a much better state of mind. Her head soon cleared, and she realized she was worried about Mel and irritated with her at the same time.

Mel had sent out a distress signal, and Rosalyn had responded with love.

She'd packed a bag and raced to the rescue and even supplied hors d'oeuvres, only to be tossed out on her ear because *Blake* didn't like the idea of her *invading his privacy*. If not for the guilty knowledge that she had, in fact, snooped through his things the day she'd laid out the bed of roses for the "happy couple", she would be plain furious.

Hard to believe that only a few weeks ago she'd been rooting for them.

She slugged back her wine and poured another.

Blake was Ashton's best friend. Ashton loved Blake like a brother, and that meant, automatically, that Blake was a good guy.

Unless it didn't.

She trusted Ashton implicitly, but were his friends to be trusted by proxy, even when their behavior seemed sketchy?

She paced the perimeter of her kitchen, cleaning up as she went. Clearing the table, putting away the salt and pepper shakers, dusting off the chairs with a broad swipe of a damp dish towel. All the while making a list of Blake's offenses in her head.

*Pushing Mel into an elopement*—to be fair, Mel hadn't ever said she'd felt pressured. It was possible she'd been in as big a hurry as Blake, but even if that were true, she'd been vulnerable and Blake had taken advantage.

*Pretending to be someone he was not. All that nonsense about loving Hemingway and classical music*—clearly a ruse to win Mel's heart. Even if Ashton had encouraged him to some extent, she'd been clear with Blake she wouldn't help him connect with Mel if he wasn't authentic. He'd *promised* to jettison the Ashton Method.

*Getting angry when Mel talked about Philip*—in Rosalyn's mind this was possibly Blake's worst offense, or at least tied with the next one on the list.

*Spying on his own wife*—Mel would probably say she didn't mind, or that it was a sign of his protectiveness and love, but it was apparent the security cameras intimidated her. Still, Blake had beefed up his home security only *after* Rosalyn had voiced concerns about a possible trespasser—and after she'd entered his domain without permission.

So, what did it all add up to?

Red flags were waving, but there was no smoking gun.

She spit chardonnay out of her mouth. "I'm freakin' worried he's married her for Philip's money!"

Until this moment, she hadn't realized or admitted that, even to herself, because *she* was the one who'd arranged their first lunch date. Blake's credibility rested on the fact that she'd vouched for him, and she'd vouched for him because Ashton had.

"I wish I had a time machine. I'd warn Melanie that Blake is a big phony and tell her to stay away from him." She crumpled into a chair, rested her head on the kitchen table, then closed her eyes...

At the sound of a crash, Rosalyn startled awake, then jumped up and moaned at the sight of her wine glass in pieces on the floor. She touched her Timex and brought it close to her face.

*3 a.m.*

She'd had too much wine and fallen asleep *naked* at her kitchen table. Rising from the chair, she considered leaving the mess until morning, but broken glass on the floor was in a much different category than dirty, wet clothes in the garage, so she took care of it right then and there.

Afterward, all she wanted to do was dive under the covers and sleep until noon, but...

*You need a bath!*

She'd been soaked to the bone by the rain, had cleaned up the kitchen in the nude, and judging by how sticky her hands and legs felt, at some point, she'd sloshed chardonnay all over herself. Adding to her discomfort, the air conditioning had switched back to its pre-programmed sleep temperature of seventy degrees.

She felt like a popsicle, but a hot bath and PJs would fix her right up.

Too bad she couldn't solve her other problems as easily.

After checking that the doors were locked, she switched off the lights and headed through her bedroom to the en suite bath, guided by the flashlight mode on her cell phone.

She pulled up short.

Was that scratching?

She whirled, trying to pinpoint the location of the noise, but the room had gone quiet. For a moment, she froze, the light from her phone vibrating in her trembling hand.

"Is someone there? Where are you?"

*Really, Ros?*

*If you have an intruder, should you politely inquire as to their whereabouts?*

She covered her laugh with one hand and flipped on the bedroom light, scanned the room, and discovered no one.

Next, she threw back the bedsheets.

*What did you expect?*

Dropping to her knees, she checked under the bed.

"Clear!" she called to herself, just like she'd done earlier when searching Mel's house.

*You're as bad as Melanie.*

But though she felt foolish about it, she had to own up to the fact that she was nervous, all alone in the house. The rapidity of her breathing, the ache in her jaw, the tightness in her gut told the tale. She needed a distraction to help her fall back to sleep... and the audiobook she was listening to in preparation for her next meeting with Sherry Anne would be just the ticket.

After putting in her earbuds and hitting play, she returned to the bath, set her phone on the countertop and switched on the light.

*Too bright!*

She dragged the dimmer to the lowest level, procured a

towel from the shelf and moved to the bath, reached for the faucet, and gingerly put one foot in the tub.

Something soft scampered over her foot and up her ankle.

Next came a quick, searing pain.

With a sharp cry, she jerked her leg out of the tub. She saw blood dripping down her ankle. Then, horrified, standing on one leg, like a paralyzed flamingo, she stared at not just one, but a good half-dozen *rats* scurrying around in the bottom of her bathtub.

# TWENTY-TWO

## NOW

Ashton tightened his grip on the wheel, steering them around a large rut on the dirt road. "Hope you like bumpy surprises."

"I love bumpy surprises." It was why she'd lobbied to get a four-wheel drive. Rosalyn reclined her seat back and maneuvered one sneakered foot onto the dashboard, firing a glance at the small wound on her ankle. "I also love the Grand Canyon."

With the jeep firmly under control, Ashton reached for her hand. "Can't sneak anything past you, I see."

She scoffed. It had been sweet of him to plan a surprise, but he'd instructed her to pack comfortable clothes suitable for layering, hiking boots, sunscreen, and a light jacket in case it got cool at night. Therefore, she'd easily guessed that this was going to be an outdoor-adventure destination in the higher elevations. For a few hours, she hadn't known where they were headed—except north. But once they'd passed Prescott, that narrowed it down. With Flagstaff in the rearview mirror, all signs pointed to the Grand Canyon. "There is one thing I haven't figured out."

"At *least*."

"I think we're going camping. But you didn't bring our tent or sleeping bags."

"Because we're not going camping."

"Then you better turn the car around because there aren't any motels out here."

"Stop being bossy. This is my surprise, and I'm in charge." He shot her a sideways smile. "Still feeling okay? You're not queasy or feverish?"

"That makes three times you've asked me in the last hour."

"And the answer?"

"Still fine."

"Did I mention I hate myself for not being there when the rats invaded?"

"Did I mention I'm not mad? There's absolutely no way you could've predicted our bathroom would turn into the set of a horror movie. We've never even seen rat droppings." She took a breath. "But I wouldn't mind having you around a little more. If I'm being honest, I had hoped that since Blake's a newlywed, you would've called off your golf weekend."

"We'd been planning it for six months. I already said I'm sorry I wasn't home. And quite frankly, given the amount of time you spend with Melanie—"

"That's not the same thing."

"Oh, but it is."

Ashton was getting defensive. Which was why she hesitated to complain about all the time he spent with Blake. At least the rats were buying them some alone time—they needed it. And although she didn't want to ruin a romantic trip, at some point she needed to get Ashton's take on what was going on between Blake and Melanie and share her concerns.

He reached for her knee. "Let's not argue. I'm super sorry, and I feel awful about this whole business. I wish I'd been the one who'd gotten bitten by rats. Are you sure you don't need a rabies shot?"

"The doctor said no." After she'd recovered from her fright, she'd called her doctor's answering service. His on-call nurse had called back right away and instructed her to wash the area with soap and water and put some antibiotic ointment on it. She was supposed to inspect the wound periodically for redness or other signs of infection. Rabies wasn't a concern, but "rat bite fever" was. Rat bite fever was easy to cure with antibiotics, but absent treatment, the sickness could be fatal.

When they'd decided to go out-of-town for Ashton's weekend surprise, Rosalyn had called her doctor again to get his blessing, which he'd given only after advising Ros to seek medical care right away for fever or other problems. As a precaution he'd prescribed amoxicillin. Rosalyn was only supposed to take it if she felt sick—which so far, she did not.

"You packed your pills?"

"I did." As worried as Ashton seemed, he'd planned an adventure that was taking them far from town, and therefore far from any urgent care centers. But they had to get out of their house. Ashton had ordered the installation of both an alarm system and a deluxe rodent package. The pest control people were, at this very moment, turning Chez Hightower into a veritable fortress—removing all the citrus trees from the backyard, fumigating, setting traps, and installing physical barriers around the house. Luckily, they didn't find rats inside anywhere except the bathroom. They'd obviously come up through the drain, but there was no evidence of rat damage in the crawl spaces beneath the floorboards—*so weird*.

But they weren't the only people with a rat problem. According to the pest people, due to all the citrus trees, there was an infestation in the area. And the noises Melanie heard had also turned out to be rats.

The same night Ros was bitten, Melanie had discovered a rat in her *bed*.

Luckily, she'd seen it in time and hadn't crawled in with it.

"Mel and Blake are staying at a four-star hotel while their place is being exorcised," Rosalyn teased.

"Would you rather? I can scrap the surprise and try to get a room at one of the hotels at the Grand Canyon, or we can turn back around and head for Flagstaff." Ashton's plaintive tone told her he would be gravely disappointed if she said yes.

"I'm only teasing. We haven't been camping in ages. I'm looking forward to a couple of nights off the grid with just you, me and the stars."

"Me too, but I told you we're not camping. We're almost there—cover your eyes for this part, okay?"

The scenery was so beautiful, the sky so blue, the trees so tall, she hated to miss even a moment of it, but she had the entire weekend to take in the glory of the high country. Dutifully, she covered her eyes. They continued to bump along, her teeth rattling as the road got rougher.

"How. Much. Longer?" The bumps punctuated her words.

At last, the jeep rattled to a stop.

The engine sputtered off. Ashton came around and opened her door for her, then helped her down.

"No peeking!"

"I swear I'm not."

With his hands on her shoulders, he guided her slowly. She could hear the sound of birds chattering. She tasted dust on her tongue, but the air was fresh and filled with the scent of pine and cedar and sunshine.

She sucked in a big, grateful breath. "I feel like the luckiest woman in the world right now."

"You're about to get luckier."

His sexy tone emphasized the double entendre, and she was glad of it. They hadn't been intimate in a while, and a bit of fun under the sheets might be just the jumpstart their marriage needed. "Impossible. I'm with the man I love in God's beautiful wilderness."

"I'm going to count to three."

Her fingers tingled in anticipation. She really didn't know

what to expect at this point, but Ashton's excitement was contagious. What more could there be?

"Three!"

"What happened to one and two?"

"I couldn't wait another second. Open your damn eyes!"

She stood there, eyes squeezed tight, a big grin stretching her cheeks. It was her turn to make him wait.

He squeezed her shoulders. Shook her gently.

"Okay. Okay." Her eyes fluttered open. She gasped, covered her mouth, and then tiptoed up to kiss her amazing husband.

After a long embrace, he said, "Did I do good?"

"So good."

About fifty feet ahead, a number of giant canvas domes encircled an outdoor area—a square covered with a bright-green awning and strung with fairy lights. Wooden tables and chairs were set up around a firepit. There were horse-shoe rings, bean-bag tosses, basketball hoops.

"I told you we weren't camping."

"We're *glamping*. Ashton, this was so thoughtful." It really showed how well he knew her, and how much he cared. Outdoor adventures had been a huge part of her family life before her parents died, and after Philip got sick, he was especially sad he could no longer go camping—sleeping on the ground would have been too painful. During his chemo, she'd read about this very place, and they'd pored over the brochures, planning, once he was through his treatment to take a family trip here. For Philip's sake, she blinked back her tears and vowed to make this the best weekend ever.

After checking in with the staff, Ashton led her by the hand to their own private "tent". The space was large—at least as big as a bedroom and living room combined, and furnished with a leather couch, chairs, a coffee table, and a wood-burning stove.

"We have our own front porch!"

But the pièce de resistance was a four-poster king-size

feather bed positioned beneath a stargazing window in the ceiling.

*Oh, yes.*

She was so ready to recharge their romance. Wasting no time, Ros crawled beneath the sheets, which smelled of lavender. "It's like a cloud."

Ashton climbed in bedside her and rolled onto his side, spooning her. "About what you said in the car..."

She snuggled her bottom into the warmth of his body. "Mm. Which part?"

"About Blake being a newlywed."

A twinge of annoyance rippled through her. She didn't want to talk about Blake in a romantic moment like this.

"I agree he should be spending more time with Melanie. And I should be spending more time with you."

She eased out of his arms and rolled to face him. Touched her forehead to his. "There's no *should* here. I want us to spend more time together because it's what we *want.*"

"I do want. I want *you.*" He dragged her hand down his body, letting her feel the proof of his declaration. Then his lips were on her neck. His hands beneath her blouse.

How she'd missed this. Missed *him.* "That feels *so* good."

She snaked her hand from his inner thigh to the snap on his jeans.

"Not so fast, sweetheart, I want to take our time, savor the—"

"Surprise!"

She rolled away and jerked her blouse down. Sat straight up on the bed.

"Sorry! We didn't mean to interrupt," Melanie said, but she didn't look a bit sorry. She was smiling.

In fact, she looked as happy as Rosalyn had seen her in months.

And that *almost* made up for the hurt she felt.

Had Ashton known they were coming?

*Please don't let that couch be a sofa bed.*

"This is your four-star hotel?" she asked, as cheerfully as she could manage.

"One of the top five hundred resorts on the planet, according to *Luxury Vacation Magazine*."

"You look underwhelmed." Blake smiled. "Don't worry, Ros. We're not bunking with you. But if you need anything, Mel and I will be right next door."

# TWENTY-THREE

## NOW

"Has everyone applied sunscreen? Pre-hydrated with Gatorade? Have you packed plenty of snacks and used the bathroom?" While they lingered at the head of the Bright Angel Trail, Melanie ran through her helicopter-mom list in a no-nonsense voice.

Blake grunted, pushed his sunglasses up and folded his arms across his chest.

Ashton saluted.

Rosalyn understood the men's impatience—she, too, was anxious to make her way into the canyon—but she also appreciated Mel's concern. Given what she'd been through, what she'd lost, her protectiveness was understandable. The switchbacks on the trail were steep and numerous, and the canyon's heat posed a real threat.

"Mules..." Mel started.

"Where?" Ashton did a three-sixty.

"Not now." Mel shook her head. "But there will be some on the trail. Does everyone know what to do if we encounter mules?"

Blake threw an arm around his wife and kissed the top of

her head. "Step aside and give them the right of way. Don't start back on the trail until the last mule is at least fifty feet ahead. This isn't anyone's first time to hike the canyon."

"Wrong. It's mine, and safety matters." She ducked out of his grasp and sent Rosalyn a stern look. "Are you *sure* you're up to this?"

"C'mon, Mel, I was bitten by a rat, not a lion."

"Did you do a temperature check before we left? I don't want to head into the canyon if there's any chance you might need medical attention. I did an internet search and it said rat bite fever can be fatal."

"No fever. No redness. I've got antibiotics in my daypack, just in case. Let's *go*."

Blake exchanged a look with Ashton, as if waiting for him to confer his blessing.

"Oh, good grief. It's my decision, not my husband's, and I feel perfectly fine. Not to mention I have more hiking experience than the three of you put together."

She had felt a little nauseous this morning, but that was normal. At an altitude of nearly 7,000 feet, it was common to feel headachy and queasy. Still, she'd hedged her bets by zipping her bottle of amoxicillin into her daypack. As Mel had just pointed out, safety matters. "We're turning around at the first rest house, so it'll only be three-miles round trip. Besides, the park rangers patrol all day. I'm every bit as safe here as I would've been if I'd stayed back at the tent—more so because we'll all be together."

A moment passed, but then Mel's shoulders dropped. "That's true. I'd much rather keep an eye on you."

"Come on," Blake started down the trail, calling back over his shoulder, "it's go-time."

The narrow trail meant they had to hike single file, and Rosalyn hung back letting Ashton and Mel go ahead of her.

If Mel felt protective of Rosalyn, the sentiment was mutual.

Ashton and Blake had cut their golf trip short and returned to Tucson the morning after the rat incident. Given Blake's all-present hovering, Rosalyn hadn't had a chance to check in with Mel. No matter how much she denied it, she could see she was cowed by her new husband.

The trail descended quickly into the Bright Angel fault, the switchbacks growing more numerous and narrower as they picked their way down the dusty path through sandstone cliffs. The men easily bested the women, and after an hour or so, they were no longer in sight—or within earshot. Rosalyn had hiked this popular trail many times and knew that, up ahead, it widened to reveal an even more magnificent view.

"I'm getting winded." Truly breathless, she called out to Mel, "Will you wait for me?"

Mel halted, whirled, and then jerked her phone out of her pocket. "You're not feeling well. We're turning around now. I'll call the guys."

"No, no, no. I just need some rest and some water. There's a spot up ahead." She reached Mel and touched her on the shoulder. "Let's see how I feel after a break."

Mel frowned at her phone. "I don't have service."

Rosalyn shrugged. "We're too far down. C'mon. There's the spot I'm talking about."

They'd reached a juncture with a space between the trail and the cliffs. With a bit of scrambling, they found two flat boulders to sit on, nestled beneath a pinyon pine, overlooking a sight fit for the gods. A blessed breeze cooled her hot skin and bunches of squirrel-tail grass waved fuzzy stems, while she and Mel slugged water and munched granola bars.

For a few minutes, they remained quiet, taking in the view of magnificent wind and water-carved cliffs that revealed the geological history of the earth. Rosalyn imagined a giant painter's trowel sweeping across the cliffs, depositing pale pinks and bright-orange stripes in textured patterns.

"Feel better?" Mel was the first to break the silence.

"Thanks. I'm breathing easier." She left out the part about feeling seasick. If she ignored it, it would pass. "How about you?"

"Me? I'm fine. I can keep going if you can."

"I meant... what we talked about the other night." Rosalyn wracked her brain, trying to recall exactly what Melanie had said to her, worried she'd confound it with what she'd learned from the letter she'd read at Philip's grave. "You said Blake was needy, I think. That you wished you hadn't eloped."

A beat passed. "Did I?"

"And that you'd only been able to give him part of your heart."

Mel frowned. "I don't remember saying that."

She pressed her hand against her stomach, which was threatening to give up the ghost. "You said you wanted to try harder... but, Mel, maybe marriage shouldn't be so much work."

"I don't think that's fair. My relationship with Philip was easy, but he was my first love. Blake pretends otherwise, but I know it hurts him to think of the love I shared with Philip." Mel's tone seemed guarded. "I don't know why you've suddenly turned on Blake. I'm trying to rebuild my life, and frankly, for you to suggest I've made a mistake, that it isn't too late to change course, feels like you're trying to sabotage us. Is it possible you don't want to see me with someone else because of Philip? Subconsciously?"

It was true—only there was nothing subconscious about it. Still, given the things she'd told her, it didn't seem fair for Melanie to keep taking offense. She was trying to find a way to say just that when the discomfort in her belly roared into full-blown cramps.

Her face felt hot, and her head went light—she doubled over.

"Rosalyn! What's happening?" Mel jumped to her feet, and then pressed a water bottle to Rosalyn's mouth.

She pushed it away, turning aside to vomit. The sour smell made her retch again. When she caught her breath and looked up, she saw Ashton and Blake running toward her.

"I need to go back," she managed as they arrived, dust swirling up from the ground at their feet.

"Thank heavens you turned around!" Melanie waved her phone in the air. "I don't have a signal, and we need to get Ros to a hospital."

"A hospital? No. It's just the heat—and the altitude," Rosalyn said.

"We're all at the same altitude, and none of the rest of us are sick." Ashton pulled her to her feet. "Can you walk or should I go ahead and bring back help?"

"I can walk," she said, as her knees buckled beneath her.

"No, you can't." Ashton propped her up against him, then guided her back to the boulder and helped her sit down, lowering himself alongside her, holding on to her tightly. "Blake, can you run it?"

"You're faster."

Rosalyn cringed at the thought of being left here without Ashton.

"She'll be safe with Blake and me. I promise to keep watch over her," Melanie said.

Rosalyn turned her head, her stomach threatening yet again. When she looked up, Ashton was already running full speed up the steep switchback. "Tell him to slow down." Her voice was too weak to cry out after him.

"He's surefooted," Blake said. "There's a water station just down the trail. Mel, will you take our bottles and refill them? I don't know how long we're going to be stuck here."

"I'd rather keep Mel." She'd feel safer with Melanie, or even by herself.

"I think she's confused. You stay with her while I go fill up the water bottles," Mel said.

"Please don't go," she begged.

But then Blake smiled kindly at her.

Maybe she'd misjudged him. This was *Blake*. Her husband's long-time friend. Melanie's husband. And here she was acting like she was afraid to be alone with him. She shook out her shoulders and raised her chin. "Sorry. I'm not thinking clearly. Go ahead, Mel."

"Are you sure?"

She nodded and held out her half-empty water bottle.

"You keep yours. I'll refill the others but you should have one on hand. And I think you should take one of your pills."

Her daypack was lying a few feet away on the ground.

Blake grabbed it, took a step toward Rosalyn but then turned and trotted down the path after Mel.

Rosalyn blew out a breath and touched her Timex. She felt totally abandoned. What was wrong with her? One minute she didn't want Blake around; the next she was scared for him to leave.

Her chin dropped to her chest, and her lids grew heavy, so she let them close. When she opened her eyes again, Blake was next to her, the contents of her pack emptied onto the dirt beneath his feet. "I don't see any pills."

"What? Oh, they're in the second zipper compartment." She'd dozed off. Who knew for how long?

"They're not. You must have left them back at the tent."

"I know I brought them. Give me my pack."

He lifted the empty daypack and dangled it upside down. "There's nothing in here."

"Give it to me, please."

"If you don't believe me, come and get it." He took a step toward the edge of the cliff and lifted her bag over his head.

She tried to climb to her feet but her legs wouldn't support her weight.

As she crumpled back down into a heap on the dirt, Blake returned and knelt over her. "Ros! Ros! Snap out of it." His hand whipped up and came toward her with a velocity and force she never expected.

The sound of a slap.

Excruciating pain shot through her jaw all the way up to her mushy brain. Her face was on fire. Where was the concerned, kind friend Blake had always presented himself to be? And where in the hell was Melanie?

"Get a grip. You were mumbling about how you can fly."

"You-you didn't have to slap me," she managed.

"You deserved it." He picked her up and carried her to the edge of the cliff. Set her back on her feet. "If you know what's good for you, you will *never* interfere with my marriage again."

"What's happening?" Her head was spinning, playing out all kinds of wild scenarios.

Then, suddenly, Blake's hand hit her shoulder.

She felt herself falling and stretched out her arms. Now she was flying—gliding, soaring above the blue ribbon that was the Colorado river.

# TWENTY-FOUR

## NOW

Rosalyn opened her eyes, grateful to see the afternoon light dancing around the familiar corners of her bedroom.

*Home.*

She'd spent two miserable days, that seemed like twenty, in the hospital. The doctors had pumped her full of fluids for dehydration and given her antibiotics to combat a potential infection from the rats, though they'd never officially diagnosed her with rat bite fever.

The hospital staff had been wonderful, but all she'd wanted was to get home.

Back to someplace she felt safe.

Her fever had been above 105 when they'd brought her in, and she'd been babbling about flying. According to Ashton, the doctors initially considered putting her in "soft restraints", but Blake had persuaded him to refuse their recommendation, saying it might make her more agitated. Blake had suggested they take turns sitting by her bedside to make sure she didn't pull out her IVs instead.

*Blake.*

Outside her room, she heard voices, and then the door

eased open and Ashton poked his head in. "You up for visitors?"

That safe feeling evaporated.

She could always say no, but one of the voices was Mel's, and she was worried about her. She wanted to verify, with her own two eyes, that she was okay. She'd had terrible, vivid dreams of Blake slapping her, accusing her of trying to destroy his marriage, and then pushing her off a cliff.

According to everyone, her first words upon coming around, had been, "Blake's trying to kill me!"

She'd gone on to insist he'd slapped her, stolen her antibiotics, and then pushed her off the rim of the Grand Canyon. She'd also insisted she'd be dead if only she hadn't *flown with the eagles* back to safety.

Obviously, Blake *did not* push her off a cliff, though he easily could have if he'd wanted to. And even if he believed she'd interfered in his marriage, he certainly wouldn't have tried to *murder* her because of it. This close call reminded her, and everyone else, of the fact that not so long ago it'd been Blake who'd saved her from a deadly rattlesnake.

The high fever had left her confused, disoriented and, unfortunately, she had to admit... delusional.

There was no denying it.

And, yet, her face was bruised, and the antibiotics she *knew* she'd packed had vanished. But could she swear she hadn't forgotten them? "Sure. Come on in, everybody."

Blake was the first to enter toting a big vase of red roses mixed with white hydrangeas and lilies.

Suddenly the stale room smelled delicious.

Melanie followed, looking perfectly safe and sound, and Ashton brought up the rear.

Blake offered her a tenuous smile. "Hope it's okay for me to be here. I'll leave if it makes you uncomfortable."

She studied him, looking contrite and worried and hurt.

Then she glanced at Melanie, who wore a pleading look on her face, and at Ashton's hopeful smile.

No, she didn't feel comfortable around Blake, and, yes, she'd like him to go. But now that he was married to Mel, he was *family*. And she couldn't honestly say she'd ever known Blake to actually hurt anyone.

Her cheek throbbed, and she gingerly touched it.

He denied slapping her, but even supposing he *had*—she'd been hysterical at the time, possibly even a danger to herself. "The flowers are beautiful."

Blake put them on an end table and stepped closer, extended his hand.

She took it. "Thank you... I'm..." she couldn't bring herself to apologize to him, though she knew Ashton and Melanie both wanted her to. Struggling to find words that were genuine, she settled for, "I'm so grateful to all of you for getting me safely off that trail."

"Thank your husband. He sprinted up the hill like an Olympian and brought back help," Blake said.

"Better to thank the mule who carried you out." Ashton smiled.

"I will if I ever bump into him, but I think it's going to be a while before I hike the canyon again."

Melanie beamed.

Blake released Rosalyn's hand, and she let out a breath.

*There's no such thing as a perfect marriage.*

# TWENTY-FIVE

## THEN

The numbers on my laptop screen fade in and out. I remove my reading glasses and rub my tired eyes.

"Blake!" A clap of hands near my ear makes me jump in my chair.

"Thanks, man." That was a dick move but at least I'm awake now. I pivot and swing one arm over the back of my chair, then rest my chin atop it.

Ashton stands before me, dressed to kill. "How do I look?"

"Like a guy who wants to get laid."

"No, I look like a guy who is *going* to get laid. My drip is epic."

"Go to her place, okay? I'm—"

"Don't tell me, I know. You're studying. My roomie is a monk. And he's trying to make a monk out of me, too."

"Bull. I'm living vicariously through you. I wish you Godspeed and an unbreakable condom. My only ask is that you do the deed elsewhere. I'm working here."

My roommate, Ashton, has a way with threads, words, and women. But his constant quest to drag me out with him is messing with my plan. I've worked too hard and given up too much.

College is my ticket to a legit life, and I will not, I cannot, afford to screw it up.

I gave up *Zoe* for college.

So, if Ashton thinks I'll sacrifice my Economics 101 grade just to go trawling for tail, he's going to be sorely disappointed. But I like the dude, and I don't want to blow him off. I know from experience that an important exam won't be a good enough excuse for him. No big deal. I've got a proven standby excuse at the ready. "You know I would, but ever since Lola ghosted me, I just can't work up the juice."

Ashton scoffs. "I don't believe there ever was a Lola. From what I can tell, you freeze around women. That chick in the bakery, for example, the one with the—"

"Pretty eyes."

"Yeah, that's the one. You turn into a zombie around 'Pretty Eyes'. It's pitiful. Gets me right here." Ashton pounded his heart.

"You caught me, man. If only I had your silver tongue."

"I could teach you some lines." He puffs out his chest.

The thing is, if I can't have Zoe, I don't want anyone. But Ashton keeps goading me to go prowling, so I came up with a way to get him off my back—pretend I'm devastated over breaking up with Lola, and that I've lost my confidence. Apparently, I'm one hell of an actor, because Ashton is now fully convinced I don't know my way around women. "Maybe another time. And kudos to you if you've already studied for your own midterms."

"You're not the only one who plans to graduate."

"But I am the only one who plans to graduate with honors." I toss out a barb.

"I wouldn't wager the farm on that." He lobs it back.

The Hightower family isn't well off. Ashton's parents

barely scraped up enough money to cover his tuition, and he has to pay his own living expenses. He works as a part-time mechanic, and he's always talking up some online art website he's building that he swears is going to make us both rich someday. The art business might be legit; Ashton seems like a stand-up guy, but something about the whole thing sounds shady to me. And I've been living outside the lines for so long, I don't want to chance it.

Zoe cut me out of her life.

She won't even hang out as friends, and there's no one else I'm willing to lie, cheat and steal for.

So, I'm reinventing myself—and that's final.

"I'm not going anywhere without you." Ashton folds his arms.

"Then you're not getting laid, so you might as well crack the books."

"I don't have a test tomorrow, and if I did, so what?"

Ashton is super smart, and so well read, he hardly needs to study at all. I admire that about him. There's more to Ashton than his frat boy image (he can't afford a fraternity and he's not in one, but you'd never know it). Ashton is the personification of today's vocab word: *erudite*. Me, on the other hand... I've been playing catch-up since the day my stepdad kicked me out of the house at fourteen. "But *I* do have a test. So, either get out of here or—"

There's a sharp knock at the door.

It's probably Kent from down the hall looking to attach himself to Ashton for the evening.

"To be continued." Ashton flings open the door with the confidence of a man who has the world by the tail.

A tall dude in a tan suit pushes his jacket aside, showing off a holstered pistol and a gold badge. The cop clears his throat. "I'm Detective Julian Van, and I'm looking for Mr. Blake Tyler. It's about a young woman. A friend of his."

A moment of panic renders me speechless, but Ashton says, "He doesn't know any women. For real. The guy's a monk."

I force myself to stand and walk toward the detective, keeping eye contact with him the entire time. "Please, come in."

My whole life, or rather the dreams of what my life could be, my *future*, flashes before my eyes.

Detective Van lets the door slam behind him. "Let's sit down, Mr. Tyler."

"All right if I stay?" Ashton ropes an arm around me in a brotherly gesture that catches me off guard. I never figured Ashton for the loyal type. But his arm across my back, in this moment, when I'm in trouble, creates a tangible bond between us.

I've never felt close to a man before. This is something new —having a guy who cares enough to stand up with me, no questions asked.

"Who are you?" Van inquires.

"I'm his best friend, Ashton Hightower," Ashton replies coolly. "And I live here. We're roommates."

*I have a best friend.*

"Then I'd like to talk to you, too."

"Shouldn't you read us our rights?"

"Take it easy. This is just an informal interview. Hightower, you said?" The detective pulls out his phone. "I'm recording this if you don't mind."

Ashton shrugs his acceptance, and I manage a stilted, "I consent."

Detective Van smirks.

I pull up a chair for the detective, and Ashton and I sit on our respective beds. Our dormitory quarters are basic. Just a double desk, two single beds and a bathroom we share with the guys next door.

Van stretches his legs. "A young woman's been badly beaten."

My heart stops. *Don't let it be Zoe.*

My teeth hurt, and I force myself to unclench my jaw.

Why did I ever let Zoe walk out of my life?

Just thirty seconds ago, I still believed it was the right thing to do.

But now I know…

I'd do *anything* for Zoe.

*I'm in love with her.*

"She says she's your girlfriend, Blake."

*It's not Zoe.*

I can feel my pulse again. I can breathe. Zoe would *never* refer to herself as my girlfriend. Besides, I doubt she'd go to the cops no matter what—she's been living incognito to keep Walter and Hannah from finding her.

*It's not her. She's okay.*

"I don't have a girlfriend."

"He's a monk." Ashton tilts his head and spreads his knees wide in the way that men do when they want to show you who's the Alpha.

Detective Van stretches out one long leg and kicks Ashton in the foot. "Oh, yeah? Lola Sampson says otherwise."

# TWENTY-SIX

## THEN

*This kid looks nervous as hell.*

Julian had guessed he'd be able to peg Blake Tyler easily. He had a face you could read like a road map—at first. He'd thought, from those initial questions, it wouldn't take much to crack him. But letting the roommate stay might have been a mistake.

Julian had hoped having Hightower in the room would put pressure on Tyler to tell the truth. It's hard to lie in front of someone who can call you out and say, *hey, bud, no you weren't home last Saturday night. You didn't come home until morning and you were wearing bloody clothes.* Of course, that would be *too* lucky a break to pin your hopes on, but he had supposed the roommate might at least offer insight into the relationship between Lola and Blake.

Julian had gone to college. He knew roommates saw and heard everything. The best friend knows all, and they often tell.

Julian slid his eyes to Ashton. It was surprising he'd volunteered to stay. Most young men would have gotten the hell out while they'd had a chance. That should have been his first clue that Ashton was a lot more loyal than your average college roommate. "Either of you gentlemen know anyone who would wish harm on Lola Sampson?"

"I've never met her," Ashton said. "Blake, what about you? You hardly know her, right?"

Julian scrunched his nose. This was going to be a problem. The roommate was coaching Blake, and Blake was following his lead. Buoyed by his friend's support, he'd suddenly grown a poker face.

"Is Lola okay?" Tyler asked.

"She'll recover, physically. But, no, she's not okay. She's very badly hurt. I need to know if she was your girlfriend, like she says, or if you barely knew her, like your buddy says."

"We went on a few dates."

"How many?" Julian already knew the answer, but he wanted to see if the kid would lie. Lying about little things means you have big things to cover up.

"Thirteen."

Points for the kid—he didn't lie. And it was notable that he'd kept track. It indicated a genuine interest in Lola. That didn't mean he didn't beat her up. Jealousy can drive a man to do all kinds of terrible things. "Thirteen dates sounds like a girlfriend to me."

"It wasn't serious."

Time to show him he had ammo. "Then why did she give you her car?"

"I bought it off her."

"She sold you a twenty-five-thousand-dollar car for five hundred dollars. Again, sounds like a serious girlfriend to me."

"Nah, she's rich, and she wanted a new one, so she gave me a good deal. Money doesn't mean much to her."

"But it does to you. When was the last time you saw Lola?"

"She's been ghosting him," Ashton interjected.

The more Ashton talked, the more time Blake had to compose his responses.

"You're pissing me off." He wasn't a jerk by nature, but a young woman had been beaten and left to die in the desert, so no way was he going to go easy on these kids. "Let the man speak for himself."

"I'm just trying to be helpful, sir."

"Then don't answer any more questions that aren't directed at you."

"Yes, sir."

"Mr. Tyler, when was the last time you saw your *not-a-serious-girlfriend*, Lola Sampson?"

"I wish I could tell you, but I don't remember."

"Yet you remember exactly how many dates you went on."

"Okay... Let me think... It had to be after spring break, because we went to Rocky Point."

"You spent spring break in Mexico with her."

"A group of us went. It wasn't like we were all coupled up."

"I don't care about the rest of your group. Were you and Lola an item at that time?"

"At that time, yes. But then we drifted apart. We didn't argue or anything, she just stopped responding to my calls and texts."

"I bet that made you real mad, when your rich girlfriend ghosted you."

"Not at all. I was relieved. I have to study hard to make my grades."

"That's funny because I checked, and you have a perfect grade-point average."

"Because he studies freakin' day and night. Believe me, this dude hasn't got time to beat anyone up," Hightower interjected.

"Didn't ask you a question, buddy." Julian pushed his jacket back to show his sidearm. Might be a bit of overkill but the guy deserved it, and kicking his foot hadn't worked.

"So, what about the ghosting, *Blake*?"

"I texted her a few times to see how she was doing. Just being a gentleman, but she never responded. So, I quit trying."

Ashton made a show of raising his hand.

"What?"

"Permission to speak?"

"Have at it."

"If Lola is recovering, and she was able to tell you Blake is her boyfriend, which he's not, by the way, why don't you just ask her who hurt her?"

Julian pressed his hands against his knees and pushed up to a stand, to loom over them. "She doesn't know. Someone came up behind her and put a cloth over her mouth and she passed out. She woke up in the middle of the desert, in bad condition, but luckily someone found her in time to get her to a hospital. She says, Blake, that you're the only one who would have any reason to be upset with her. I wonder if you'd be willing to take a lie detector test?"

"No way," Ashton said. "Those things are unreliable and there's nothing in it for him. If he passes it won't prove he's innocent, and if he fails, it will damn him even if it's inadmissible in a court of a law."

Julian didn't trust polygraph results as far as he could throw them, but he did want to know if Tyler would agree to one or would try to dodge it.

"Not your question, Hightower." Julian turned an unflinching stare on Tyler. "What do you say, Blake? Will you take a lie detector test for me?"

"I've got nothing to hide, sir. Bring it on."

# TWENTY-SEVEN

## NOW

Rosalyn paused the video she'd been watching. She grabbed the binoculars she kept in the top drawer of her home office desk to focus on a cactus wren perched atop a giant saguaro. The chunky brown bird flaunted its spotted breast and fanned its tail like a skirt before dipping its beak into the center of a creamy white saguaro blossom. Rosalyn watched, transported by the show. At all times of year, she loved the view from her west-facing study, but never more than when the saguaros were in bloom. Their beautiful flowers were a rare treat, appearing only a few months out of the year, and the life of a blossom was only a single short day.

This morning she'd entered her study with a heavy heart and a worried mind. Then she'd noticed a cluster of open flowers on the giant cactus outside her window and had felt an immediate sense of peace. The world wasn't a perfect place, but there was order in the universe. A rhythm, a destiny. Flowers bloomed, birds pollinated, life moved on. She felt lucky to enjoy these blossoms, however short their lives might be—in fact, it made her appreciate their beauty all the more.

If she'd known how brief her brother's life would turn out to be, she would have cherished each moment. They'd been close, but like every brother and sister, there'd been plenty of missed opportunities in the form of postponed gatherings. And how many times had she been too busy to speak with him on the phone? What in her life had been so important she'd had to say, "Sorry, can't talk"?

*I miss you, Philip.*

She took one last look at her industrious cactus wren. Imagined it arching its striking white eyebrows at her and saying, *you promised Philip to look out for Mel, so get on with it.*

Lowering her binoculars, she set her jaw. Snooping or spying, or however one might characterize her behavior, did not come naturally to her. And trying to get information about Blake out of Ashton had yielded little fruit while causing lots of friction.

The internet was her next step. And so, she'd queued up a video on how to conduct a private investigation online. She'd found names of some companies that would search public records—but they weren't free, and the last thing she needed was for Ashton to spot a payment on their credit card to *Digital Sleuths.*

But, she reasoned, if the records were *public* she could search them herself.

Maybe she should make herself lunch first though, to fuel her brain.

*Stop stalling.*

*Start with something easy.*

She navigated to the Pima County Recorder website.

Cracked her knuckles.

*You're not doing anything wrong.*

If it were illegal to sleuth Blake Tyler's records, she wouldn't be able to go to an official website and simply type in his name...

*Boom!*

She hit the search button.

"No items found."

That wasn't right. The deed to Blake's home had to be recorded. Had she misspelled his name? She checked all the boxes, and all the information looked correct so she tried her search again.

"No items found."

She hovered over the search boxes and found a *search-by-address* link. After being directed away from the county recorder to the county assessor, she searched again. This time plugging in the name and street number of Blake's home in Catalina Foothills Manor Estates.

*Results 1 of 1 – bingo!*

She let out a breath. This just might work. There might be a learning curve, but nothing she couldn't manage. She clicked the link and waited for Blake's name and address to populate. Then she tipped back in her chair, and an uneasy feeling made her breath catch. The address was correct—but Blake Tyler was *not* the property owner. The house was titled under a name she'd never heard of.

She touched her watch for luck, and also noted the time. Ashton was due home—past due. Without thinking twice, she quickly found his location on her phone app.

One mile from home and the circle was moving quickly.

She had no more than a minute or two to finish up if she didn't want to get caught.

And she did *not* want to get caught—sharing her suspicions with Ashton about his *best friend* before she had any proof would only make him angry. He might even feel obligated to tell Blake.

Her fingers poised mid-air over the keyboard, and then she began typing fast and furiously. Last year, she'd used an online realty site to help Mel search for houses, and it allowed users to see a property's history.

She filled in Blake's address.

The last sale noted for the property was dated *nine* years earlier. Blake had purchased the home *three* years ago. But according to these records, three years ago, the house had been listed *for rent,* not *for sale*.

Bile rose in her throat.

Her stomach clenched.

She heard the sound of Ashton's car pulling into the drive, the garage door opening. She scanned the webpage, her breathing accelerating as the garage entry opened, and footsteps sounded in the hallway.

"Hon, where are you?"

She hit a drop-down menu and sent the property history to her printer, then slammed her laptop shut. "In here, babe. Can you turn on the patio misters? I'd love to sit outside and watch the sunset with you. The saguaros are blooming, the birds are posing, and the sky is like a painting."

# TWENTY-EIGHT

## NOW

Lola pulled up the online book page she and Rosalyn were considering for their next read. "It sounds intriguing, but I've never heard of the author."

This was her third "book club" with Rosalyn, and so far Lola had scored a big goose egg. The only thing she'd accomplished to date was enjoying Rosalyn's company—and developing a genuine friendship with Ashton's wife was *not* part of the plan, to the extent she had one.

If she was honest with herself, her "plan" hadn't yet moved past the information gathering stage, and she needed to come up with something more concrete, soon, before the men figured out who Rosalyn's new friend, "Sherry Anne", really was.

"Ooh, I love the cover," Rosalyn said. She'd been viewing the same page, across the table, on her own laptop.

"A sweeping family saga. Buried secrets. Loaded with twists. And it's on sale for ninety-nine cents. Let's commit." Lola looked up at Rosalyn.

"Just one-clicked it."

"Sherry Anne! Rosalyn!" a barista called out.

"Be right back." Before Lola could offer, Rosalyn struck off to grab their lattes.

She thought Rosalyn seemed to be trying too hard to have fun today. She could sense that underneath all that verve and enthusiasm, her new "friend" was troubled. And if something was bothering Ros, she wanted to hear about it. Not because it mattered, one way or the other, how Ros felt, but because her mood probably had to do with her husband. And where Ashton went, Blake followed. Anything Lola could learn about them might give her an advantage—inform her, so far, very *uninformed* mission.

Rosalyn returned, a cup in each hand.

The latte spilled a little when Ros passed it to her. "Thanks. This is the second time you've paid. Next time's on me."

"If you like." Ros smiled, a big forced grin—something was definitely up with her.

A twinge of unwelcome sympathy made Lola put down her cup. "How's the freelance writing going? Did you hear back from that magazine you submitted to?"

"*Around Our Town*? Oh, yes. I can't believe I forgot to mention that they bought my article on local botanical attractions. It's not much money, but the editor says she's interested in seeing more pieces from me. And they may even have an opening for a columnist soon."

"Congratulations! *Around Our Town* is quite a coup."

"*Home and Gardens* would be a bigger one. I'm still waiting to hear back from them."

"Hopefully, we'll have that to celebrate next time. I guess that's why you're so bubbly, today."

Rosalyn's smile deflated. "Can I be honest?"

"Of course."

"This week has been good, workwise, but on a personal level, I could really use someone to talk to."

"I'm flattered. And I'm here for whatever you want to discuss, but what about your husband? Can't you talk to him?"

"Normally I would. I'm lucky to be married to my best friend. But in this case, I can't confide in him, because my problem has to do with *his* best friend."

"Ashton's your best friend, but you're not his?"

"Oh, gosh. I see what you're saying but..."

Lola tilted her head, hoping to indicate empathy and interest, but in a nonintrusive way that would encourage Ros to open up—the way Dr. Gainey used to do with her. She missed her therapist. And, unfortunately, she found herself looking forward to her talks with Rosalyn for all the wrong reasons. She must remember to not allow the *pretense* of friendship to become real. She mustn't allow herself to actually care about Ros or she wouldn't be able to do what was necessary.

"I shouldn't be telling you this, but since you don't spend time in the same social circles as Philip's wife, I know you won't repeat what I'm saying to anyone," Rosalyn said.

Lola almost spit her coffee. Philip Monroe had made a small fortune off that wearable phone charger he'd invented—the Chuckle. When she'd first come up with the story of meeting him in a coffee shop, she'd kicked herself because she was sure no one would buy it. But as it turned out, Philip was, apparently, down to earth; and Rosalyn had no trouble believing he'd befriended a lowly woman like the one she was pretending to be. "My social circle is limited. I don't think you have to worry about me spilling the beans to Melanie Monroe or anyone she knows."

"It's Melanie Tyler now."

"Right, I forgot." She covered her mouth. Not a good habit as she'd read it's a clue that you're lying. But Rosalyn was no human lie detector or else she wouldn't be having coffee with Lola. "So, this is about Melanie's new husband? Ashton's friend, Blake? Did I get everybody's name right?"

"Yes. And as for Blake... I don't trust him."

"I'm surprised to hear that. Does Melanie know your opinion of her husband? You're family. Whatever's bothering you about him, you should tell her."

"The problem is I'm not sure of my facts. I've known Blake a long time, but he doesn't seem to be the man I thought I knew. It's almost like he has a split personality. And, I realized that after all these years, I know very little about his finances or personal history. I do know he runs a nonprofit called Opportunity Knocks, but that's about it. Apparently, he's not close to his parents. Ashton says he *never* talks about them."

"That doesn't sound too strange. A lot of people don't talk about their families or discuss their jobs when they're socializing."

"I'm one hundred percent certain he told Ashton and me that he owned the house he lived in before he married Melanie. It's in an upscale part of town, and it's worth several million dollars."

"Sounds like he'll be a good provider." Not that Philip Monroe's widow had to worry about money.

"*Sounds* like. But I did some investigating, and it turns out he was renting his house. Now, he's moved into Mel's place. What if he doesn't have the kind of money he claims? What if he married Mel to access Philip's wealth?"

"I can see how you wouldn't want to make an accusation like that without proof."

"I can't believe I'm saying this, but I think Blake Tyler might be a con man. I found out about his house from the internet, and I want to keep digging into his background. I'm good at some types of research, but I don't think I'm up to this level of snooping."

With her laptop's back to Rosalyn, Lola typed in *private investigation* and hit search. "We haven't talked much about me and my background."

"Oh, I'm so sorry. I shouldn't keep going on about my problems. Please, I want to hear about you."

"No. No. I want to hear *everything* about this Blake Tyler character. I mentioned my own background only because, as it happens, *I'm* a private investigator. I work for..." She glanced at the website whose page was loading as she spoke. "*Digital Sleuths.* Have you heard of them?"

"I have! Are you serious?"

"I certainly am. Tell you what, because this is for Philip's widow's benefit, I'll take the case free of charge."

"And any information you find is confidential?"

"One hundred percent. Not only that, I can keep it off my books. This is simply a favor for a family friend."

"Thanks for this, so much, but I can pay you. I'd insist on it, as long as you'll accept cash so my husband doesn't find out."

"Your money is no good with me, Rosalyn. But I am going to need some things from you: Blake's social security number, driver's license if possible, and any information you can get on his schedule for the next few weeks."

"I don't think I can get his social security number. That wouldn't be right."

"This is to protect Melanie, isn't it?" Lola could not believe her luck. But it wasn't only luck. She deserved credit for thinking on her feet. "The results of the investigation will depend on how much you give me to work with. Whatever you want to volunteer is fine, but just know that."

Rosalyn looked down, and then back up again. "I'll find out his schedule... and his social security number."

"Don't worry about this getting back to your husband or anyone else," Lola said. "You can trust me one hundred percent. In fact, I could lose my license if I violate confidentiality. There's no reason to worry. Blake Tyler's secrets will be safe with me."

# TWENTY-NINE

## NOW

The dating app specialized in matching handsome men with wealthy women who had no qualms about the transactional nature of the relationship. It wouldn't have surprised Lola if Blake had, in reality, been a site member; but the fact that she hadn't found a profile for him wasn't going to stop her. It'd taken her less than an hour to create a fake one for him.

*I enjoy sunsets*
*Long walks on the beach*
*Living fast*
*Loving slow*
*You pamper me*
*I'll pamper you*
*Please reply to @BoyToyBlake*

She'd uploaded a mirror selfie of a man's bare chest she'd grabbed off the internet along with an actual head shot of Blake and a couple of photos of him golfing. She'd taken photos of Ashton on the greens that very same day, and it was tempting to create a fake profile for him, too, but she didn't want to stretch credulity.

Rosalyn seemed resistant to all attacks on her husband's

character, and she would probably be much more receptive, more likely to believe the profile was genuine if Lola kept Ashton out of it.

She confirmed the username *BoyToyBlake*, created a password, tapped *join*, and then *print profile*.

Stretching her arms overhead, she smiled.

She didn't want to simply ruin Blake and Ashton. She wanted to *obliterate* them.

This wasn't enough. Not nearly enough. But...

*It's a start.*

# THIRTY

## NOW

Rosalyn stared at the frothy foam swirls atop her cappuccino.

It'd been a mere three days since Sherry Anne had volunteered to investigate Blake, and, apparently, she'd already found
something. Hence their second "book club" this week. She was
grateful, incredibly grateful, to Sherry Anne for her help, and
she didn't want her to think she didn't trust her. But Sherry
Anne's insistence that Ros steal Blake's bank account info was a
bridge too far. "I don't think I should do it."

"But why not?"

Rosalyn had already managed to sleuth Blake's social security number off a document she'd found in Ashton's desk and
had called Sherry Anne with it. She simply could not steal his
bank account number, too. "I understand that the more information you have about Blake, the better the chance of uncov-
ering criminal activity. But Melanie and Blake are married.
Their bank accounts are community property, which means I'd
be stealing Melanie's information along with Blake's. So, no. I'm
sorry. I just can't."

"Look at me."

Ros lifted her eyes. The way Sherry Anne tilted her head

seemed oddly comforting, but then her hands contracted in a claw-like motion. It was a strange habit, and even over the course of their short friendship, Ros had come to recognize it as a quintessential *Sherry-Anne-in-distress* signal. "Please don't take it personally. I trust you implicitly, but I can't betray Melanie. She's like my sister and—"

"I know. I know. You promised Philip you'd look out for her. But don't you see? This is how we accomplish that."

"We?"

"Yes, *we*. I'm not trying to usurp your role as protector of Philip's widow. But Philip was my friend, and I believe he'd want me to do all I can to keep Melanie safe. Our mission is the same."

Rosalyn hadn't been looking at it as a mission, exactly, but the description fit, and it was a comfort to have a partner in Sherry Anne. Someone who also felt a strong allegiance to Philip. "You're right that we have a mutual interest. But there must be some way to help Melanie without committing a crime and breaking into her financial accounts."

"*Save* is a better word than help. Blake seems like a snake. And you said you were worried he's after her money."

"Philip left her very well off, so I have to consider the possibility. If I hadn't married Ashton before Philip made his fortune, I might even be worried that my own husband is a gold-digger."

"Oh, I wouldn't worry about Ashton. You're such a good judge of character—you would never fall for a con man."

She didn't need another person to confirm Ashton's character for her, but it was nice to hear Sherry Anne give him her vote of confidence. "Thanks. So, what did you come up with? You said you had something to show me."

Sherry Anne slid a manilla envelope across the table.

Rosalyn picked it up reluctantly, as if it might scorch her fingers. "Should I open it here, or at home?"

"Up to you, of course, but, if I were you, I wouldn't wait."

"Is it... something really bad?"

Sherry Anne sent her a sympathetic look. "I guess that depends on your definition of *really bad*, but it's definitely not good."

Ros tapped the envelope on the table. Shook it like a mystery gift. Bit her lower lip, and then opened it, pulling out the contents—a sheet of paper—with her eyes squeezed shut.

She dreaded finding the very proof she'd been looking for.

She opened her eyes and commanded her hands to stop shaking, then scanned the page, which contained what looked to be some kind of dating profile. "Okay. It's a skeevy dating profile. But maybe this was before he started going out with Melanie."

"Look at the date the profile was created."

"Two days ago!"

"It's from an app that caters to older, wealthy women looking for younger men. You need to show this to Melanie right away. Unless you've changed your mind about getting me that bank info so we can gather even more evidence first."

"I'm still a 'no' on the bank account. And I don't think now is the time to show this to her."

"Every day we delay is a day he can damage her. And remember what you told me about his behavior after you got bitten by a rat? That he was aggressive and threatening."

"I think he did slap me, because of the bruise on my face, but remember, I also said I was very confused that day because of a high fever."

"You're doubting your own two eyes and ears. But you shouldn't. Melanie doesn't want to believe anything bad about her husband, and what she needs is a wake-up call."

"I need more evidence. I need proof of bad intent before I go to her."

"This *is* proof of bad intent, or at least bad character," Sherry Anne said.

"Maybe or maybe not." A shadow of a doubt was ping-ponging in her brain. "A profile isn't *proof*. It could be catfishing, or spoofing or whatever they call it when someone steals your identity and creates a phony account."

Sherry Anne did that claw thing with her hands. "It seems like you don't want to find out bad news. Blake gaslights you on the hiking trail when you're sick. He lies about owning his home. I bring you damning evidence of probably infidelity and certainly money lust, and you still want more. What will it take for you to believe that Blake Tyler is the wrong man for Philip's widow?"

"If someone brought me evidence like this about Ashton, I'd want irrefutable proof that it wasn't spoofed. So, I suppose I need to hear it from Blake, himself."

"That's a great idea... only you'll need to be careful."

She shivered in the air-conditioned coffee shop and dragged on her sweater. She hadn't been expecting Sherry Anne to agree with her. The minute the words came out of her mouth, she'd had second thoughts. In all likelihood Blake *was* a con man. He might even be dangerous when backed into a corner. "You think he'll admit it?"

"I think he'll deny it. But if he's innocent in all of this, if there's been some kind of misunderstanding, he'll have a chance to explain. Not just about *BoyToyBlake* but about pretending to own his house, and about that day you were sick from the rat bite."

"And if he's guilty, even if he doesn't admit it, he'll do what he did before: he'll threaten me. But why would Melanie believe *this* when she refuses to even believe he slapped me?"

"Because this time you've got me. And I just came up with a brilliant idea. I know a way we can catch Blake Tyler in the act, and get Melanie to kick him to the curb where he belongs."

# THIRTY-ONE

## NOW

Zoe applied a second coat of deep red and blotted her lips with a tissue. She snapped her compact shut and dropped it, along with the lipstick, into her purse, then twisted around in the booth to blow a kiss at the teenager she'd caught gaping at her. His eyes widened and his face turned almost the same shade as her lips.

His mommy looked mad as hell and a little bit terrified.

Zoe found that gratifying.

Sometimes, she worried she'd lost *it*. That magic that kept men in general, and Blake in particular, spellbound; made them willing to break any rule, cross any line to please her.

As she sipped her beer, she tapped the toe of one Choca Lux Louboutin sandal.

It'd been a long time since she and Blake had shared a meal at Applebee's.

In the old days, it had been a big deal to "dine" here—a treat reserved for special occasions like a birthday or a big score.

They'd come so far since then, but sometimes it was good to remind Blake of his roots, where his real loyalties lay. She didn't like the idea of him getting soft and spoiled, living in that big house with Melanie. A frisson of anxiety rippled through her at the thought of Blake's saccharine-sweet wife. Did he prefer that boring woman, that boring *life*, to the excitement Zoe offered?

"Can I get you another Dos Equis?" asked the server, an older gentleman, who seemed to be having a hard time keeping his eyes off her cleavage. She'd make sure Blake left him a generous tip. A fellow his age should be relaxing on a beach, enjoying his pension, not setting out drinks with shaky hands—a good portion of her beer had spilt thanks to the man's tremor.

Just then she spotted Blake.

He rounded the corner and slid into the booth across from her. "Make mine a Michelob."

Zoe smiled sweetly and said, "Bill, this is Blake, the man who's dared to keep me waiting. I believe I will have another beer, and we'll have an order of wings—extra spicy—to start."

"Of course. Would you like to hear about our limited-time offers?"

Zoe plucked a cardboard insert with the words "limited-time offers" printed at the top, from between the pages of a giant plastic menu. "We're okay reading them, here. But thanks."

"I'll be back with beer and wings, then. Extra *spicy*."

Once Bill was out of earshot, Zoe leaned in, showing a bit more of her ample décolletage to Blake. "What's his story, do you think?"

"You mean what's he doing waiting tables at his age?" He shrugged. "Maybe his granddaughter duped him out of his life savings."

"Ouch."

"Just a theory."

"That was so mean."

"Sorry." He reached for her hand. "It *was* a low blow. But I can't help thinking about Walter sometimes. I wonder how he's doing."

"Walter's fine."

"You don't know that."

"Yeah, I do."

"Have you been sending him money? I thought you said we couldn't because he'd know it was you—which frankly doesn't seem like it would be so terrible."

"You must be kidding. If he found me it would ruin *everything*. But to answer your question, yes. Now that we've scored big, I decided to get creative. Last week I had a messenger deliver an envelope with twenty grand inside, along with a phony letter saying the money was part of a settlement from a class action suit against the makers of his heartburn medication. That should hold him for a little bit. Later we can pretend he won a contest or something. We can make a game out of coming up with ways to funnel cash to him."

"It's always a scam with you. Even when you're doing the right thing."

"It's not 'the right thing'. That implies I owe him something, which I don't. But we've got Melanie's trust fund to draw on, so why not?"

"Whatever. I don't want to fight. If you insist you don't care what happens to Walter, and that this is just a new game, I'm not going to beat you up about it. But, about Melanie—that's something I want to discuss."

Bill returned with their beers and a plate of wings, then shuffled off, after taking their order for two burgers with chili cheese fries.

Zoe used a cocktail napkin to wipe spilled buffalo sauce off the tablecloth and then forked two wings onto an appetizer plate. That tickle of anxiety returned but she distracted herself with a hot juicy bite of spicy chicken that burned her tongue. "What about *Melanie*?"

He arched one eyebrow. "Why do you always say the name 'Melanie' like you're spitting out poison?"

"Spitting out artificial sweetener is more like it. So syrupy." She shuddered from her toes to her head.

"Mel's not so bad. She grows on you after a while."

"You like her." That was obvious. "Too much, if you ask me. You need to be careful, keep your eye on the prize, instead of chasing some phony baloney life in the suburbs. Those people are only pretending to be happy."

"I can't believe I'm saying this, but just now, you sounded jealous of my wife—which would be beyond absurd."

"Don't be ridiculous. Melanie isn't even in the vicinity of my league. I'm the one you can't live without."

"You don't have to sell me on that, Zoe. Those years we spent apart were the worst in my life. Being on the streets was nothing compared to how I felt when I thought I'd lost you forever."

She wanted to ask, *Do you mean that?*, but that wasn't her. The Melanies of the world might beg their men for reassurance but Zoe would never. "Good. Bear that in mind when you're tempted to turn back from our plan."

"Right. About the plan. Philip Monroe's trust fund is so *big*. And unlike Rosalyn, poor darling Melanie has the trustee wrapped around her little finger."

"Your point?"

"I'm happy you sent money to Walter, and I'm wondering, since we're being generous—"

"If you want something for your family, I don't have a problem with that."

"That's not it. I don't have a Walter. My stepdad kicked me out on the streets and my mother let him. They've been dead to me since I was fourteen. You're the one who took me in. You're my family. My *only* family."

She jerked her gaze to her hands, concentrating on the specks of orange sauce that dotted her fingertips.

*You're my family, too.* "So, what's the play, then? Whatever you want, just ask. The buildup isn't needed. Not between us."

"I don't want to eliminate Rosalyn."

It was worse than she thought. He really had gone soft.

"Because Ashton's your friend." *Give him rope.*

"He *is* a friend—a good one. Those times when you wanted nothing to do with me, he stood by me. For most of college, Ashton was the only person I could turn to."

"And yet, you use him. You're happy enough to position him to take the fall in case you get caught."

"If *we* get caught. I always do what you tell me even if it doesn't make sense to me. I don't question you."

"You're questioning me now. Where does your loyalty lie?"

"With you, Zoe. You're the love of my life and you know it. But here's the thing—Ashton's my friend. The only friend I've ever had. We don't need to set him up to take the fall because we don't need to get rid of Rosalyn. There's plenty of money to go around."

"Half of Philip's trust fund belongs to Rosalyn... until her death, at which time anything remaining in the trust reverts to Melanie, and, may I remind you, what's Melanie's is Blake's. Is *ours*. Rosalyn *has* to die, and soon. As annoying as it is to have the bank doling out the dollars over the course of decades, it benefits us in one regard. We can't get our hands on all of Melanie's share at once, but neither can Rosalyn. Poor thing couldn't even convince the banker to give her anything extra to pay for Ashton's legal troubles."

"You predicted he'd turn her down. In the trustee's mind, since that art scandal, Ashton's been tainted. Now the trustee's hellbent on keeping Rosalyn's money locked safely away, so that her disreputable husband can't get his hands on any of it."

"Ironic."

"Isn't it? But, like you said, we shouldn't have to build up to things so I'll say it straight out. Again. I don't want to eliminate Rosalyn. Why take an unnecessary risk?"

"It's the only way we can get her share of the money."

"We don't *need* Rosalyn's share. You promised me that if we worked together and managed to get our hands on Philip Monroe's money, it would be our last scam."

"I lied. I love a good con."

"I don't want to go to prison."

"No one is going to prison. But if anyone did, it wouldn't be you or me. It would be Ashton. He's the perfect foil. And he'll never suspect that you're the one who framed him, because you really do care about him. That's the genius of it."

"I don't want more blood on my hands."

"More? Since when is there blood on *your* hands?" She held hers up, now covered in wing sauce. "I'm the one who did the dirty work. I'm the one who tampered with Philip Monroe's medicine because you were too squeamish—and it was such a piddly little thing to ask of you."

"Murder is definitely not a piddly little thing."

"Oh, please. Euthanasia is legal in some states."

"Not in Arizona. And it's not euthanasia if the patient wants to live. But I agree with you that getting rid of Philip was relatively low risk. And we didn't actually take his life—cancer did. We just helped it along." He took a deep breath.

"You think killing Rosalyn is different. Congratulations on your moral high ground." She scoffed.

"It *is* different, not to mention a lot riskier. It'll be very hard to make it look natural. Your rat-bite fever plan was about the most harebrained scheme I've ever heard of and a lot less likely to succeed than the rattlesnake, which was not exactly a sure thing either. You should've dropped that plan after she spotted the snake in her garage before it could strike. I told you I thought putting it in her jeep, just a few days later, was far too suspicious. That we needed to cool it for a while."

"It would've worked if you hadn't gotten cold feet and pulled her out of the car. But death by rats? Please, that wasn't supposed to kill her—although it damn near did. That was just for fun, and I thought it might teach her a lesson."

"I don't think it did. She's trying harder than ever to convince Melanie to leave me."

"Exactly why we can't back down. Why you didn't grab the chance to push her off a cliff, I'll never understand."

"Too popular a trail. Someone could've come around a blind corner at any minute. Besides, we never planned for me to push her."

"You never heard of seizing the moment?"

"I told you—it was too risky."

"Maybe. But you know, her death doesn't have to look like natural causes. It could even be an obvious murder, so long as we make it appear that *Ashton's* the one who did it."

Blake was squirming in the booth like a little boy.

"Why are you suddenly so skittish? Has something happened? Something you're not telling me?"

He reached for the hand that held a chicken wing and pushed her arm down. "Promise you won't overreact."

She dropped the wing. Apparently, he thought she might choke on it whenever she heard whatever this news of his was. After all these years, he should know she reacted the exact right amount to every situation. She did what was necessary to keep herself and *him* safe. Nothing more and nothing less.

"Rosalyn's got a new friend who goes by the name of Sherry Anne."

"So what?"

"Sherry Anne is tall."

Zoe took a swig of beer demonstrating her calm by not spewing it all over him.

"Ashton and I both thought Lola might be back. We were going to spy on Rosalyn and her, but then Ashton backed out.

Said it wasn't right. So, I went by myself. I waited across the street from the coffee shop until 'Sherry Anne' came out. Then I reported back to Ashton that Sherry Anne was *not* Lola, so we didn't have to worry about her causing problems for us again."

"When was this?"

"A few weeks ago."

"So, it wasn't her? I'm confused. Is Lola hanging around again or not?"

"I told Ashton that *Sherry Anne* isn't Lola because I can't count on him to keep secrets from Rosalyn anymore. Even though he doesn't want her to know a woman accused us of beating her up in our college days, he might tell her about Lola if he knows she's back. But, Zoe, Ros knows *nothing*. Why not just keep things as they are and live a good life off Melanie's share of Philip's money? What's wrong with *that* plan?"

*Everything.*

This wasn't the first time Blake Tyler had forgotten where his loyalty lay. She reached for his hand as a reminder that he was hers, and hers alone. He didn't belong to *Melanie*, and he damn sure didn't belong to Lola. "You should have told me Lola was back right away. But don't worry about it. We'll just add her to the list."

# THIRTY-TWO

## NOW

Rosalyn glanced at her wrist. Earlier, Sherry Anne had given her a different watch that contained a tiny listening device for today's sting operation in Carousel Park. That meant Rosalyn had to leave Philip's Timex at home.

Hopefully, Blake wouldn't notice.

Now, brass horns buzzed, piano keys tinkled, and Rosalyn's nerves jangled as the merry-go-round turned. She needed to either get a grip or call this whole thing off. Last night she'd dreamed that Blake had ripped off her shirt and found a recorder secured onto her chest with duct tape. Then he'd chased her, wielding a knife and cackling like a maniac. She'd awakened with her hair damp from sweat and her skin covered in goose bumps.

Of course, there was no chance she'd actually be caught wearing a wire. In the digital age, wearing a wire was archaic, but try telling that to her dream self.

"Let a smile be your umbrella," Bing Crosby crooned over the carousel's speakers.

Rosalyn had a creepy feeling she'd be hearing that song playing in her nightmares for years to come.

She checked the watch/recording device again.

*3 p.m.*

*Maybe he's not coming.*

"Oh, he'll come." Sherry Anne had been confident. "He needs to find out what you know."

And... Sherry Anne was right. Up ahead, Blake strode toward her, with a smile on his face.

*An evil grin.*

Man, she'd seen one too many thriller movies. She really, really needed to get control of these wild thoughts.

She was here to have a mature conversation.

There was still a chance Blake could clear this whole thing up, and if he did, she'd walk away a happy woman. The last thing she wanted was for Melanie's husband to turn out to be a liar and a cheat. The next to the last thing she wanted was to have to tell Melanie and Ashton about it.

Her mind could find an excuse for each piece of evidence against Blake—but not for the totality. So, she'd come prepared to face the truth and to get the goods to prove it.

Sherry Anne was out there somewhere with a telephoto lens. As soon as Ros tapped her watch, it would start recording and streaming the conversation back to Sherry Anne.

She shook out her fingers. They were in a public place—Carousel Park—and while it wasn't too busy on such a hot day, there were a few witnesses around. There would be no chasing her with a knife, just like there was no "wire" to give her away if he gave her a bear hug.

*Ugh.*

The thought of Blake touching her made her want to scratch her skin off.

Fortunately, he didn't lean in for a hug.

"Hot out," he opened with the weather. "Should we buy a ticket for the carousel? It'll be fun."

She considered this. On the merry-go-round, they would

have guaranteed privacy, since no parent in their right mind would put a child on a horse in this heat. The aluminum saddles would burn their legs and the brass poles would incinerate the skin off their palms. But it would be equally uncomfortable for Ros and Blake, and the music on the ride might be loud enough to obscure the recording.

Was that the reason he'd suggested it?

He suspected what she was up to?

"Let's have a seat on that bench, if you don't mind. I don't want to have to shout over the music." She kept her eyes on his face, trying to gauge his reaction. If he insisted on staying near the music, she'd have her answer.

"Great idea." He motioned for her to follow and headed for a bench yards away.

She had to trot to keep up with him.

And then it dawned on her. Sherry Anne would have to take up a new position to get good photographs. But she was going to have to let Sherry Anne worry about the photos. She needed to focus on getting the truth out of him and recording it.

"Here." Blake offered her his handkerchief, and they both sat down on the bench.

"Thanks." She took his offering reluctantly. She was sweating profusely, and also, she didn't want to antagonize him, so she dabbed her forehead, pretending it didn't bother her that something that had been in his pocket was touching her face.

"What are we doing, here, Rosalyn? You used the word 'urgent' on the phone. Is this about Melanie? Is she unhappy... or ill?"

He sounded genuinely concerned. She liked that his first thought was of his wife.

"I'll get straight to the point. I have some questions for you."

He lifted a shoulder. "I hope I have the answers."

"Did you, or did you not, tell me to stay out of your marriage if I knew what was good for me?"

"When?"

"Ever! But specifically, I'm referring to our glamping trip, after I was bitten by rats."

"I might have said something similar—but I'm sure I didn't use the phrase 'if you know what's good for you'—that would be a threat. I do remember wishing you would stop interfering. It's hard enough playing second fiddle to a deceased, sainted husband without his sister whispering to your wife behind your back—I'm just being honest. That's what you want, isn't it?"

"Yes. Let's move on."

"I'm ready."

If only he were—ready with a good explanation so she could drop the whole thing and they could get on with their lives. "I wish things could be good between us again."

"Me too. There's nothing I want more than for us to be a normal family."

A look of vulnerability, like she'd never seen on Blake's face before, made her regret this whole plan. But she'd come too far to turn back. And if he could somehow dig himself out of this, it would all be worth it. "Why haven't you put your house on the market? Now that you've moved into Mel's place. Or why aren't you at least renting it out?"

"What are you talking about? It's not my house. I'd been leasing it from the owner for three years before Mel and I eloped."

"You said you bought it. I *remember*."

"No, Ros. *You* said I bought it, and I didn't correct you, because I felt embarrassed that I couldn't afford a place like that. But I can assure you, Melanie knows I don't own that house. She's always known."

Ros crinkled the handkerchief in her hands. Maybe she *had* been assuming things. And it had been wrong but human of him to let her go on thinking he had that kind of money. She pulled out the manilla envelope containing the dating profile and passed it to him. Watched in silence as he scanned the page, slowly, his face reddening, his expression growing dour.

"Where did you get this?"

"I downloaded it from an app—the one for rich women seeking younger men."

"I'm not going to ask what you were doing on an app like that, but I can tell you right now, this isn't me."

"You're saying that's not your face."

"No. That is my face. But it's not my chest." He unbuttoned his shirt and revealed a tattoo with the initials Z.W.

"Who's Z.W.?"

"It's not your business, but for Melanie's sake, and for Ashton's, I'll tell you. Z.W. is a woman I knew a long time ago. My first love. And yes, before you ask, Melanie knows all about her."

Given the fact the tattoo was over his heart, Rosalyn had to assume the subject had come up.

*He's telling the truth.*

"Then someone faked your profile." Not Sherry Anne. She would have no reason.

"That someone is trying to ruin my marriage, Rosalyn. My question is—and I need you to think very carefully before you give me an answer because it's going to determine everything moving forward—are you going to let this go or do you and I have a problem?"

Zoe itched to get closer to her prey. She tread carefully, not making a sound—not even the rustle of a leaf or the slap of shoes against dirt. A few yards ahead, Lola knelt, aiming a camera with a telephoto lens. Lola was spying on Blake and Rosalyn, just as Zoe had known she would be.

Whirring. Non-stop clicking.

Zoe wanted to scream at the fool: *Leave us alone.*

Ironically, it had been Zoe's idea for Blake to target Lola back in college. Her father had been a prominent attorney. According to the obituaries, Timothy Sampson died of a stroke. He was survived by his wife, Mary, and his only child, Lola. Zoe and Blake assumed, rightly, that Lola would have access to plenty of money, and be vulnerable after having recently lost a parent. So, after a bit of surveillance on Zoe's part, Blake managed to keep bumping into Lola, at her various haunts around town.

It had all gone according to plan.

But then Blake and Zoe had called things off because Blake insisted on "going legit".

Zoe would have let things go at that, if only Blake hadn't

decided to patch things up with Lola and try to make her part of his so-called "normal" life.

Back then, Lola had been lucky to survive Zoe's wrath.

She remembered clearly, viscerally, how it felt to kick an unconscious Lola in the ribs, to punch her in the face until it turned into a bloody pulp, to leave her under a scorching desert sun to die.

That was a little more than ten years ago, on a sunny day like today.

Lola had been rushing through a parking lot, her long hair bouncing from side to side, shimmering in the morning sun. Zoe remembered the seductive swing of Lola's hips, the tan lines popping in and out of view as her shirt slid off her shoulder.

Lola wouldn't walk like *that*, she wouldn't have put on a strapless bra, unless she was looking for a certain something— and that something had been Blake Tyler.

For months, Zoe had watched her in action.

The way she tossed her hair when she laughed.

The way she slowly crossed and uncrossed her legs, inviting hungry eyes.

That long-ago morning, Lola had been putting on a show in a soft, stretchy skirt that showed off her perfect backside. She'd seemed to be saying, "Look at me. Look at me. I'm yours for the taking."

*Then* Zoe had tugged on gloves and moved close enough to sniff Lola's perfume.

*Now*, she did so again.

# THIRTY-FOUR

## NOW

This was the first time Rosalyn had ever been inside a police station. And, so far, it was hardly exciting.

You sign in.

You wait a long time, and then someone directs you to a different window, and you wait some more.

It took nearly an hour for her to finally get her turn to speak to an officer—an officer who did *not* want to take her report. But she wasn't walking out this door until someone did. There was simply no way Sherry Anne would miss their meeting without contacting her. For the past forty-eight hours, Rosalyn had been replaying, in her head, Sherry Anne's promise:

*If I can't make it to book club, I'll text you. I won't leave you waiting and wondering what happened to me. I give you my word on that.*

It was almost as if Sherry Anne had had a premonition.

In any case, she wasn't going anywhere until someone listened. *Really* listened.

"I'd like to report a missing person," Rosalyn repeated, and then stuck her chin up.

"Mrs. Hightower, like I said before, I can't file a report without more to go on."

"Then I'd like to speak to someone who can. I'd like to speak to a detective."

Officer Thurgood steepled his fingers. "I'm happy to find you a detective, ma'am, but that won't change anything. I'm sure your friend will turn up."

"And if she doesn't?"

"Then maybe she wasn't such a good friend. You don't even know her last name."

"No, but I do know Sherry Anne, and she wouldn't just disappear on me. I know that much for a fact."

"I'm trying to help you. If I could do more, I would, but you want to go over my head."

"No. I want to report a missing person."

Officer Thurgood splayed his fingers and bent them back.

His hands must be sore from all the reports he *wasn't* typing up.

"Look, I know a guy who might be able to help—if he's around. Detective Julian Van. We call him 'Detective Lost Cause', but don't tell him I told you."

A lanky man, fiftyish, with a pleasing face, youthful haircut, and eyes too gentle for the job tapped Officer Thurgood on the shoulder. "If you don't want him to know, don't announce it in the reception area." Then he turned to Rosalyn. "I'm Detective Julian Van. How may I help?"

"I'd like to report a missing person," Rosalyn repeated the mantra, keeping her voice cool, and her spine straight. She was aware of how her story sounded, and she didn't want to give the police any reason to discount her. Tears were pricking her eyes and her throat was so tight it hurt, but she would not let these men see her emotion, risk having them dismiss her as a hysterical female.

Minutes later, after fetching her a bottled water—the detective said he didn't want her throat to get parched—he led her to a room the size of a large closet and directed her to a seat in the corner.

He took a chair facing her. "I'm recording our conversation. Okay by you?"

"Please do."

"State your name for the record."

"Rosalyn Monroe Hightower."

His eyebrows lifted and then relaxed but she could've sworn she saw a glimmer of recognition cross his face. "Rosalyn Hightower. And you're here to report a missing person?"

"Officer Thurgood says the police can't do anything. I know it sounds like nothing, but I'm sure it's something."

"Relax and tell me, in your own words, what's happened. Just tell the truth and don't worry about how it sounds."

Maybe this detective was humoring her, or maybe he was for real. Either way, at the moment, he was all she had. "A few weeks ago, I met a woman at the Bug Springs trailhead. She said her name was Sherry Anne and that she had been a friend to my late brother, Philip Monroe."

Detective Van's eyebrows rose again.

He recognized Philip's name. This time, she was sure of it. "You may have heard of him. He's not famous or anything but I suppose he's known in certain circles in Tucson. He invented The Chuckle, and when he passed away from cancer, it was in the local news."

"I'm sorry for your loss."

"Thank you." She took a breath. "Anyway, Sherry Anne explained to me that she'd met my brother in a coffee shop and they got to talking about books and then became friends. They'd meet about twice a month, and they grew close, but then one day Philip stopped coming. He never told her why, but it was around the time he met Melanie—a woman he later married. That's how I know that Sherry Anne would never stand me up.

She was hurt when Philip did it to her, and she made a point of promising me she would always be there or else let me know the reason why. She assured me I could count on her. And I believe her."

"And now she's ghosting you?"

"I think it's fair to say Sherry Anne and I bonded. She would never no-show." Especially not now, while they were investigating Blake.

"Because Philip ghosted her, and she promised she wouldn't do that to you?"

"Right." She hesitated. This detective seemed so willing to listen, she wondered if she should confide in him about Blake—but at the park, Blake had a good explanation for everything she'd confronted him with. Best not to drag him into this—it would feel like a betrayal of family, and what if it distracted the detective from finding Sherry Anne? "When I suggested she and I meet regularly, she was as eager as I was. We were both invested."

"So, you met for coffee how many times, again?"

"Three times—no, four—and then, this past Wednesday, we had scheduled another meet-up." *To review the photos and recordings from Carousel Park.* "And she didn't show."

He put his hands behind his head. "Only two days ago? I assume you've tried calling and texting her?"

"Of course. I know she wouldn't ignore me. She understands how it feels to be left wondering what on earth happened. Whether your friend is okay or lying in a ditch somewhere." This was the part where Detective Van would handle her. Tell her the failure to appear at a coffee date, by a woman she'd met only a few weeks ago, did not warrant making a report, much less a formal investigation.

He dropped his hands, pushed the recorder closer. "May I call you, Rosalyn?"

"Of course."

"Rosalyn, your brother was Philip Monroe. I presume Hightower is your married name?"

"Yes, my husband is Ashton Hightower."

"If your husband is the Ashton Hightower I'm thinking of, then I'm familiar with your family."

Something like hope filled her chest. "You are?"

"Yes. Not long ago, your husband was involved in a case of online art fraud."

Her chest deflated. "That was a misunderstanding. Ashton has made restitution, and he's settled the whole thing already. There were no charges filed."

"I hadn't heard about the outcome, but that's good. Do you know a Blake Tyler?"

She shifted uneasily in her seat. *What's going on?* "He's my husband's best friend. And he married my brother's widow, Melanie."

"Okay. How would you describe the missing woman, Sherry Anne?"

"Gorgeous. A knock-out platinum blonde with wavy hair."

"Age?"

"Not sure, but about the same as me, I suppose, and I'm thirty-two. And tall, Sherry Anne is super-model tall."

The detective picked up his cell and punched in a number. "Cancel my one o'clock." Then he turned to her and planted his hands on his knees. "I need you to tell me every detail you remember, no matter how small, about your friend Sherry Anne."

"You believe something bad might have happened to her."

"Think hard, Rosalyn. Sherry Anne told you she knew your brother, Philip. Did she ever say anything to you about knowing Blake Tyler?"

"No. Why would she know Blake?"

"I can't divulge that, ma'am."

"It sounds like you think he has a connection to my friend... and her disappearance. Why?"

"Sorry, I'm not free to divulge—"

"Got it." Her hands were shaking, but she held her head high. She knew what she had to do. "In that case, after I tell you everything I know about Sherry Anne, I have a lot more to say on the subject of Blake Tyler."

# THIRTY-FIVE

## NOW

Awareness seeped in bit by bit: unidentified smells, flickers of light penetrating her eyelids, needles pricking her back... and an overwhelming sense of claustrophobia.

Lola opened her eyes. She was in a huge, open space, and yet, it felt as though she'd awakened in a coffin.

She blinked against the source of light—sun leaking through cracks in the pitched wooden slats above her and the weathered walls surrounding her. Her arms felt heavy, weighted down. When she tried to lift them, something clanked. She turned her head toward the sound.

Her breath froze in her lungs.

*Chains!*

Adrenaline flooded her body.

Her brain kicked into gear, and now, fully conscious, she assessed her surroundings in a flash.

Sun high.

Dirt floor.

Empty stalls.

A saddle.

*Barn. I'm in an old horse barn.*

How the hell she'd gotten here didn't matter nearly as much as how the hell she was going to get out. She was sprawled on her back on some type of makeshift mattress. The sheet beneath her was frayed with bits of hay sticking through the holes. Her back felt like a million ants were crawling over her skin. One hand and both of her feet were shackled to iron rings set into the concrete platform beneath her "bed".

She'd been beat to hell and left for dead once before, and she'd survived.

If they thought she would succumb this time, they'd sorely underestimated her.

Sweat dripped from her hairline into her eyes. Her head throbbed. Her dry mouth begged for water.

But her heart had an easy beat, a regular rhythm.

Her chest rose and fell with deep solid breaths.

Like climbing onto a bicycle, fighting for her life came back naturally.

If she was going to go down, it would be swinging. She'd never known for certain whether Blake had kidnapped her all on his own, how big a part Ashton had played. Did he do more than give Blake a false alibi? Maybe, now, she'd find out if that psychopathic bastard, Blake, had acted alone or if he and Ashton had taken turns using her as a punching bag.

How she wanted to shout and curse, but she needed to conserve energy. Better not scream until there was someone around to hear her.

*First step—stay calm.*

*Second step—get off your back.*

Even with her feet shackled, the chains were long enough to allow her to bend her knees and sit up, taking some of the strain off her stretched arm. She ran her free hand across her chest and her neck but found no wounds. She flipped the sheet that covered her body and yelped in relief—she was fully clothed. Beside her, within easy reach, was a water bottle.

She grabbed it, then screwed off the cap and slugged its contents. The water was hot as the day, but it felt like ice on her parched tongue, worked magic on her desiccated throat. She gargled the next gulp before swallowing, and her throat muscles relaxed. She had no immediate plans to scream, but it was good to know she'd be able to, should the moment arise.

Her thirst quenched, she scanned the area near the bed, looking for any sharp objects that might've been carelessly left within reach. Maybe a stray nail had been dropped, unnoticed, near the "bed".

She squinted, pretending she was Superman with X-ray vision. If there was an implement around anywhere, she'd find it.

*Okay, nothing within reach.*

But the old barn yielded up at least one potential weapon— a pitchfork. Oh, what she could do with that once she got free of these chains...

And she *would* get free.

"You're awake." A long shadow followed Blake into the room.

Her heart stuttered, and she punched her own chest like a medic reviving a fallen soldier.

In one hand, Blake held a paper bag. "Did you find your water?"

"Thank you." She lifted the nearly empty bottle. Whatever he expected from her, it wouldn't be this calm demeanor.

*You're a survivor.*

*First kill him with kindness, then with a pitchfork.*

He sent her a shaky smile.

*He's nervous. Good.*

"I brought lunch. I don't remember you having one of those deathly peanut allergies. You don't, do you?"

At that, she actually laughed. Not a little chuckle but a big, hearty, rolling laugh that took her awhile to get under control.

"What's so funny?"

"Nothing," she sputtered. Apparently, he didn't see the irony in saving her from the dangers of peanut butter while keeping her shackled in a barn. "And, no. I love peanuts."

His face relaxed. "One PB and J coming right up. I peeled you a tangerine, too. And I've got wet wipes in the bag. You'll have enough of them to clean up a little."

*How very thoughtful.* "Maybe I could take a shower? This hay is super itchy."

His face reddened. "Look, I'm trying to make you as comfortable as I can, but I'm not here to play games."

Realizing her shoulders were hunched defensively, she lowered them. "Okay. I don't want to play games either. I want to go home. Can you help me with that or not?"

"No."

"At least tell me how I got here and what the plan is."

"We chloroformed you and put you in my car and drove you here."

"Is that how you did it ten years ago? When you beat me and left me to die in the desert?"

"I had nothing to do with that. I would never do that to you, Lola. I'm not a bad guy. I really care about you. And now, the worst part is you're probably going to die believing I'm the one who beat you up back then."

*No, pal, that's definitely not the worst part.* "And I care about you. So now that we're having a real conversation, more than a decade later, I think I deserve to know what happened to me then, and what's about to happen to me now."

He moved closer and tossed the sack lunch onto the bed. "It was Ashton. All of it. Now, eat."

Her stomach roiled like she'd been force fed a dozen rotten eggs, but she wanted to show him she was cooperative, and she would need nourishment if she was going to get out of this alive. She stretched her arm, pretending not to be able to reach the lunch, but decided that was too obvious a ploy—like the request for a shower. She inched the bag to her with outstretched fingers, and then fished out a mashed sandwich. She took a bite, grateful to have gargled water earlier. Otherwise, she couldn't have swallowed the sticky mess.

Next, she sat back, trying to get into a position that wasn't excruciatingly painful. "It would be a lot more comfortable if I didn't have one arm chained to the floor. If you unlock my arm, my feet will still be chained, and at least I could prop myself up on my elbows."

"Next time you're unconscious, I'll unshackle that arm," he said, as if he'd just commented on the weather. "You'll have to take a sleeping pill if you want me to be able to get close enough to you to release your hand. But just so you know, I dissolved one in your water."

"You shouldn't have told me that, Blake. Now I won't drink anymore."

"Yes, you will. If you don't, you'll die."

Killing him with kindness didn't seem to be a winning strategy. She dropped the pretense. "That doesn't sound like someone who had nothing to do with beating me up. Kidnapping me and locking me in a barn doesn't make you look so good either."

He turned and headed toward the door.

"Do you have any idea what you've done to me? What it was like waking up naked in the desert, knowing someone hated me. That someone wanted me dead? I survived, but that experience changed me forever. I've never been the same, Blake. And now this?" She took a deep breath.

He halted, his back to her, his hands clenching at his sides.

Was she making him angry? Were things about to get worse?

*No.*

They couldn't get worse, and she wasn't going to die

without saying her piece, without forcing him to see what he'd done to her. "I was in therapy for a decade, Blake. Because of you, I still have to sleep with the lights on. I wake up multiple times a night to check my closets and under my bed. I'm not the happy, outgoing person you knew in college. I dropped out of school. I don't have a career. I lost all ambition, and I became alienated from my mother. I don't have any friends, Blake. I feel alone in this world, even when other people are around me."

"I-I'm so sorry." His voice was low.

"I do not forgive you."

He whirled, then paced toward her.

She stuck up her chin. "Blake, if you ever cared about me, you'll let me go."

"I can't do that. But I'm telling you I'm not the one who beat you up and left you to die. It was all Ashton back then."

"What about now? Why did you bring me here? What's it all about, Blake? What do you and Ashton have planned for me this time?"

# THIRTY-SIX

## NOW

Blake planted his feet wide and watched his wife bustling about the kitchen. Melanie was kind and vulnerable, and he loved that about her. Zoe had caught on that Melanie was soft and loving in a way she never could be, and as ridiculous as it seemed, Zoe had become jealous of his relationship with Melanie.

Zoe was impossible.

And yet, he did love her. He always had. There was nothing he wouldn't do for her—but she was pushing his limits, demanding things of him that made his insides crawl.

*If you love me, you'll do it*, Zoe had said.

He'd fallen to his knees in front of her, tears pouring down his face. *I can't.*

She'd turned her back, and that had been enough to get him up on his feet. If she left him again, he didn't want to go on living.

Then Zoe had turned back to him. *Look at me, baby. You've got to do it. It's the only way.*

That was a lie. There were other ways to gain total control of the money.

He'd offered Zoe a whole list of alternatives, but she'd

rejected them all. And that's when he'd understood this wasn't about the money at all.

This was some kind of sick loyalty test.

Zoe wanted him to prove his devotion to her by doing the unforgivable.

And if he didn't, she wouldn't believe in his love.

He set his jaw. "Melanie."

"Yes, dear?" She approached him, with soft, loving eyes and tiptoed up to peck his cheek.

"You've been going behind my back with Rosalyn again." First, he put his hand on her throat, then he made a fist and punched down.

# THIRTY-SEVEN

## NOW

Melanie checked her phone. No messages from Blake, but there was another, the third one today, from Ros. This one was in all caps:

*URGENT*

*NEED TO MEET WITH YOU ALONE*

Melanie's hands trembled as she set down the phone without responding. She had to be very careful from here on out. Even though she'd tried to reassure Blake that everything was fine between them, she could feel the suspicion building within him.

After punching her the other night, he'd fallen to his knees. Sworn his undying devotion to her. He'd cried... and she'd told him she loved him.

Perhaps she had, once.

*No more.*

He'd left her no choice.

She knew she had to end things between them, once and for

all. But even after what he'd done, it was incredibly hard to let go. How could she have been so foolish? She'd let him convince her that fate had brought them together. And she'd hoped that even if she wasn't able to love him completely, the way he loved her, they could still build a life together.

Now, that hope was lost.

The dream in ruins.

*There's no such thing as fate.*

*No such thing as a happy ending.*

She wiped away the moisture on her cheeks.

*Enough.*

Resolved to never shed another tear for Blake Tyler, she headed to the en suite bath to toss the crumpled tissue into the waste basket and run a comb through her hair. Her image in the mirror was ghoulish, her complexion drained of color, her eyes bloodshot from the full bottle of wine she'd consumed last night before allowing Blake to make love to her.

Staring at the fist-shaped imprint on her chest, she buttoned her blouse to the top, hiding most of the damage. The bluish bruise, spreading from below her left eye to her temple, looked like someone had finger-painted it on.

She covered it with concealer.

Blake had left her for a golf date with Ashton.

The time was upon her.

As much as her heart ached for him, she couldn't lie to herself any longer. Pretend that he would never betray her again.

Still, her thoughts were swirling, her plans unsettled.

She pulled out a pen and stationery and sat down to put words on paper.

*My darling Philip,*

*I am desolate.*

*A few nights ago, I went out to meet Rosalyn without telling Blake where I'd gone, and when I got home, he went crazy. He called me names, and the more times I apologized the more vile his curses became. He went for a walk. He was gone over an hour, which gave me a chance to start cooking a nice dinner, and when he came back, I thought, at first, that he'd calmed down, like the other times he'd lost his temper with me.*

*But no.*

*It was all an act. A way to tease and torture me. He let me think all was forgiven. We sat down, and I served him his favorite dinner—pot roast braised in mustard-cream sauce, hot rolls, and a cherry pie.*

*He ate it all and then asked for seconds, but, later, when I was clearing up the dishes, he put his hands on my throat. I was so startled I dropped the plate I was holding.*

*That's when he lost all control.*

*He punched me in the face and I fell onto the kitchen floor.*

*He got on top of me and punched me in the chest, and put his hands on my throat once again. I don't know what stopped him from strangling me. Maybe it was my tears, or my promises of love and fidelity, or maybe the punches were enough to satisfy his sadistic urges... this time.*

*The next morning, he begged for forgiveness.*

*He brought me breakfast in bed, and would not allow me to lift a finger around the house. But he refused to take me to the hospital.*

*It hurt to breathe, and for a while I thought I might have a broken rib, but by the second day, I was breathing easier.*

*He wouldn't allow us to leave the house—I suppose he was fearful of my trying to flee.*

*On day three, a florist delivered two dozen roses.*

*I made such a fuss over those flowers, I even shed tears—*

*that was the easiest part of the pretense—and I seem to have finally convinced him that all is well between us again.*

*Because he left me on my own and went to golf with Ashton, although who knows where he actually goes. When I try to track his phone, the shared location services are somehow always "accidentally" disabled.*

*He swears he'll never hurt me again.*

*And he seems so sincere, it's hard to turn away from his promises.*

*But I'm not stupid.*

*I know that just as his anger escalated into physical violence, soon that violence will escalate into deadly force.*

*He put his hands on my throat.*

*I will not take a chance that next time he will resist his worst urges.*

*I'm coming to say goodbye to you today, and then I'm leaving town, leaving Blake.*

*I don't know how long I'll have to stay in hiding.*

*You were right about him all along.*

*I don't blame Rosalyn for making the match between us.*

*She is entirely innocent in this—she didn't know his true character.*

*But I'm struggling here, working it out as the ink fills this paper, what action to take that will keep me safe, without endangering Ros.*

*On the one hand, I want to confide in her. In part, because I owe her the truth, but also because it would be a great help to have someone to assist me with the details as I make my escape. But if I enlist her aid, if I tell her the whole truth, I fear it will put her in harm's way.*

*And if she knows where I am, Blake will sense it. He's very good at sniffing out lies, and Rosalyn is far from a practiced liar.*

*He'd beat it out of her, or worse.*

*Ah—there's my answer. I cannot confide in her. It's far too dangerous for us both.*

*Thank you, Philip.*

*I knew you would help me find the right path.*

*I'll go quietly. I'll sneak away and hide until I figure out the rest. But Rosalyn will play no part in my escape.*

*Rosalyn will be safe.*

*This may be the last time I can visit your grave, but you are always with me in my heart.*

*I love you, always and forever, Philip.*

*Your Melanie*

# THIRTY-EIGHT

## NOW

Julian was definitely onto something.

He had a sixth sense about these things. Most people are boringly predictable. You often hear defense attorneys trying to persuade juries that the opposite is true: "Everyone handles grief in their own way."

That's the kind of hogwash usually paraded around when a guilty-as-hell murdering spouse is caught partying shortly after the loss of the deceased spouse. There might be exceptions, but *most* folks who are grieving show it. They cry, they wail, they withdraw from the world.

The corollary to that principle is also true. Most people who are *happy*, show it. They smile, they laugh, they dance, they sing.

But if it doesn't walk like a duck, if it doesn't quack like a duck—it's probably *not* a duck.

*Not-a-duck* is what he seemed to have stumbled onto, now, in the form of Mrs. Blake Tyler, the widow bride.

While Melanie Tyler did, indeed, appear to be a grieving widow, she did *not* seem like a happy bride. Very little smiling and dancing going on with that woman. He'd been following her, and she'd led him to the cemetery. Now, from his hilltop perch, he watched her through a pair of high-powered binoculars.

Mrs. Tyler was sitting cross-legged on the ground in front of her first husband's grave. She lifted her hand, seeming to wipe tears from her eyes.

Nothing unusual there.

Grieving widows are expected to cry when they visit their husband's graves.

He could also see the numbers she dialed into a combination lock, her hand shaking as she placed a folded piece of stationery on top of other folded papers inside a marble box.

That was different.

There was something amiss in the Tyler household. And that something had driven Mrs. Tyler to the unusual act of writing letters to a dead man.

He'd love to get his hands on those letters—if that's what the papers were.

And since he'd seen the combination, it would be quite easy.

If only he weren't an ethical cop.

He lowered his binoculars.

*Not without a warrant.*

He lifted the binoculars again. Melanie Tyler was on her feet, literally running away from the gravesite. Something had upset her in a big way, and it most likely was not the familiar wound of her husband's death. This must be some new event, and it was no doubt connected to Blake Tyler.

If only he could get his hands on those letters. But he couldn't get a warrant based on a hunch about an unhappy bride who was married to a man who'd once been accused of beating a different woman ten years ago.

Even if that other woman was now missing.

What he needed was evidence.

Watching in frustration as Melanie Tyler climbed into her car and drove away, he decided he'd better wait ten minutes before leaving, just to be sure not to bump into her on the road. He started down the hill to get a closer look at that box—from the outside and strictly legal of course.

He'd made it halfway down the embankment when he spotted yet another *not-a-duck*.

Rosalyn Hightower had just beat him to the grave. She must've been spying on Melanie, too. There was no way she could have gotten to Philip Monroe's grave ahead of him unless she'd been close by.

He let out a breath.

*Not a duck.*

Not a duck, at all.

Rosalyn Hightower opened the box, and, hand on her heart, read the secret letter.

# THIRTY-NINE

## NOW

Blake remotely unlocked the doors to his Mercedes, and then slipped behind the wheel. Ashton got in the passenger seat, slapped a cooling cloth across the back of his neck and pulled out his cell. "Let me check in with Ros and make sure she's okay with me staying overnight. I hope this place doesn't turn out to be a dump."

It wasn't such a long drive back to Tucson that they couldn't have gone home, slept in their own beds, and then driven back to the golf course in the morning. But Blake had made sure to book an early tee time. It hadn't been hard to convince Ashton to stay at a local hotel rather than schedule a 3 a.m. wake-up call. What had proved more difficult was surprising him with the idea of another day of golf. Apparently, Rosalyn had some kind of discussion with him about wanting him to be away from home less often.

"No service," Ashton reported.

"They've got a landline at the hotel. You can call from there."

"A landline? Does that mean there's no cell service? What about Wi-Fi?"

"I brought cards and poker chips."

"I take it that's a *no* to the internet? How does this place stay in business?" Ashton seemed to be wavering.

"Trust me. It's super nice. You'll see when we get there. I, uh, I want to say I'm really glad we got to spend this time together." He was sincere in that. You never fully appreciate the little things, like a sunny morning on the greens with someone who genuinely likes you, laughs at your joke, confides in you, *trusts* you—until it comes to an end.

"Same." Ashton took a slug of the soft drink Blake had bought him at the pro shop and secretly laced with chloral hydrate. "Man, this tastes like crap. Too sweet."

Maybe he wouldn't drink it, and then Blake would be off the hook.

*He has to drink it.*

The next time he saw Zoe, Ashton better be dead—she'd made that frighteningly clear. This whole "brilliant" plan of hers was heartlessly cruel, and way too complex, and had him on edge.

Ashton took another slug of soda.

Blake's heart sank. "I thought you said it was too sweet."

"It's wet. That's all that matters."

Blake tightened his grip on the steering wheel. There was no turning back. He had his marching orders. Zoe was furious with him for not getting rid of Lola right away, and he'd sworn he wouldn't let her down again.

Zoe said this was the only way.

And if Blake didn't follow her orders to the letter, he was going to lose her forever.

# FORTY

## NOW

Rosalyn pressed the doorbell, and then rapped, gently, at the door.

Though her heart was racing, her blood raging through her veins, the best thing to do was to appear calm. Melanie had been ghosting her, and now she knew the reason—she was trying to protect Rosalyn from the awful truth.

And from a dangerous man.

"Mel? Please answer the door." She called out and waved at the doorbell camera. She must be home. Her car was parked on the street. It seemed odd she hadn't parked her electric vehicle in the garage for charging, but she probably wanted to be sure Blake wouldn't park behind her, blocking her escape.

She rapped at the door again, this time more insistently, and followed that up with a text message.

*I'm outside. Please let me in. Urgent.*

Staring down at the phone in her hand, she counted to thirty.

Scrolling dots rewarded her patience. Melanie was finally sending a response.

Then the dots disappeared but no message was transmitted. She tried again.

*Check your doorbell camera. It's me. I came ALONE.*

Another thirty seconds went by, and her imagination started to go wild. What if Blake was home, his car concealed in the garage? What if he'd locked Mel in a room and had taken her phone? What if it was Blake who started a response and then changed his mind?

*I'm calling 911!*

She hit send and then pressed the doorbell, holding down her index finger, listening to it chime continuously.

At last, the door flew open and she rushed inside, wrapped Mel in her arms and heard her wince. She let go and took a step back.

"Oh no. Oh no." Mel's left eye was swollen with a cut and bruise, half hidden by concealer. The other half of the bruise was exposed, as if her makeup had been washed away by tears. A macabre smile was fixed on her lips.

"Please don't call nine-one-one. Everything's perfectly fine. And if you don't mind, can you manage a smile for the cameras?" Mel whispered.

*The security cameras.*

She'd forgotten, momentarily. "Can he hear us?" she asked softly, forcing a giant smile that must have looked as bizarre as Melanie's.

"I don't think he's live-streaming. But, if you keep your voice low, it's hard to make out the words. The microphone distorts the sound."

So, they should keep smiling, whispering and mumbling. She covered her mouth with her hand, just to be safe. What if Blake could read lips? "Did I hurt you just now? I'm so sorry."

"Not at all. Would you like to come in for a cup of tea?"

Hand still over her mouth she said, "You winced when I hugged you." Then she uncovered her lips. "Tea sounds lovely."

"Great!" Mel chirped, smiling even wider. "Follow me!"

She shook out her hands, her knuckles buzzing from all the knocking. Mel was acting, but for whose benefit? For Blake's when he reviewed the indoor camera footage, or for hers? In a flash, she realized Mel didn't know she'd read the letters. Her black eye was obvious. If Rosalyn gave her a chance, she might confide in her on her own. That way Rosalyn wouldn't have to admit to reading the letters.

"I must look a fright. You'll never believe what happened." Mel touched her finger to her cheek and then unbuttoned the top of her blouse to reveal a bruise the size of a fist. "I was running on my treadmill the other day and my phone slipped off that little shelf it sits on. I don't know what they call that thing, do you? Well, never mind, that's not important. The thing is, my phone fell, and I'm such a ditz! I tried to grab it before it hit the floor, and I caught it, but then I hit the floor instead. I went flying off my treadmill. Too bad it's not on camera. It's one for *America's Funniest Home Videos* for sure."

"You don't have cameras in the workout room?"

Melanie's smile dissolved. "We do. I don't know why I said that. I erased the footage because I was embarrassed and ashamed."

"You have *nothing* to be ashamed of."

Melanie reached to open a cabinet and, once again, winced. After pulling down cups and a box of tea, she put a kettle of water on the stove, prattling on about chamomile versus orange spice, whether or not she had cookies to go with them.

By the time they sat down across from one another at the kitchen table, with piping hot cups and a box of animal crackers, Rosalyn understood that Melanie did not plan to drop her ruse. Even if it angered Melanie, even if it embarrassed both of them, there was no way around it. The only way to get Melanie to tell the truth was for Rosalyn to go first. "I read your letters to Philip."

Mel's lips went white, matching her pale complexion.

"All of them. Including the one you left today," she whispered. "I won't let you do this on your own. I'm here to help."

Mel brought out a beauty queen smile. "I don't need your help. And frankly, your being here is slowing me down. Obviously, I don't need to recount the story. You've read all my secrets so I don't need to air them again."

"I get that you're angry. We can work through that later. The important thing is to get you to a safe place. Now that we're not playing games, we don't need to sit and chat over tea. I won't slow you down. I'll help you."

"I don't want your help." She climbed to her feet slowly, still with a phony smile for the cameras, still speaking in a hushed voice. To anyone watching it would appear they were having a lovely time.

"It's possible you can get away all by yourself. A lot of women do. But two people executing a plan is better than one. It will maximize your chances. I'm not going to take no for an answer. I *read* the letter. I know you're only trying to protect me from Blake's wrath. Well, guess what, I can handle him."

"You don't know him. He can be brutal."

"I know that now." She wished she could hug Melanie, and hold her, and cry with her, and tell her she felt horrible to be the one who'd brought such a terrible person into her life. But they didn't have time for any of that. "I suggest you pack a small bag with the bare essentials. Like you said, Blake's probably not watching us live. Not from the golf course. But we don't want to waste any more time. Give me your car keys and I'll pull your car off the street into the driveway."

"But I need my car."

"We'll take mine, and then I'll leave it with you. I can grab a ride-share home. Blake might have a tracking device on your car."

She faked another laugh. "I should've thought of that. Thank you. And when he comes home and finds me gone, if my car is in the drive and all my clothes are in the closet, he'll watch the tapes and see us laughing together. He'll think I've gone out for drinks with you. That will buy me a few extra hours."

Rosalyn grabbed her gut as if doubling over with laughter. "But he'll see you packing a bag."

"I'll pack in the closet. No cameras there. Then I'll turn the security cameras and doorbell feeds off from the app on my phone, and we'll run like hell out the door. Once we're in your car I'll turn the cameras back on. That will look like a momentary glitch in the feed. If we smile *just enough*, he might not figure it out. The more time I have before he discovers I'm gone, the better."

Rosalyn nodded, letting her aching cheeks relax. "Just enough is the ticket. I think we may be overdoing the giggles. Especially since he knows you're not feeling well."

"You're right. No more belly laughs. But I hope I've convinced him, for now, that I'm still his bamboozled, goo-goo-eyed bride. I don't think he would leave me alone if he didn't buy it."

She followed Mel into the huge walk-in closet.

Mel suddenly swung around, wide-eyed. "You can't tell Ashton."

"Of course not." Part of her wanted to protest that Mel should know she would never do such a thing. But she knew, in her heart, she had every right to worry. "I give you my word. Anything I can do to reassure you, I will."

"I trust you."

Tears stung her eyes, but she blinked them away. She could not make this about her and her remorse. "I promise to live up to that trust. I've already called a hotline and arranged to get you into a shelter, in case you didn't have time."

"I'm done here. I can buy anything else I need later. I just want to get out of this house as fast as possible."

Rosalyn watched as Mel navigated on her phone. "Cameras off. Run!"

Melanie went first.

Rosalyn flew behind her, adrenaline fueling every cell in her body. Then her brain caught up, and she jerked to a stop—she'd left her purse in the kitchen. "Go. Go. Go."

She veered into the kitchen, grabbed her purse off the counter and trotted to the porch to join Mel who stood poised to lock the front door.

"Now, we walk," Mel huffed breathlessly. "For the neighbors' sake."

*Right.*

That walk from the front steps to Rosalyn's car seemed an eternity. The neighbor from across the street was outside, checking her mail, and waved them over. They exchanged glances, and then, in silent agreement strolled across the street.

Blake might well grill the neighbors.

As the minutes ticked by, Rosalyn's back grew damp with sweat. Mel was unbelievably calm. She actually recited a recipe for pound cake by heart and gave the woman a brilliant smile before Rosalyn intervened with a too-detailed explanation of "girls' night out" plans. But the woman was easily duped, and at last, they made it to the car.

"You were great, just now. I'm so proud of you." Ros fired

up the ignition, checked her mirrors, eased the car away from the curb, driving just *under* the speed limit.

Nothing to see here.

Just two ladies leisurely escaping the devil.

Mel pointed. "Make a left on Bailey."

"But we need to turn right on Bailey." They hadn't finished the shelter conversation. Maybe Mel had already arranged her own placement?

"I'm not going to a shelter. I don't want to involve the police or social workers. Sooner or later, I'm going to have to see Blake and work out a divorce. If I involve the authorities, it will enrage him."

"My advice is to do this the right way. There's a system in place that can keep you safe. The folks at the shelter have experience with cases like yours."

"I'm glad you think you know the 'right' way to escape Blake Tyler. But since I'm the one taking all the risks, I'll make my own decisions."

"I'm sorry. I just thought—"

"It's fine. I apologize if that was too blunt. I really, really appreciate this, and I don't want to fight."

"Me either."

"Get on I10 toward Phoenix. How are you fixed for gas?"

"Full tank."

Mel couldn't be staying with friends because... this was so strange to think about, but Mel didn't really have any friends besides Rosalyn and Ashton, and she couldn't risk staying with them. That would be the first place Blake looked for her. Rosalyn had a million questions. Where were they going? Did she have enough money? What was the next step? What about a long-term plan?

"Philip's friend has a ranch house east of Phoenix—near Gold Canyon," Mel volunteered. "I've still got the key. I'm staying there a day or two tops. When we get there, I'll answer all your questions. Rosalyn, I know you feel badly about setting me up with Blake, but you shouldn't. He had his eye on me for so long, he would have pursued me with or without your help."

"Thanks for saying that." Rosalyn tried not to, but she couldn't stop her tears. "I love you, Melanie, and no matter what happens, we'll always be family."

# FORTY-ONE

## NOW

"I'm not a bad person, Lola." Blake hovered at the edge of the straw bed.

Unfortunately, still out of her reach.

"I know that." If only she could lure him closer. "Do you remember that time we laid out beneath the stars and talked for hours. You told me all your plans for after graduation. How you wanted a decent job with good money, enough to support your family, but not too much because you didn't want to turn into someone who took everything for granted. You were a good man then, and you're a good man now."

"I know you don't really believe that. And I don't blame you. You don't understand why I have to do this, and I can't explain it to you. But it would be better for both of us if you stopped lying."

*You first.*

"Drink your water now."

"No."

"I kept my promise, didn't I? I unchained your arm. So now you need to do what I tell you to do."

"Or else what? You'll beat me like you did ten years ago?"

His hands clenched into fists. "Stop saying that. I told you it wasn't me. I've told you a thousand times. And if you'd had the decency to believe me, to let it go, we wouldn't be here now. This is on you."

"If *I* had the decency? You want the truth? Then, buckle up. I will *never* let it go. I want *revenge*. And I will get it. Because even if you kill me, which you're going to have to do if you don't let me go, you will be caught and convicted. And if you spend the rest of your life in prison, it will be worth dying for."

A muscle twitched beneath his eye. "You're insane. I never hurt you. I even covered up *your* stalking for as long as I could. I didn't want anyone to find out you were back because I was worried she—I mean *he*, I was worried *Ashton*, would kill you."

"You're a team. A sadistic team of men who prey on weak women. Whose idea was it to kidnap me? If it was Ashton's then I really, really don't understand your blind loyalty to him. You say you care for me. If that's true, and you want out, I have a way." She wasn't going to let up on the pressure. As long as she was breathing, she still had a chance.

"There's no way out of this that I can figure. Believe me, if there were, I'd take it. I don't want to kill you. I'm already in big trouble with... I'm in trouble with *Ashton* for not doing it already. He thinks I've betrayed him. He's not giving me a choice. Why couldn't you have stayed away? Why did you have to come back?"

She felt her entire body go numb. It was obvious Blake didn't intend for her to leave here alive, but this was the first time he'd *admitted* it.

It took her a few seconds to get her wind back, and her bravado. "If you really want out, then listen to me with an open mind. You can make a plea bargain. If you let me go, I'll testify that you treated me well. Brought me food and unchained my arm to make me comfortable. I'll say you saved me from Ashton.

That he forced you to kidnap me because I was hanging around his wife and he didn't want her to find out what he'd done to me in college. I'll explain that his wife's money is protected by a trust fund, and there'd be precious little for him in a divorce. That's the truth, isn't it? That's why he wants me dead. To keep Rosalyn from finding out about college? To keep her from leaving him?"

"He ordered me to kill you. And yes, everything is because of Philip's trust. Honest-to-God I don't give a damn about Philip Monroe's money. I wish I'd never heard the man's name!"

"So let me go. Cut a deal with the cops."

"I can't."

"You mean you won't."

"I mean I *can't*. I don't know what to do anymore, Lola. I wasn't supposed to chain you up in a barn. I was supposed to strangle you. I did try, but I couldn't go through with it. And now Ashton is *furious*. He's going to be here soon, and he warned me that when he gets here, you'd better be dead."

"I'm not going to fall on my sword for you, Blake. If you want me dead, you're going to have to do it yourself. If you don't want my blood on your hands then give me the key and let me go. Make a deal with the cops."

"I can't."

"Why do you keep saying that?"

"Because... I've got blood on my hands already. Nothing anyone does or says, including me, can change that."

# FORTY-TWO

## NOW

"That's the exit up ahead," Mel said.

Rosalyn pulled off of Highway 60 onto King's Ranch Road. Gold Canyon was a small town nestled at the foot of the Superstition Mountains, reputed home to the legendary Lost Dutchman's Gold Mine. Many an adventurer had lost his shirt or even his life on the hunt for a mine that most likely never existed.

"Funny, I never heard Philip talk about this place. You're positive Blake doesn't know about it?"

"I might have mentioned it to him once, in passing. But unless he was on the lookout for a perfect hideaway, he wouldn't have given it a second thought. It was the briefest of discussions, months ago, and I didn't give a lot of details. Even *if* he remembers there's a ranch, I highly doubt he knows where to find it."

They passed a Walgreens, then a church, then a golf course with towering saguaro cacti and desert chollas dotting the lush greens. The Superstition mountains loomed forebodingly on the horizon, and middle-class houses were interspersed with sprawling, resort-like retreats.

Philip, being a wealthy man, had friends among the rich and famous.

Was Mel's hideout one of these hillside mansions?

"You're sure the owner won't be home? I'm not suggesting we ask his permission—I think it's best if *no one* knows where you are. Later, when you're safe and this is all settled, we'll ask the trustee to compensate the owner."

"Out of *my* share. This is too minor a point to argue over but I won't have you paying for any part of this. It's not your fault. All you did was set up a lunch date between Blake and me. I'm the fool who married a man I barely knew."

*After I gave him my stamp of approval.* "You're right about one thing. We aren't going to waste our breath disagreeing about the little things—like whether you'll accept my money. Let's just focus on getting you whatever you need, and we'll settle the tab later. Deal?"

"Deal."

"Good, because I've got five thousand dollars in the glove compartment. I can get you more as needed. Just in case the owner's home, you'll be able to get a hotel room until we figure out next steps."

Melanie snorted. "Highly unlikely. This is his second home, his escape from the harsh Minnesota winters. Snowbirds like him don't gravitate to extreme temperatures. He'll be fishing on a Minnesota lake about now, not sweating it out in the desert in August."

Rosalyn glanced at the dash. The outdoor temperature gauge read 109. "A snowbird? You're right, then, he's definitely flown north for the summer."

As the miles wore on, the houses got fewer and farther between, older, and more dilapidated.

They passed a few ranches, and Rosalyn slowed up for the curves and the rough spots in the road. "Are we almost there?"

"A little way further."

"We're getting pretty far out. We're practically off the grid."

"That's why they call it a hideaway."

"But you need cell service. That's an essential."

"Rosalyn, I know you mean well, and I am grateful for your help—it's a relief to have you here. I love you and you're the only person in my life I trust. So don't take offense when I say that if I want your advice—"

"You're going to get it whether you want it or not. In case Blake shows up, you have to be able to call nine-one-one."

"The point is to be so far out of sight, he won't find me. But if he does, I'm prepared."

"What does that mean?"

"I have a pistol in my purse."

"Do you know how to use it?"

"I know how to point it, and that should be enough to get him to turn tail and run. Make a right at the next intersection, and then get ready for a bumpy ride."

After another three or four miles, that took a good half an hour due to the horrible, rutted road, Rosalyn spotted a run-down old house.

Really old.

Really run-down.

Then an old weathered barn.

"You should see the look on your face." Mel said. "I'm not above sleeping in a place like that if it means getting away from Blake, but don't worry, I won't have to. Back when this was a working ranch, that building next to the barn was a bunk house for hired hands. The main house, where we're going, is a mile up the road, and it's been completely remodeled."

Rosalyn blew out a breath.

"I had a few days to think about this while Blake had me imprisoned in my own home. I've got a plan. Just try to relax and trust me."

"I don't know how you can be so calm, but I'm impressed," Rosalyn said. "I do trust you. And I'm proud of you."

Melanie seemed to be catching her breath, then answered, "I'm proud of *us*."

"I feel a little like Thelma and Louise."

"That's the spirit. But don't drive us off a cliff please."

"I see it!" Rosalyn slowed and veered onto a side road barely wide enough for her vehicle. A few minutes later she pulled up the concrete drive. Mel hadn't been kidding when she said this place had been remodeled. The one-story ranch house stretched across a well-maintained lot with traditional desert xeriscaping to conserve water. Giant saguaro's instead of trees, gravel instead of grass, and desert wildflowers instead of petunias. The timber framed home featured an expansive porch with deep overhangs, and a style that perfectly blended old-west tradition with modern efficiency. "It's stunning. Like something out of a movie."

"They do have a few movie sets in the area. I think *The Guns of Navarone* was shot against the backdrop of the Superstitions."

"Try to think of this as a well-deserved vacation. I feel a lot better knowing you'll be comfortable. I was beginning to worry there wouldn't be indoor plumbing."

"Not an issue. There are four bathrooms."

"Great. My bladder's about to burst."

They hurried inside with the few belongings Mel brought with her, and after finding one of the advertised bathrooms and splashing water on her face, Ros joined Mel in an open-style great room. It was luxuriously furnished, boasting modern pieces mixed with antler chandeliers and faux kerosene lamps. "I wish I could spend the night. I was thinking of making some excuse to Ashton. What if we call and say we decided, on the spur of the moment, to drive to Flagstaff to get out of the heat for the weekend. That would buy you even more time."

"Too suspicious. And Blake would insist I drive directly home. The minute he guesses I've flown the coop, he's going to start looking. Besides, there's no cell service out here. We're officially off the grid, my friend."

Pacing the room, Rosalyn kept her eyes on her phone. No bars. No bars. No bars.

She walked out onto the porch and back indoors.

Still no bars.

"That's weird. Philip's friend must have plenty of money— this place is off the hook. I'm surprised he put so much into remodeling a place with no services. It's going to be hard to sell, later on."

"My guess is he doesn't care about resale value. And he probably *wanted* to be off the grid. I think Philip said he was an artist—or a writer, someone who craves privacy."

Rosalyn frowned. She'd already advised Mel to find a place to stay with cell service, and this ranch was both luxurious and well off the beaten path; she could see the appeal. "I'm sorry. I don't mean to sound like a broken record but your phone is your lifeline. Let's go back to Gold Canyon and get you a hotel room."

"No cell service means Blake can't track my phone."

There were so many things to consider. Rosalyn had worried Blake might have a tracking device on Melanie's car, but totally overlooked the fact that he could've been tracking Mel's phone this whole time. "We should've thought of that before. He could have found your phone at any point along the way... before we went off the grid."

"I turned off location sharing before we left. That will make Blake suspicious, but I'm hoping it will seem like an innocent glitch, and besides, what choice did I have? Only Ashton can track you. He wouldn't, would he?"

"Highly doubtful. When he golfs, he's totally focused on the game."

"Good. But just in case Ashton does try to track you at some point, let's be tricky about the route you take home and turn it to our advantage. I'll drop you in town—if you're still agreeable to leaving me your car."

"Of course."

"Then you can get a ride to Apache Junction, then to Phoenix, maybe even north to Prescott and *then* take a shuttle back to Tucson."

"Smart. Only for all those Ubers I might need a thousand dollars of the emergency cash I just gave you."

"Take all of it."

"I'm joking."

"I'm not. I don't want your money."

"You'll pay me back."

"I promise." Mel's eyes moistened and for a split second she dropped the brave warrior face, and in those sweet honey-brown eyes, Rosalyn could read the desolation, the naked fear. Like a little girl—a terrified little girl. Then as quickly as it had dropped, the façade returned.

"The only promise I need is for you to be careful. You said you had a pistol."

Mel retrieved her purse from where she'd left it on the kitchen island. "Right here." She pulled it out and held it timidly in both hands, aimed toward the floor.

"Is it loaded?"

"Yup."

"So, what's the plan?"

"Sorry?"

"You said you had a plan."

Mel returned her pistol to her purse and set it on the coffee table. "I lied, but don't worry. Something will come to me."

*Promise me you'll look out for Melanie. Treat her like your sister.*

At this point, she wasn't sure she could keep Melanie safe. But one thing was certain: she would never leave her own sister alone in the boondocks with no phone service and a gun and tell her to fend for herself. "I know you think it's too risky, but Blake is going to figure out you're gone before long anyway—if he hasn't already. I'm going to drive down the road until I get service, and then I'm going to call Ashton and tell him you and I went to Flagstaff for the weekend. I'm spending the night. I'm not going to leave you here all alone."

Mel crumpled onto the couch. "Philip would hate me for putting you in danger."

"Stop it. I promise not to say another word about how I'm to blame for bringing Blake into your life if you promise not to say another word about not wanting to put me in danger. We are in this together... we're sisters."

Mel blew her nose and looked up, then smiled weakly. "Sisters."

"I'm going to get something with ice to drink—cross fingers the owner keeps the water on when he's away."

"I'll take one too, since you're up."

Rosalyn grabbed two cups and opened the freezer. "Jackpot! We not only have ice, we have frozen meals. I wonder if he left any bottled water." She opened the fridge and covered her mouth. "I'm afraid the owner must be staying here after all. This fridge is loaded with fresh food. But, maybe he'll let us stay. You said he was a good friend of Philip's."

"Hello, darling," said a voice deep enough to make a woman swoon.

Rosalyn turned, a sick feeling in her stomach.

"And Rosalyn, so nice of you to join us." Blake waved a pistol in her direction. "I thought Melanie might turn up here, but I wasn't expecting her to bring a guest. Good thing I stocked plenty of food. Now, please pick your jaw up off the floor and join my beautiful bride on the couch. Bring the waters with you."

The room was spinning, her vision wavering. She took a deep breath and walked woodenly to the couch where she took a place next to Mel, their shoulders and hips touching.

She set the bottles of water in front of them, and then clasped Melanie's hand in hers.

"Good girl." Blake pulled a prescription bottle from his pocket and emptied some pills onto the coffee table. "Three for each of you. These will help you relax."

"No thank you, darling," Melanie said. "Will you please put that thing away so we can talk?"

"Take your medicine, my love, and nothing bad will happen to you."

Mel squeezed Ros's hand and scooped up three pills, washed them quickly down with water. "I'm going to do everything you want me to, Blake. I promise. So, you can let Rosalyn go home to Ashton. You haven't done anything wrong. I fell off a treadmill. That's all. Rosalyn saw it happen, didn't you, Ros?"

"That's right, this is all just a big misunderstanding. Put the gun down, and we can all go back to normal. It will be like nothing ever happened. Just like after you put those rats in my bathtub. We carried on perfectly after that, didn't we? We can do it again."

"Your turn, Ros." He jerked his pistol toward the remaining pills.

"I can't. I have a long drive back. You two need privacy to work things out."

"Take them, now, or I'll blow her brains out in front of you."

Rosalyn steeled her spine. "I don't believe you, Blake. You're hurting, but you don't really want to kill Melanie. You love her. I can see it written all over your face."

"You think you know everything, Ros. But you know nothing. Nothing about who I am. Where I came from. Who I truly love."

Melanie's hand was growing limp in her grasp.

Blake strolled behind the couch and pressed his pistol to the back of Melanie's head. "Take your medicine, Ros, or don't. Whether Melanie lives or dies doesn't really matter to me. I leave the decision to you."

# FORTY-THREE

## NOW

The case of wet food wasn't heavy so much as awkward, banging against Julian's knees with every step he took toward Walter's kitchen. No space on the counter. "Where should I put this?"

"Just set it down next to Whiskers' bowl."

"Can opener?"

Walter pulled a rusted one from a drawer. Whiskers rubbed up against Julian's leg, mewing while he twisted the can open, his fingers sore from the force it took. No wonder Walter had been feeding Whiskers nothing but dry food—he probably couldn't open a can with his arthritis.

"I'll open another and put it in the fridge. I'm going to order an electric can opener for you from—"

"Don't bother."

"It's not a bother. Dr. Ginger said Whiskers hasn't been getting enough wet food."

"I've got it covered. Thank you for taking us to the vet again, and for bringing over this case of prescription food, but I've got plenty." Walter shuffled over to the pantry and flung open the door to reveal three cases of prescription cat food stacked underneath neatly organized shelves. Shelves filled with canned goods and spices, and bags and bags of pasta. "My new electric can opener is scheduled for delivery tomorrow."

Julian dumped the cat food into the bowl. It squished as it slid out of the can in one slimy piece.

Walter sat down at the kitchen table—a nice oak one with four chairs.

Julian took a place across from him and put his hands behind his head. "You got a new table."

"And a new sofa and a new bed." Walter pulled a checkbook out of his pocket. "What do I owe you for the vet bills? I know the visits weren't free."

"Not a thing."

"I want to pay."

"Walter it's not—"

"I got money." He flicked his pen across his teeth. "A letter came in the mail. It said I was entitled to money from a class action lawsuit, and then, the next week, a check arrived."

"Look, Walter, unless that check was for a million dollars, I think you should use the money for expenses going forward. The vet visits and the food are my gift to Whiskers. But you can pay his way from now on if you can afford it."

Walter nodded. "If you're sure… I was thinking I should keep a little in the bank for emergencies."

"That's right. But I'm glad you got a windfall." He wanted to ask how much but that didn't seem proper.

"Twenty thousand dollars." Walter grinned. "Can you believe it?"

"Wow. I'm happy for you, and this must be your lucky week, because, I've got something to tell you."

Walter leaned on his elbows, fixed his eyes on Julian.

"It's not much. Just information that might lead to more information that might lead to—"

"I understand. You haven't found her."

"It's a fresh road to travel, Walter. And that's thanks to you telling me you gave Zoe money and letting me look through her things. So, I want to be transparent with you. But I don't want you getting your hopes up."

"I like hope."

So did Julian. "Here's the deal. I got a hit on Zoe's friend. The young woman in the picture we found—the one who moved to Germany." He needed to put this carefully. "I researched her name, because I wanted to speak to her, find out if she was back in the states and when was the last time she heard from Zoe."

"You talked to her?"

"By phone."

"So, what's the news, then?"

"I found out that Mrs. Hill—that's her married name— hasn't seen or heard from Zoe since she moved to Germany. And she's still living there."

"That's no good."

"I'm not done."

Walter clapped his hands and Whiskers leaped into his lap.

"It seems that some years ago, she doesn't recall how many, Mrs. Hill got a notice from the Arizona Corporation Commission regarding registration for a company under her maiden name—which was Greene."

Walter stopped petting the cat.

"But Mrs. Hill doesn't own any corporations in Arizona or anywhere else. It made her a little nervous, but she checked her bank accounts and credit score and everything was fine. She figured it was just a mistake. The name 'Greene' is so common. So, she threw away the notice and never got another one. She doesn't remember the company name, but I've already reached out to a contact at the Arizona Corporation Commission. I expect to get a list from them, by tomorrow, if not sooner, of all the people with the last name 'Greene' who have registered a corporation in Arizona for the past ten years."

"You think Zoe's living under her friend's name! You think she started Zoe's Closet after all!"

"There's no Zoe's Closet registered in Arizona—I checked that first thing. It's a big leap to conclude Zoe assumed her friend's identity for the purposes of starting a business, but it's worth looking into. That notice might have been a simple error, but it might signal identity theft. If Zoe left on her own, which, Walter, is what I lean toward, now that I know she had ten thousand dollars for a new start; she would likely be living under an assumed name. And since her friend is out of the country, hers would be a natural choice. They looked like sisters in that old photograph. Maybe Zoe got her hands on her friend's driver's license and then used that to get other identification."

"What's next?" Walter's eyes filled up.

Julian didn't want to crush him if the outcome wasn't what they hoped—but Walter deserved honesty. "Unfortunately, it is, indeed, a common name. But when I get that list from the Arizona Corporation Commission, I can narrow it down."

"You're really going to find her, aren't you? I'm going to live to see my granddaughter again." A tear rolled down Walter's cheek and splashed onto his crepe-skinned neck.

"I'd say the odds are better than they've been." If Zoe was still alive, she might very well be living in Arizona, right under their noses, and Julian was determined to find her.

# FORTY-FOUR

## NOW

The whispers drifting her way sounded like exploding grenades. Melanie bolted upright and forced her heavy eyelids open. When she tried to lift her hands to cover her ears, she found them bound by rope. The world lurched into focus, as if she'd been driving in the dark without headlights, and then suddenly switched them on. She set to work immediately, biting at the rope to loosen her wrist restraints. "What's happening?"

"Shh. We're okay. We're all okay," Rosalyn said in a soothing voice.

Melanie cast her gaze around, slowly remembering where she was—the ranch. "He locked us in the old horse barn, didn't he?"

"Yes," Ros answered.

"Who's that on the bed with you? Did Blake—"

"My name is Lola."

"I'm sorry, but who are you?" Melanie stared at the rusted rings on the floor attached to chains leading up to Lola's feet. Rosalyn was bound by a second set of shackles. They sat back-to-back on opposite sides of a straw mattress covered with an old sheet.

"This is the woman I knew as Sherry Anne," Ros said. "But it turns out that's not her real name."

"I'm Lola Sampson. Mine is a long story, and I don't think now is the right time to go into it all, but Blake kidnapped me. It's not the first time, and unless he's changed his stripes, Ashton is part of it, too. I think he's the one calling the shots. The more dangerous of the pair."

Mel searched Rosalyn's face to gauge her reaction. It remained stoic.

"Ashton has nothing to do with this," Ros said. "When he realizes I'm missing, he'll go to the police right away. He'll find us. Wait and see."

"If now's not the right time to tell your story, Lola, I don't know when would be. It sounds like you know some things about both my husband *and* Rosalyn's. Something we both need to hear."

Lola nodded. "Of course, you're right. In case you two make it out of here alive, and I don't, you need to understand how dangerous they are."

Melanie tried to get off the dirt floor, but her knees were too weak, her head too groggy.

"Blake was my college sweetheart, but he was into some kind of illegal schemes with Ashton," Lola began. "The two of them scammed me out of my money with a fake charity called Opportunity Knocks. After a while, Blake confessed the whole thing to me. I forgave him, because he'd had an awful past that had left him vulnerable. Then, one day, someone came up behind me in a parking lot and put a cloth over my mouth. They beat me up and left me for dead but I survived. When I went to the police, Blake and Ashton gave each other an alibi. Ashton was definitely part of it—and now... Blake swears Ashton forced him to bring me here."

Melanie was feeling stronger. She wrangled her way back

onto her feet. "I'm sorry to say so, Ros, but I agree that Ashton's always been the leader of that duo."

Rosalyn shook her head. "I trust my husband."

"Like I trusted mine. Open your eyes. What this woman says makes sense. Think about the phony art Ashton was peddling."

"It was only the one time, and he didn't know it was a forgery."

"We can debate that later," Mel said. "Right now, we need to figure a way out of this barn."

"I don't think Blake wants to kill us," Lola interjected. "I've been locked in here for a long time—seems like forever—and he hasn't hurt me yet, even though he's had every chance. He brings me food and water. He unshackled my hands when I promised to be good. It took me a couple of days to convince him, but I finally managed. I've known Blake a long time, and he's weak—a follower, not a leader. If we tread lightly, we might be able to convince him to let us go. I've been talking to him about turning himself in. He seemed to be softening to the idea before he brought you two here. But we've got to convince him before Ashton gets back."

"Ashton was here? When?" For the first time, Rosalyn sounded doubtful about her husband.

"Before Blake brought you both to the barn—the same day, but earlier. I didn't see Ashton, but I *heard* him speaking. He and Blake were outside."

"Did you call for help? Did you scream?" Rosalyn asked.

"It was *Ashton*. If I would have screamed, he would've come in here and killed me on the spot. So I stayed completely quiet, and I haven't heard his voice since. But I'm one hundred percent sure it was him. He has to be the one giving Blake his orders."

Melanie had been tugging at the rope around her wrists with her teeth, and, at last, there was just enough slack to wiggle her hands. Moments later, she jerked them free. "The last thing I remember is Blake forcing Rosalyn and me to take pills at gunpoint. How long ago do you think that was?"

"You two were knocked out a long time," Lola said. "Nearly twenty-four hours, I bet. The door is locked from the outside—I hear the bolt drop every time Blake leaves, but the good news is he didn't chain you up like he did Rosalyn and me."

"My husband, a prince among men."

"There aren't enough shackles for three people," Rosalyn observed matter-of-factly.

"And he thinks I'm the least resourceful." Melanie reached her hand out to the wall to keep from falling. Her legs felt boneless, but she managed to make her way over to Lola and Ros. "But he's underestimating me. If I can somehow pry these rings out of the floor and get you free, maybe the three of us can break down the door."

"There's a pitchfork in one of the horse stalls—or at least the top of one. It's covered with a blanket, but in the mornings, I can see sunlight reflecting off the prongs. I don't think Blake knows it's there," Lola said.

Melanie wobbled to the stall and quickly spotted the gleaming points sticking out from under a dirty quilt. "Big mistake."

She dragged the corner of the quilt, her arms so weak it seemed the fabric was woven from lead. Bit by bit she revealed her weapon: the top half of a rusty pitchfork, its handle split into a perfect spear.

# FORTY-FIVE

## NOW

Rosalyn's ankles burned from the friction of the iron shackles. She smiled encouragement at Melanie, who'd been working a long time. Melanie had tugged a loose prong from the pitchfork. She'd been using that to try to pick the lock on Rosalyn's shackles, with no apparent progress, for ages. But they'd had plenty of time for discussion, and Ros had explained the "Sherry Anne" story to Mel in detail.

Mel sighed.

*She has to be getting tired and frustrated.* "Try Lola's. Maybe hers is easier."

"I'll switch to your other foot." Melanie gritted her teeth. "I'm going to get us out of this one way or the other."

It was understood she meant all three of them, Lola included, but it would have been nice for her to say so explicitly. There was some kind of weird tension between Lola and Melanie. Either Rosalyn was imagining it—very possible—or it had to do with the *fake* story about Lola having a book club with Philip. Maybe Mel didn't understand it was completely fabricated and saw Lola as an old rival—she was eyeing her like she didn't trust her.

"So, Lola never knew Philip at all," Rosalyn offered.

"I followed that when you told me the story." Melanie didn't look up.

"Okay, just thought I'd clear that up, in case."

"In case what?"

"In case you were upset about her connection to Philip. I mean the three of us are in this together, and we need to have each other's backs one hundred percent."

Mel rocked back on her haunches. "I understand it was a ruse. What I'm not thrilled about, Lola, is that you lied to Rosalyn. You inserted yourself into our family circle under false pretenses, calling yourself Sherry Anne. Not trying to be rude, but I don't have the energy right now to be diplomatic. You shouldn't have lied to Ros. With that said, you don't deserve any of this. And I'm so, so sorry for what happened to you when you were younger. I can't imagine what you've suffered."

"I'm the one who's sorry. Instead of trying to get revenge, I should have told both you and Rosalyn about your husbands, so that you could've protected yourselves from those monsters."

Ros wanted to defend Ashton, to protest, again, that he wasn't a monster. But she couldn't account for his presence at the ranch earlier. And she didn't doubt that Lola could easily recognize his voice. Then there was the fact that, the same day she and Melanie came to the ranch, he'd told her himself he planned to hang out with Blake.

Suddenly, the door rattled, and then creaked on its hinges.

"Hide the pitchfork!" Ros hissed under her breath, praying it wasn't too late.

Blake stood in the doorway, silhouetted by the light from the sinking sun. His gaze arrowed to the loose prong in Melanie's hand.

Rosalyn's pulse pounded in her ears.

Melanie catapulted to her feet.

Dropped the prong. Grabbed the pitchfork. "You bastard!"

*He has a pistol.*

Eyes blazing, Melanie lifted the pitchfork over her head, and Rosalyn's stomach dropped. "Melanie! No! He's got a gun!"

Blake took giant strides across the barn, his gaze locked on Melanie, his shadow following him like a black cape.

Melanie lunged at Blake with the pitchfork, and, for Rosalyn, time slowed to an excruciating pace.

Mel tripped.

Lunged again.

Stumbled and fell onto her back.

Mel was completely vulnerable, now—they all were.

*You promised Philip to protect her!*

Shackled and physically helpless, Rosalyn tried begging. "No! Please, Blake. Don't hurt her! You love her!"

Blake raised his arm.

Pointed his pistol at Mel.

The shackles cut into her flesh as Rosalyn strained against them. "No! No! No!"

A deafening crack followed a flash of light.

Melanie cried out, then her body jerked, and blood pooled around her. An eternity passed before her spasms finally stopped, and then Blake fell to his knees beside her.

# FORTY-SIX

## NOW

Sobbing. Moaning. Shrieking.

The entire barn rang with the sounds of despair. The cries rose to the lofty ceiling and bounced off the rafters, dove down to the floor, swooped back up to the roof like hawks carrying prey in their talons.

The stench of sweat and blood filled Rosalyn's mouth. Unable to bring herself to watch as Blake dragged Melanie's body from the barn, she stared, instead, transfixed in horror, at the bloody marks left in her wake.

A wave of hate filled her.

She emptied her stomach, and the sour smell of vomit mingled with the rest of the foul odors in the air.

The barn door thundered shut... but she didn't hear the bolt drop.

Like a slap in the face, the absence of that thud snapped her out of her delirium.

*He forgot to bolt the door!*

*Do not shut down.*

*Do not give up.*

Melanie had shown such courage, charging the devil with

his own pitchfork. And, though she hadn't prevailed, there had been a moment when she'd had a chance. It had been a risky move, and it had cost her life—but there was nothing more dangerous than doing nothing. Rosalyn refused to wait, like a pet, for Blake to deliver them food and water. She would rather die than live by his mercy.

Wiping snot and tears from her face, she spit out the bad taste in her mouth. "Lola, honey, we've got to get out of here."

At some point, Lola must have crawled off the straw mattress onto the floor. She lay curled up, hugging her knees to her chest, her bare feet looking tiny and childlike, protruding from the shackles. Her face was splotched with fat red blobs, streaked with dirt and tear trails. Her chest heaved with panting breaths, strangled whimpers, wailing cries. Beneath her creased brow, her lids fluttered as if she was afraid to open her eyes.

"Lola! Lola! Look at me!"

Lola's lids slowly opened and her gaze connected with Rosalyn's.

"We've got to get out of here. Lola, you *must* stop crying," Rosalyn commanded.

Lola's rounded back straightened, and, little by little, her weeping ceased.

"We've got to get out of here," Lola repeated Ros's words.

"That's right. There's no reasoning with Blake. We'll never convince him to let us go. He's shown us who he truly is, and we cannot wait for him to come back for us."

"What will we do?"

Ros took a fortifying breath and willed herself to shut off the feeling part of her brain, to let reason instruct her instead. "We pick the locks on our shackles and then find a way to open the door. We'll use whatever slack we have in the chains to drag..."

"To drag what?" Lola followed Rosalyn's gaze across the floor.

Ros had been about to say they could use their chains to lasso the pitchfork, then go back to picking the locks with its prongs, when her eyes alighted on a small, shiny object.

Unless her mind was playing a trick on her... no, the look on Lola's face told Ros she'd seen it, too.

It wasn't a mirage.

It was a miracle.

"A key!" Lola shouted. "It must have fallen out of Blake's pocket. Do you think it will unlock our chains?"

"I don't know, but we have to get it."

"It's too far away."

"Maybe, but we can drag *the pitchfork* to us using our chains —it's closer. And once we get hold of that—"

"We use the pitchfork to reach the key."

Rosalyn and Lola set to work. There was no further discussion. No mention of the terror that had unfolded in this barn mere moments ago.

No mention of the tragic loss of life.

No mention of their own fates if they should fail.

Instead, they focused solely on their mission.

*Get the pitchfork, then get the key.*

The repetitive sounds of chains slapping against the dirt floor filled the barn and every clank lifted Rosalyn's spirits.

When hope turns into action it makes quite a racket.

# FORTY-SEVEN

## NOW

Zoe sprawled naked on the big fluffy bed inside the largest suite on the ranch. Swimming in the sheets, she stroked their soft fabric, delighting in the feel of the luxury she'd always craved and, at last, possessed.

This ranch was hers—it said so right on the deed, which was titled in the name of her nonprofit, Opportunity Knocks. Buying this place was one of the first things she'd done after she and Blake got access to Melanie's inheritance.

She slipped her hands between her legs, enjoying every sensation, reveling in what she had accomplished, anticipating the final time she would join her body with Blake's. The blood in her veins was singing, her senses heightened, her heart revving. Sex with Blake, tonight, was going to be exquisite, and all the sweeter, because it would be their swan song.

"Darling? What's taking so long? I'm getting lonely in this big bed all by myself." Her voice cracked on the word "lonely".

All the more reason for them to part ways. Before she'd met Blake—only a boy at the time, and not so dangerous for her heart as he was now—she'd never been lonely a day.

Because she'd never truly cared for another human being.

Zoe had been on her own her entire life up until she'd rescued Blake from that horrible shopkeeper. She was on her own with her mother's corpse when she was just a toddler. She was on her own when she was under the "care" of Walter and Hannah who thought they could make up for the mistakes they'd made with her mother by imposing loads of suffocating rules on Zoe.

Alone—always.

Lonely—never.

Not until the day Blake Tyler decided his wish to lead a so-called "normal" life trumped her need to survive. She craved excitement—but that wasn't the issue. She didn't know how to be "normal". It was impossible for her to function in a world of nine-to-five jobs and kids' soccer games. She'd considered it, for his sake. At one point, she'd thought she could do it. But there was simply no way.

Blake wanted children.

And Zoe refused to ruin an innocent life the way hers had been ruined. She didn't have what it took to nurture a child.

Blake's actions proved he wanted his "ordinary life" more than he wanted Zoe Wessex.

She'd forgiven him that sin once, when he came crawling back, during his college years—shortly after she'd beaten Lola and dumped her in the desert.

After breaking up with Zoe, Blake had taken Lola to Rocky Point for a lover's weekend, and the notion of them together, not for the sake of a scam they were pulling, but because he wanted Lola by his side, had made her physically ill.

Blake had planned to replace *her* with Lola.

She couldn't live with that. Either she had to take her own life or Lola's and she'd made the only sane choice.

Zoe wasn't a religious person, but when a shaman found Lola in the desert and brought her home alive, and then Blake begged Zoe to take him back, it seemed like fate.

And fate was something she *did* believe in.

She'd been fate's victim her entire life until she learned to take matters into her own hands.

Fate was real.

But Zoe knew how to get around it.

The bathroom door creaked open.

Blake emerged, his damp skin glistening, the muscles in his arms rippling as he rubbed his hair with a towel. She ran her eyes, greedily, over every inch of him and posed invitingly, allowing him a view no one else had ever been granted.

*One last time, sweetheart.*

"I missed you," she drawled. He'd taken nearly an hour in the bathroom. "Did you enjoy your shower? If all that hot water didn't relax you, I could give you a massage. You've earned it."

"No, Zoe. I did not enjoy my shower. I did not enjoy scrubbing Melanie's blood off my body and scraping it out from under my fingernails."

She sighed, disappointed that he was still focused on Melanie when he had Zoe ready and waiting for action in front of him. "I guess that was difficult for you."

"Difficult? It was insane. You made me execute my wife in front of Rosalyn and Lola as some kind of loyalty test."

"And you passed. Now you get to come to bed."

"I'm not in the mood."

Blake was too sensitive—which was exactly why he'd failed her. Now he had to pay the price. He'd forced her hand. Left her no choice. "I'll take care of that in a flash. Come here, my love."

"Ros and Lola are even more terrified than before. They're sobbing, suffering. It was cruel to make them witness her death. I don't understand why you made me do that."

"Because you didn't strangle Lola like you were supposed to. You chained her up in the barn, instead of killing her and dumping her body. If they find her DNA on the property, that puts Opportunity Knocks, and both of us, in jeopardy. And you *lied* to me about it."

"I did tell you, eventually. I said I was sorry."

"I had to know if I could trust you. And now I do. You're in too deep. You can't back out of this now. I know you won't let Ros and Lola live, no matter how hard they beg for their lives, because you've killed Melanie right before their eyes."

"It was a heartless thing to do." He tossed the towel on the floor and came and laid down beside her, put his hands behind his head, staring at the ceiling instead of the feast that awaited him. "I love you, Zoe. But I don't like this side of you."

And to think she'd been worried this would be too difficult. That she wouldn't be able to go through with it. "You mean you don't like *me*."

"Not in this particular moment, no."

"Well, then, I guess you're going to have to close your eyes and think of *Melanie*." She climbed on top of him and rubbed the full length of her body against the full length of his. He lay motionless for a while, until at last, he moaned and stirred beneath her. "There you go, my love, I'm all yours tonight. I'll be whoever you want me to be, but just this once."

"I only want you, Zoe," he whispered as he closed his eyes.

When she lifted her hand and stroked his cheek, she felt moisture. "Don't cry. Don't cry. You're the love of my life."

When they were finished, she pulled the covers around them and let him hold her against him until he groaned drowsily and rolled away. Then she tiptoed into the kitchen and poured them both a neat whiskey.

She sat at the edge of the bed, watching the shadow of his lashes on his cheeks, and then traced the curve of his jaw with one finger. "Ready for round two?"

He reached for her, and she laughed. "I'll take that as a yes. Let's take our time though."

He propped up on one elbow and accepted the drink she'd

brought him. Slugged it back in a few gulps. "Great idea. I was parched."

"You worked hard today."

"I don't want to fight anymore." He sat straight up in bed.

They were staring each other in the eyes, naked, when he put his hands on her shoulders.

"I'm sorry," she whispered.

He nodded. "Me too. All I ever wanted was to live like other people. I never wanted to hurt anyone. I never wanted to kill anyone. I only wanted us to live a normal, happy life *together*. But I've finally realized, after all these years, that's not possible."

"Really?" It was too bad he hadn't figured that out before. Maybe things wouldn't have had to end this way. "Are you saying we don't have to get a minivan and kids and a dog?"

He pulled her close, wrapped his arms tightly around her, and she buried her face in his chest. "No minivan. No family. Only you and me, forever."

"Just us?" Her mind began to race. Was there still time? No. It was too late. "Blake, I need to tell you something. I want to be totally honest with you because you are the only person who truly loves me. I hope you can forgive me for what I'm about to tell you."

"There's nothing you can say that will stop me from loving you."

"You know how the plan was to set up Ashton to take the fall for killing Ros and Lola? After you brought Lola here, instead of getting rid of her, I felt so betrayed. I thought I couldn't trust you, so I went with plan B instead. I've arranged things, by various means, to make it seem like you and Ashton were partners in all of this."

He kissed her neck. "I already know that."

"You do?" She lifted her head to see his reaction. "How?"

"I may not understand the finer points. But I'm not stupid. You ordered me to kill Melanie in front of Ros and Lola, and the only reason I can figure is that you plan to frame *me* instead of Ashton for the murders."

She tried to jerk away, but his hands dug into her flesh.

"I'd like to know all the details, every turn of your twisted brain—plan B must be brilliant—but I'm afraid we've run out of time for talking," he rasped.

His breathing was slowing, his words slurring. Blake *knew* she'd poisoned him. "Yes, I think we have."

"I placed a key to the shackles on the floor of the barn. It will probably take Ros and Lola a while to spot it, and even more time to drag it to them, but by now, they've probably freed themselves and made a run for it."

His hands wrapped around her throat. His fingers began to squeeze.

"Let me go, Blake! You're hurting me."

She grabbed his wrists, tried to pry his hands off her throat, but... she had no strength, no air. As the world faded away, she heard him whispering in her ear over and over again.

*I love you.*

# FORTY-EIGHT

## NOW

Zoe coughed, sputtered, gasped for air. As her brain fog lifted, an excruciating sensation replaced the fingers around her throat, a sensation worse than any physical pain.

*Betrayal.*

The only person she'd ever loved had tried to murder her.

And Blake damn well would have succeeded if she hadn't poisoned his whiskey.

He must have succumbed to the strychnine just after she lost consciousness, otherwise she was sure he would've finished her off.

*Poor Blake.*

He hadn't seen it coming until it was too late. He should have known that after all the ways he'd failed her—especially the way he continued to put his bond with Lola and Ashton over his loyalty to her—that she couldn't trust him. And then there was the matter of the spoils of victory.

She'd never relished the idea of splitting all that money with Blake, but she had given the idea of sharing a life with him a real chance.

A real chance was more than anyone had ever given her.

In the end, she'd granted Blake's every wish, and he'd let her down when she'd asked him, for once, to be the one who got his hands dirty.

If there had been a small pang of guilt as she'd added strychnine into his drink, he'd choked it out of her with his bare hands.

No more regrets.

No more attachments.

Not to Walter.

Not to Hannah.

Most definitely not to Blake, or any other man.

Zoe Wessex was flying solo forever and ever, amen.

She rolled off the bed and landed on the floor with a satisfying crack. And there, her lover, her confidant, her one and only friend—his face blue, his eyes open—sprawled lifeless.

"Damn you, Blake Tyler. Why did you give them the key?" She rose and stepped over his corpse. "Doesn't matter. I'll find them. Lola and Ros will pay."

Even if they'd escaped the barn, and who knew if they'd managed that feat, they couldn't have gotten far.

She went to the closet and grabbed a flashlight and a pistol.

*Time to go hunting.*

# FORTY-NINE

## NOW

The heat was their foe, Rosalyn thought.

The darkness a mighty impediment. But their worst enemy was their bare feet.

Blake had removed their shoes and socks before chaining them up, and, even at night, the hot desert sand burned the tender skin on the bottom of their feet. The danger from cactus needles and scorpions and snakes meant they had to be smart where they stepped.

As tempting as it was to run for her life, Rosalyn knew the only chance they had to traverse the desert at night, barefoot, was to move carefully and quietly.

"Lola," she hissed, "slow down."

Ahead, Lola raced through the night. Rosalyn didn't want to shout. Didn't want to risk the sound of her voice alerting Blake to their escape. But what choice did she have? They needed to stick together. It was too easy, too dangerous, to get lost in the desert.

"Lola! Please, slow down! Wait for me!"

## FIFTY

### NOW

Lola's thoughts were a fire blazing across her brain. She'd been here before. Left to die in the desert. Back then, she hadn't been able to stand, to walk, to run. She'd been at the mercy of fate, and fate had rescued her in the form of a shaman. But this time she would not rely on miracles.

This time she would save herself.

"Lola!" Rosalyn called after her.

*Keep running!*

The voice in her head commanded her to flee. To disappear. To fight for her life, and *only* her life.

*You have a right to survive.*

*You owe her nothing.*

But something deeper than flesh, deeper even than bone, something at her very core, slowed her down. She could *not* abandon Rosalyn in the wilderness the way she had once been abandoned.

Waiting for Rosalyn wasn't the smart thing to do.

It was the *human* thing.

*Help her.*

*We have to help each other.*

"Hurry up, Ros!" she cried, looking back over her shoulder. Then her foot slammed against a rock. Her ankle twisted, and she flew forward, landing face first onto the dirt and scree. She bounded back to her feet and limped to a boulder; resting, panting, waiting for Rosalyn.

# FIFTY-ONE

## NOW

"Are you hurt?" Rosalyn trotted to Lola's side, devastated by the thought Lola might be seriously injured. "We mustn't run," she whispered.

"You ran over here, just now," Lola whispered back.

"I shouldn't have. It was instinct when I saw you fall, but we have to be smarter than our instincts if we're going to survive. And we should keep our voices low. Stick together."

"I shouldn't have run off like that. I shouldn't have left you."

"Never mind that. Are you hurt?"

Lola was leaning against a boulder with one foot lifted off the ground. "Just my ankle."

"Can you put weight on it?"

Lola, tried to stand and let out a soft yelp. "Yes."

"Put your arm around me."

Together, they shuffled a few steps forward. The moon emerged from behind the clouds and Rosalyn glanced at the ground. They were leaving quite a trail for anyone who came looking.

They struggled a few yards more and then Lola stopped

short. "I changed my mind. You should go ahead and get help, it's our best chance."

"I won't leave you."

"You're the one who said we have to be smarter than our instincts," Lola fired back.

"We will be. We just have to figure this out. We're not going to make it to the road tonight. We can't see well enough to get our bearings. I have no idea which direction to go. I think we should find a place to hide and wait for daybreak. We can take turns sleeping and keeping watch," Ros said.

"We can't stop here. We're too close to the ranch. He'll find us. You have to keep moving."

"*We* have to keep moving. You're wasting time arguing with me. We stick together. End of discussion. But how can we make sure we don't just go in circles?"

"Find the Big Dipper and look for the North Star?" Lola said, doubtfully.

Thank goodness Lola seemed to have dropped the idea of going it alone. Time was too precious to waste arguing. "The North Star isn't a bad idea." Rosalyn looked up at the sky and the twinkling stars, scanning the horizon for the Big Dipper. "It will show us true north, then we can keep moving in one direction, but *which* direction should we head? I don't want to wind up back at the ranch. Let me think for a minute."

Tomorrow morning, the Lost Dutchman state park would be full of hikers and tourists. Rangers! And there were water spigots there.

"On the way to the ranch, Mel and I drove past the Lost Dutchman trailhead. That means the park is nearby. We know that park is at the base of the Superstitions. We can't be more than a few miles away. We'll use the North Star to keep us straight and head toward the mountains. The Superstitions and the stars will be our map."

"I don't know if I can make it, Rosalyn. I can't move fast enough."

"Blake probably won't discover we're gone until morning. We'll be at the park by then. Slow and steady is the only way in this terrain at night anyway. You beat the desert once, Lola. You can do it again."

"You make it sound like the state park's a sure thing, but people get lost out there and die."

"*We* won't get lost. When the sun comes up, we'll find a trail. We'll find help. But what I need you to do right now is put one foot in front of the other."

Leaning on Rosalyn's shoulder, Lola did just that.

"There you go. Easy does it. Whenever you get tired, we'll stop and rest. We can make it, Lola—fear is our fuel and we have plenty of that. All we have to do is stay alive until sunrise."

# FIFTY-TWO

## NOW

There was something about the desert at night. The solitude, the howling coyotes, the snakes coiling unseen, waiting to strike anyone or anything that threatened their survival. The whole of it made Zoe feel at peace with herself and one with the universe. Tonight, in the company of the other animals, she tracked her prey—with a flashlight in hand and a pistol stuffed into the back of her pants.

She felt a deep sense of purpose, of belonging.

Something she'd never felt in the company of people.

Except for Blake.

He'd been the one person she'd thought was like her. But it was all an illusion. What did the books call it? *Trauma bonding.* They had their hard-knock life in common, but little else.

That magnetic pull they'd felt toward one another was never going to be enough to overcome their differences.

She'd suspected that when he'd refused to get his hands dirty with Philip.

She'd wanted *Blake* to switch Philip's medications, but he'd refused, and she'd had to take on the risk herself. But after

Philip was out of the way, Blake had been eager to reap the rewards of *her* labor.

He was like a pleading puppy who'd melted her heart and then peed on the carpet. She should never have involved him in her schemes. If it weren't for him tossing the key behind him when he'd dragged Melanie from the barn, Lola and Rosalyn wouldn't have gotten free. She had hoped he'd been lying about that. But when she'd checked the barn, they were gone, and who knew how much of a head start they'd had.

But no matter.

They couldn't get far without water.

Without shoes.

She'd find them—she had the advantage.

A rustling in a nearby bush caught her attention. A rattlesnake, alerting her to keep away. When a snake gives you a warning, it's a kindness. It's doing you a favor. If you don't heed the warning, you deserve the consequence.

Blake hadn't heeded her warnings.

Now he was dead, and without him to hold her back, to make her doubt herself, to question whether the things she did were right or wrong, she was more powerful than ever.

Zoe swept her flashlight over the rocky terrain.

It'd been hours since she'd started searching with no luck... until now. She lifted her chin and yowled like the wild creature she was.

Footprints!

Human tracks.

Distinct and easy to follow.

She'd find Rosalyn and Lola easily, and then do what she must. It wasn't personal; it was nature's way. Survival of the fittest. Nothing more, nothing less. She wasn't a good person or a bad person—she was an animal fighting for her life.

# FIFTY-THREE

## NOW

*Footprints!*

Followed by bootprints.

Two sets of bare feet—most likely two women, judging by their size. And the bootprints could belong to either a small man or a tall woman. In this case, Julian had a sick certainty the boots belonged to a woman named Zoe Wessex, and the bare feet to Rosalyn Hightower and Lola Sampson.

After finding a corporation, Opportunity Knocks, registered under Zoe's assumed name—and Blake Tyler's, he'd learned that same nonprofit held the title to The Rocking Z Ranch.

That had led him, here, to the spread at Gold Canyon, where he'd discovered the body of Blake Tyler on a bedroom floor. A quick search of the premises revealed an empty barn with evidence someone had been holding prisoners there, and in the old bunkhouse, he'd found Ashton Hightower.

Bound, gagged, drugged, unconscious—but alive.

Julian had called for backup, but he couldn't waste time waiting on them.

Now, leading with his pistol, he followed the footprints.

*I have to bring* all *of them home alive.*

If he was forced to kill Zoe, it would be the end of Walter Wessex, and Julian couldn't bear to do that to his friend.

# FIFTY-FOUR

"I need to rest," Lola said.

They were so close. Rosalyn could tell by the clumps of desert poppies at their feet. "Do you think you can make it to that boulder?" It wasn't a question, really. They had to be able to take cover in case Blake was tracking them.

"I don't think so."

The sun had barely risen, but there was light enough for Ros to see that Lola's legs were shaking, and that her ankle was bruised and swollen to the size of a small melon.

She knelt on the dirt. "Climb on."

"No. You can't carry me on your back into the park."

"Not all the way, just to that big boulder over there, so we can rest. Then you're going to have to do your best. You'll walk if you can, but if not, I *will* carry you on my back. We'll go a few yards and stop and rest and then go again."

"That will never work."

"We'll make it work. We're not going to curl up and die out here."

"Be reasonable, Ros. We're a long way from the ranch now.

I'll let you carry me to the boulder, and I'll hide. Then you go get help. It's the best way for *both* of us."

"Climb on. Let's get to cover. Get a minute or two of rest, and then we can argue about the plan."

Rosalyn's mouth was dry, her legs aching, her back sore, but it was her feet that screamed in agony under Lola's weight. She didn't want to admit it, but in reality, it was unlikely she could make it the rest of the way with Lola on her back, and if she tripped and injured herself, they'd both be doomed. The few yards she had to travel to get to the giant crop of boulders seemed like miles.

But the boulders gave perfect cover.

*Too perfect.*

It would be obvious to Blake, if he tracked them this far, where they were hiding.

*A few more steps.*

Her legs refused to move.

*Keep going.*

And then, somehow, they were there. In the shadow of the boulders hidden from view. Lola slid off her back, and the relief was immediate. Exquisite.

"Thank you." Lola huddled behind the largest rock and reached for her hand. "Forgive me."

"Nothing to forgive. It's not your fault you're injured."

"It is in some ways, but that's not what I mean. Please forgive me for not warning you years ago about Ashton and Blake. I knew what they were. I could've saved you. But now, you're the one who's saving me. I'm not sure I deserve it."

Rosalyn's heart tore at the thought that Ashton could be involved, and deep down, she still didn't believe it. The man she loved was more than capable of making mistakes. And he'd been too loyal, *blindly loyal*, to his friend, Blake. But he would never hurt another person intentionally, much less cover up a beating or take part in a kidnapping scheme. "You deserve *everything*, Lola. Especially justice for what Blake did to you."

Lola's eyes widened.

Ros paused and pricked her ears. "What was that?"

"Rosalyn! Lola!"

A *woman's* voice carried on the wind.

## FIFTY-FIVE

### NOW

Rosalyn and Lola must be behind that crop of boulders. Zoe could see footprints leading that way and then disappearing. Of course, they might have stopped and left again, somehow covering their tracks to make the trail end at the rocks. But if they had the time and means to wipe away their prints, they would have done so before now.

This might be some kind of trick.

*No.*

Zoe was the one with the trick up her sleeve.

She needed to lure them out from behind those rocks, in order to shoot them. She forced herself to alter her voice into one that was syrupy and weak—a voice she *hated*. "Rosalyn! Lola! Please come out. It's me! Melanie. I'm alive!"

She heard movement, and then, Rosalyn's forehead appeared, for a split second above the boulder. More noises, and then, Rosalyn stepped out from her hiding place and limped at an admirably fast pace toward her.

"Melanie! How? Never mind! But hurry up and take cover. Can you walk? Are you all right? I can't believe it. There was so much blood."

Oh, how satisfying Zoe found the sob in Ros's voice, the shocked relief written on her face at the sight of her dear *Melanie.*

"I'm fine, Rosalyn." Zoe pulled her pistol from her waist band and aimed it at her sister-in-law. "That was stage blood. Blake took it from the movie set outside of town. Too bad I can't collect an award for my role as a corpse, or for my portrayal of Melanie Monroe Tyler—grieving widow."

"Melanie, what—"

"Don't call me Melanie again, or I'll shoot Lola first and make you watch. I hate the sound of that insipid name. Of course, Melanie is an insipid woman so it suited her perfectly. But it does not suit *me.*"

Zoe was glad the sun had come up and it was light enough to see each nuanced expression flicker across Rosalyn's face. First relief, then confusion, then fear, and now... "You're angry. As you should be."

"I-I... put the gun down. Talk to me, Melanie, help me to understand."

"I'm not Melanie! My name is Zoe Wessex. And, before I kill you, there is one thing I really, really want you to know. I am not your sister. I am not even your friend. And I would never use your brother's birthday as a combination unless I *wanted* you to read those ridiculous letters. I never loved your precious Philip. I didn't hate him, but I didn't care about him, either. I married him for his money, and I hated every single minute I had to spend playing the role of spoiled, silly Melanie Monroe. When Philip got cancer, I bought a bottle of Dom to celebrate. But I couldn't wait for him to die. I switched his medications for sugar pills and watched him wither away. He was really suffering at the end, and when he called for me to bring his pain medication, I denied him that, too. A man like Philip, who made so much money from an absurd invention, didn't deserve anything better. A man who would marry a simpering fool like 'Melanie' deserves to get played."

Telling the truth was a rush. Revealing her true self to another human being was like a drug. She'd never allowed anyone to *see* her except Blake. Euphoria swept through her, lifting her up, and then suddenly left her bereft. She was only able to reveal herself to Rosalyn because Rosalyn was about to die.

Zoe didn't need to be loved, but she did need to be seen.

Without Blake, Zoe would be truly alone.

Forever locked in the role of Melanie Greene Monroe Tyler, widow to Blake and Philip.

She shrugged—*wealthy widow* to Blake and Philip.

"On your knees." She waved the pistol. "Do it or I'll drag Lola out here and kill her first."

Rosalyn lifted her hands in the air. "Nice meeting you, Zoe. I'm going to do everything you tell me to do."

"Fabulous. Get on your knees."

Rosalyn's chin came up, and she locked her eyes with Zoe.

Zoe frowned at Rosalyn's hand, curled into a fist. "What have you got?"

"Nothing."

"In your hand. Show me what's in your hand."

Rosalyn opened her left palm, and then with her right fist, landed an upper cut to Zoe's jaw.

Zoe stumbled and fell to the ground.

Suddenly, a flurry of rocks sailed from behind the boulder.

Zoe covered her head.

*Lola!*

Rosalyn leapt on top of Zoe, wrestling with her, trying to wrench the pistol from her grip. The gun flew from Zoe's grasp, landing out of reach. Rosalyn raised her chest, and Zoe pushed up, flipping Rosalyn onto her back.

Combat crawling on her elbows, Lola dragged her body toward them.

With Zoe's weight on her chest, Rosalyn couldn't move, couldn't fight, couldn't *breathe.*

Lola reached them and began pounding Zoe on the back with her fists, pulling her hair, gouging her eyes, until, finally, Zoe rolled off of Rosalyn and life-saving air moved through her lungs.

Zoe jumped up.

*The gun!*

*Zoe was running for the gun!*

"Stop! Police!"

Rosalyn's heart split wide open—she knew that voice...

A man emerged from the shadows, his pistol straight-armed in front of him.

Melanie—*Zoe*—stopped in her tracks and raised both hands in the air.

"Now place your hands behind your head, turn around and get on your knees," Detective Julian Van commanded. "Zoe Wessex, you're under arrest. You have the right to remain silent."

# FIFTY-EIGHT

## NOW

Rosalyn stared at the taillights on the police SUV as they disappeared into the night, taking Melanie with them.

*No, not Melanie.*

Apparently, her sister-in-law's real name was Zoe Wessex.

"Lola's injuries appear to be limited to her ankle. What about you? Are you hurt?" Detective Van asked her.

Rosalyn's entire body was buzzing with adrenaline. "If I am, I'm not feeling it at the moment."

Van lifted her hand and turned it over, then released it. "Your knuckles are swollen and scraped. We definitely need to get an X-ray. The pain will probably hit you later—after your endorphin high wears off."

*Endorphins.* "You're probably right."

"You think you can wait for the hospital a bit? Not dizzy or confused?"

"Not dizzy. I can definitely wait."

"Good. I won't call for a medevac helicopter, then. We'll drive you and Lola to the ER." Detective Van inclined his head toward a second SUV with a uniformed officer behind the wheel and Lola resting in the back.

Then another vehicle pulled up, and before it even came to a complete stop, a side door opened and Ashton leaped out of the car.

Rosalyn's heart flipped.

She dove into her husband's arms. He hugged her, and then she did feel the pain. But she didn't wince—she didn't want him to ever stop holding her.

He stroked her hair and kissed her eyelids, all the while whispering, "I'm sorry. I'm so sorry."

"This isn't your fault. But how did you get here?" She pulled away, suddenly fearful.

"Blake. He drugged me, tied me up, drugged me again. According to the officer who's been babysitting me, Detective Van found me and called for backup, then went hunting for you. Thank God you're okay."

"Ashton, what about Blake? Have they caught him?"

"Blake Tyler's dead," Van supplied. "Looks like Zoe double-crossed him. But we'll know more soon. We found his cell phone back at the ranch, and he recorded something on it. We'll have to authenticate it, but it appears he left some sort of confession."

## FIFTY-NINE

### NOW

"Did you sleep?" Rosalyn asked, as Lola hobbled into the conference room that Detective Van had secured for their meeting. "Where're your crutches?"

Rosalyn and Ashton had been discharged from the emergency room, about twelve hours ago, with the admonition to hydrate and rest. Lola, whose ankle was confirmed to be sprained but not broken, had been given a pair of crutches and the same firm instruction.

"No sleep," Lola said. "And the crutches are more hindrance than help. What about you guys? Did you get any rest?"

Ashton slid his rolling chair over to Rosalyn and threw an arm over the back of her shoulders. "We tried."

Rosalyn had lain awake in his arms until the alarm went off. She'd been in tune to his breathing, his heartbeat, the tension in his body, and based on that, she doubted Ashton slept either, though they'd both lain very still, each not wanting to move in case the other was dozing. "I don't think I'll be able to sleep until I hear Blake's confession."

Lola's gaze traveled around the plain room—beige walls,

beige carpet, long, laminated wood table, faux leather chairs with silver bases on wheels. There was little to capture anyone's interest, so either Lola was a fan of the world's most boring décor or she was avoiding looking at them. "Lola, I hope you realize I don't bear any ill will toward you for—"

"Lying to you. Stalking you and your husband."

"Exactly," Ros said. "I understand, or at least I want to. We've been through so much together, and now that the danger has passed, I want us to remain friends. We were on the same team yesterday, and we should be on the same team from here on out."

Lola's lip quivered, and she covered her face. Then she dropped her arm and allowed them to see the tears streaming down her cheeks. "I could use friends. I've been on my own a long time. I really believed it was Blake who beat me and left me for dead. And when Ashton swore he was with him the day I was attacked, I thought he was part of it. Ashton, I thought you helped him. And now that I know that, for all his sins, Blake was *not* the one who dragged me out to the desert—"

"Wait," Ashton held up one hand, "I really was with Blake that day, just like I told the police. I know it wasn't him. But why are *you* suddenly convinced?"

"Because after he kidnapped me, he never hurt me. He unshackled my hands. He showed compassion. The person who beat me and left me for dead isn't capable of compassion. It wasn't Blake, and I know it wasn't you, either."

"Thank God," Ashton said. "I feel awful knowing that you, that *anyone*, thought I could be that kind of a monster."

"I wanted to destroy you once—both you and Blake—but I didn't get very far. I did manage one act of revenge, though, which I deeply regret. I'm the one who switched your company's original artwork for a forgery, and I'm going to make amends for it. I've got money, an inheritance of my own, and I can pay you whatever damages I owe. Plus, I intend to publish a public apology to help your company rebuild its reputation."

Rosalyn reached out her hand, and Ashton grasped it.

"I hope someday you can forgive me."

The room was silent, and then, Ashton said, "Lola, my wife's life is far more precious to me than my reputation as a businessman. There are no words for how grateful I am to you for helping save her life. What you suffered in college... we may never know who's responsible, but they don't deserve to be walking around on this planet. I hope, someday, you'll find out the truth about your attacker. As for what you did to me, I forgive you—with all my heart."

There was a knock at the door.

Detective Van pushed through. "Oh, good. I see you're all here. Everyone get some sleep?"

He took his place at the head of table. "No?"

"Not really," Rosalyn sighed. "We're all anxious to hear Blake's confession, and we want to know what's going to happen to Zoe."

"What happens to Zoe will be for a jury to decide. But I can tell you the D.A. is not planning to seek the death penalty."

"Why not?" Ashton raised his voice.

It was clear enough how he felt, but Rosalyn wasn't certain —she was still trying to come to grips with the fact that the woman she'd been trying to protect, for Philip's sake, had caused his death by withholding his medication. That Zoe had apparently murdered Blake, and then tried to kill three of the four people sitting around this table.

"The D.A. thinks there are mitigating circumstances—her life's been a difficult one, as you'll soon find out. But you will all get an opportunity to give a victim's impact statement before sentencing—if she's convicted."

For her own sake, Rosalyn wanted to confront Zoe. And she wanted the judge to know what she'd stolen from her when she'd killed her brother. But what would Philip want? Suddenly it felt like a hot rock was lodged in her throat. She didn't believe he would want "Melanie" to get the maximum penalty.

Yet the woman Philip knew as Melanie was a myth, not a real person.

"We're so grateful you showed up at the ranch when you did, Detective Van. But how did you know that Melanie was really Zoe? How did you know where to find us?" Ashton asked what they'd all been wondering.

"I might not have ever solved the case of Zoe Wessex if not for Lola showing up and then disappearing again. In a catch-up visit with Walter Wessex, I looked through some of Zoe's old things and found an old photograph of her with her best friend. That best friend's name was Melanie Greene, and Walter told me that friend had moved to Germany."

Rosalyn couldn't help her startle response. *Greene* was Melanie's maiden name.

"That was how the cases eventually intersected. 'Melanie Greene' turned out to be a co-owner of 'Opportunity Knocks' and I recognized that name because I'd been looking into Blake, again, in connection with 'Sherry Anne's' disappearance. I realized Zoe had probably been living under an assumed name—that of her old friend who was out of the country. I dug around some more and found out Opportunity Knocks held title to a remote ranch, and you know the rest of the story."

"I'm surprised you didn't recognize Melanie as Zoe when you met her," Lola said.

"That's just it. I never actually met her. Maybe if I'd interviewed her in person, but I only surveilled her from afar at Philip's grave.

"Did Blake admit his part in everything?" Lola twisted her hands. "I don't think I can wait any longer. Please, tell us what's in the confession."

"What if I play it for you instead? You can hear it in his own words, like he requests in the recording. Is everyone okay with that? Or will it be too much to hear his voice?"

"Please, play the recording," Rosalyn said, and Ashton and Lola nodded.

Detective Van held up a small device. He pressed a button and there was a click, followed by a voice from the grave.

# SIXTY

## NOW

*My name is Blake Robert Tyler and I am of sound mind and body. My last request is that this recording be played for Ashton Hightower, Rosalyn Hightower, and Lola Sampson. My friends, you are the only people who ever cared about me, and I want to confess my sins, not to a priest, but to you.*

*I guess you can consider this confession my last will and testament. I have no money that I've come by honestly, therefore I have no monetary assets to leave my family. And I have no family, none who care about me. And, so, to you, my friends, I bequeath the only thing of value I possess—the truth.*

*I do not have the right to call you friends, but you mean more to me than anyone except Zoe. It seems, in the end, you meant more to me than she did.*

*I will not kill you in order to keep her.*

*To give you a bit of background, I met Zoe when I was a boy.*

*I was fourteen and she sixteen when we threw our lots in together.*

*In the beginning, we lived as friends, but I fell in love with her on the day we met.*

We started a company, a nonprofit to avoid taxes, and we scammed a lot of people into donating money to our 'charity'. Lola, when I first pursued you, it was to get my hands on as much of your inheritance as I could. But after spending time with you, I grew to care for you, and I was grateful for the affection you showed me.

Zoe and I parted ways once we had enough money for her to make it in the world on her own, and for me to go to college. I enrolled at the university, and that's when Ashton came into my life. Then I got back together with Lola, and it was all real. I thought Lola and I could have a future. I wanted to get an education, succeed in a legitimate business, start a family, enjoy my friends.

I'm sorry it didn't work out that way.

Zoe had a hard life—trust me on that—and she needed my complete devotion, even though she was unable to fully return it. I only learned that later, though.

I promise, Lola, I did not know!

I did not know how enraged Zoe became when she learned I was back with you. I did not know that it was Zoe who drugged you and beat you and left you in the desert until much, much later.

What I did know was that, suddenly, Zoe wanted me again, and I was blinded by my love for her.

I swore I would do anything for her, and I almost did.

I told Zoe, who was then going by Melanie Greene, that my friend, Ashton, had a wealthy brother-in-law. I'm so sorry, Ashton. I'm so sorry, Rosalyn. Please believe me that the plan was never to kill Philip. The plan was for Zoe to con him out of money for our charity. But then Philip proposed, and the scam changed. Zoe planned to marry and divorce him; take him for half of his wealth.

Until fate stepped in.

When Philip was diagnosed with cancer, Zoe saw a chance

to have it all. For months, she dumped out his medications and filled his prescription bottles with various pills she bought at the store—like vitamins and such.

I convinced myself that this wasn't the same as murdering him, but when he died, I had to stop lying to myself because, then, she turned her sights on Rosalyn. She promised me the one thing I'd always longed for, if I'd go along with her plan.

She promised to marry me.

She kept her word.

After we married, I thought it might really work, but life as "Melanie" stifled Zoe, and then Lola showed up again.

Zoe was always jealous of Lola, and I was afraid of what she would do to her. I lied to Ashton and told him Sherry Anne was not Lola, to keep him from spilling the secret.

But in the end, I realized that Zoe would eventually find out about Rosalyn's mysterious friend, and I decided to come clean.

Turns out I was right to be afraid of what Zoe would do to Lola.

Zoe chloroformed Lola, stuffed her in the trunk of my car and told me to get rid of her. I drove her to a ranch we'd bought through our nonprofit—the ranch was a place Zoe went to escape her role as Melanie. She said when she was in the suburbs, she could feel herself becoming more and more like Melanie—like a zombie.

I loved Zoe, but I couldn't kill Lola.

When I told Zoe that Lola was at the ranch, locked in the barn, Zoe was furious with me. Then she decided to lure Rosalyn to the ranch, too. She suggested she should pretend she was fleeing my abuse.

The second hardest thing I've ever done was punch "Melanie" in the face and chest. But Zoe said it was the only way to trap Rosalyn, and a fitting punishment for me, because

I had once again betrayed her by keeping Lola alive in the barn.

Zoe insisted that I drug Ashton and bring him to the ranch, too. She wanted me to kill my best friend. She said she was to be my only friend, and I was to prove my loyalty to her by killing you all.

I tried. But I couldn't do it.

When she came up with a nonsensical plan for me to pretend to shoot 'Melanie' in front of Rosalyn and Lola and use movie blood to make it look real, I finally figured it out. Zoe invented all kinds of excuses for why I needed to do this to make 'our' plan work.

But I'm not stupid.

Supposedly, the plan was for us to make it look like Ashton killed Lola and Rosalyn and then shot himself.

But if that was the real plan, there was no logical reason for me to pretend to shoot 'Melanie' in front of the women.

There was no logical reason to make me beat 'Melanie' up in order to get Rosalyn out to the ranch.

And no logical reason for Zoe to write letters to Philip (she didn't know I knew about them) that made Melanie look like an angel, but made me look like the devil.

None of it made sense.

Except...

It all made sense if Zoe was setting me up instead of Ashton, to take the fall for everything.

I remembered an incident from our past. The very first time I met her, Zoe tricked a shopkeeper into doing something terrible in front of his own security cameras. So, I searched the ranch and found that, yes indeed, she'd hidden cameras in the barn.

She had me on camera punching her in our kitchen. She had me on camera dragging three unconscious women into the barn and then 'shooting' 'Melanie'!

*I figure after everyone else is dead, Zoe plans to murder me, then shoot herself in the leg and act like she's the only survivor of my killing spree.*

*Maybe I'm wrong about her trying to frame me.*

*Maybe what she truly wants is for me to kill the three of you and pin it on Ashton, like she claims.*

*But I can't let that happen, either.*

*I no longer believe there is a normal life waiting for Zoe and me.*

*I can no longer live with what we did to Philip, and I damn sure won't kill the only three people who have shown me kindness. Lola explained to me how she changed because of what Zoe did to her. What she believed Ashton and I did. Nothing Lola did wrong is her fault.*

*Everyone has suffered enough, including Zoe.*

*Including me.*

*I love Zoe, but I can't make her happy.*

*I don't think she's capable of happiness.*

*I dropped the key to the shackles so the women can get free and go for help. I left it just out of their reach. It may take them awhile to get it, but I have faith they will find a way.*

*I need a little time before they escape in order to do what I must.*

*There's going to be a murder-suicide tonight, but not the one Zoe planned.*

*I can't let her keep hurting people, and I can't go on living without her.*

# SIXTY-ONE

## NOW

"You can all be seated." Judge Frank Jessup pushed up the sleeves of his robe as he slid behind the bench.

Ashton let out a long breath.

He'd wondered if the D.A. made the right call when she decided not to pursue the death penalty against Zoe. But, as promised, she'd secured a quick conviction—it had taken the jury only two hours to render a guilty verdict.

He and Rosalyn had attended every day of the trial, and afterwards, the sentencing hearing.

Yesterday, Ashton barely managed to keep from tearing up during Lola's gut-wrenching victim's impact statement. Rosalyn had prepared her own statement, but then, despite Ashton's urgings, she'd changed her mind. Incredibly, Rosalyn said she felt torn because of her promise to Philip to protect his widow. She was grappling with what *he* would want, and knowing his forgiving heart, she worried he might hope the judge would show Zoe mercy. In the end, not feeling sure of the right course to take, she chose to remain silent. Still, after Lola's statement, the judge had been visibly moved, and Ashton had thought, surely, he'd give Zoe the maximum sentence: life without a chance for parole.

But then came the defense's turn—and Walter Wessex broke everyone's heart with his plea for mercy. When he'd recounted the story of Zoe being found as a toddler, curled up next to her mother's corpse, the judge had wiped moisture from his eyes and ordered a recess.

Now, a day later, court had reconvened for the moment of truth.

The judge was about to hand down Zoe's sentence—without hearing from Rosalyn.

Ashton stiffened his shoulders and swallowed down a mouthful of bile.

# SIXTY-TWO

## NOW

Zoe's defense attorney touched her arm—preparing her for sentencing—offering moral support that was not only unwanted but unnecessary.

*I am an island.*

Without Blake around to confuse her with his messy emotions, Zoe had returned to her natural state—alone and dependent upon no one else in the world.

She folded her hands, pasted on a meek expression—the one she'd practiced with her attorney—and looked directly at Judge Jessup.

His mouth was moving, but she'd already muted him in her head. By freeing herself of Blake, she'd taken back her power. And now no one, not even *his honor*, could strip it from her.

The judge's eyes met hers and held.

An indication, she thought, that he'd believed her show of remorse.

Sometimes she wished she wasn't such a good actress. She'd played the role of Melanie so well she'd almost lost herself. Some nights she'd fallen asleep and woken up the next morning still in character—and oh how Blake's eyes had shone with adoration when she'd spoken to him, or touched him as Melanie.

Her heart clenched at the memory.

This was his fault.

None of this would've happened if he'd remained true to her—the *real* her.

But he'd chosen his so-called friends, Ashton, Lola and Rosalyn, over her—Zoe—and that was the *real* reason she'd been determined to get rid of them all. To her, it was about much more than the money.

It was about taking back what was rightfully hers.

Blake Tyler told her over and over and over again that he loved her, and only *her*, but that had been a lie. He'd wanted his friends, and worst of all, *Melanie*, more than he'd wanted the real Zoe.

The girl who'd saved him from the streets.

Grown up with him.

Done her damnedest to be a true partner and never betrayed him... until the very end.

*So much for love.*

Her eyes felt ridiculously wet—like she was an ordinary person.

*This* was what Blake had done to her.

She cast a sideways glance at the other side of the aisle, where Lola, Ashton and Rosalyn huddled, apparently rapt, hanging on the judge's every word.

Perhaps she did bear some responsibility. She had to admit it had been a mistake to indulge Blake's ridiculous dreams, allowing him to seduce her into half-believing them herself.

If she hadn't married him on a beach at sunset like they were characters in a romance novel, and so soon after Philip died, maybe Rosalyn wouldn't have caught onto him and made their plans that much more difficult to carry out.

But she'd promised to give him what he'd been begging of

her for years, right after they'd scored with Philip. And in all their years together, she'd never broken a promise to Blake. Besides, she'd assumed that after they married, his insecurities would fade.

Instead, he became more insecure, more possessive.

He was even jealous of *Philip*.

As it turned out, there was nothing she could do to convince Blake that she preferred a street kid like him to a sophisticated man like Philip Monroe.

If murdering Philip and marrying Blake hadn't persuaded him, what would have?

She would never have killed Blake, though, if he hadn't discarded *her* first.

He'd betrayed her not just once, but many, many times.

With Lola, with Ashton, with Rosalyn, and yes, with Melanie—the woman she could read in his eyes he wanted her to become.

And though killing Blake had been far more difficult than she'd ever imagined, she didn't regret it.

It had been an act of self-preservation.

Now, her attorney motioned for her to rise. It must be time for the formal pronouncement of her sentence.

The judge's mouth kept moving. He went on for what seemed like an eternity. She was starting to feel light-headed. Her legs grew unsteady.

Then, at last, the judge stopped talking.

She felt eyes boring into her and turned to meet them.

*Rosalyn.*

# EPILOGUE

Lola walked briskly, head held high, into the visitor area at the women's correctional institution.

She stowed her valuables in the provided lockers, and then followed Ashton down the hallway.

Even though she had him with her for moral support, her nerves were jangling.

It all seemed so unjust.

If only Rosalyn had taken the stand and read her victim's impact statement, maybe the judge would have gone a different way. But he'd taken Walter's plea to heart and handed down the minimum sentence, leaving at least a possibility for Zoe to be paroled after fifteen years.

"Do you wonder what would've happened if Rosalyn had taken the stand?" she asked Ashton.

"We can't turn back the clock. And we don't have the right to second-guess Rosalyn's decision. She said she didn't think Philip would've wanted Zoe to get the maximum sentence. He would've wanted the judge to give her a chance to reform herself." His face went pale, and Lola followed his gaze.

They were bringing the prisoner in now.

Her hands were cuffed, her feet shackled, but she raised her chin as she shuffled toward them.

* * *

Rosalyn's heart pounded. The key clanked as the guard unlocked a heavy metal door and escorted her into the family visitation room.

Rosalyn took tiny steps—the iron cuffs on her legs and the coarse fabric of her prison issue pants chaffing her sensitive skin. Like the prison cell block, the walls were painted shiny gray, but it was as if she'd stepped into a different world. The smells of body odor and snacks from the vending machine were a welcome change from the stale, antiseptic air in her cell, and the visitors' room reeked of hope—not despair.

Here, for a short time, the prisoners, like Rosalyn, were no longer inmates—they were mothers, daughters, sisters, and friends.

Over in the far corner, she spotted Ashton and Lola already seated at a metal picnic-style table that, like all the other "furniture" in the room, had been bolted to the floor. Her body shook with the effort of containing her tears as she and the guard made their way over and she slid onto the bench, allowing the guard to cuff one wrist onto the iron ring on the tabletop.

Ashton reached for her hand.

"No touching the prisoner," the guard warned.

He withdrew his hand, but not before his fingers grazed hers, sending a wave of calm rippling through her.

"I miss you, sweetheart," Ashton said.

"I miss you, too." Those simple words could not convey the profound love in her heart, but she hoped the look in her eyes did. She took a breath and managed a smile for Lola. "I'm so glad you came, Lola. I've been telling Ashton how worried I've been about you. But I must say, you look well."

Lola lifted her hand, as if to reach out, but quickly lowered it when the guard sent her a stern look. "No need to worry about me. I'm better than I've been in years. Believe it or not, I've befriended Walter Wessex... or we've befriended each other. If I'd had a grandfather like him in my life, maybe I wouldn't have needed Dr. Gainey all these years."

"You've gone back to therapy, though, right?" Rosalyn hoped the answer would be "yes". Lola had been twice traumatized, and she was perhaps the most vulnerable of all of them, even if Rosalyn was the one behind bars.

"Oh, yes. Dr. Gainey says I'm making great strides... and I don't sleep with the light on anymore. I wish I'd been honest with her a long time ago. If I hadn't been interfering in your life, you wouldn't be in prison, now. I'm sorry, Rosalyn. I'm so, so sorry."

Rosalyn shook her head. "Zoe's dead because *I* lost control. I'm here because of my own actions, not yours."

"But it's so unjust. It's not like you *murdered* her," Lola protested. "You didn't mean for her to die—"

"I think I got a fair enough deal," Rosalyn interrupted. But Lola was right about one thing. She hadn't meant to kill Zoe. What happened at Zoe's sentencing wasn't the product of thought or reason on Rosalyn's part—much less premeditation.

She hadn't *planned* to leap out of her seat and charge at Zoe. Only a fool would do that in front of the judge, and onlookers, and armed bailiffs.

She hadn't *planned* for Zoe to fall back and hit her head against the rail, any more than she'd planned for the bailiff to spring into action, pull her off of Zoe and place her under arrest.

"Whether I meant to or not, I caused Zoe's death. So, it's right for me to face the consequences."

"No," Lola said. "I *wanted* her to die. The only reason I didn't kill her is because I didn't know how to pull it off with all those bailiffs and metal detectors. And yet I'm free and you're the one behind bars. You don't deserve this."

"I do." Rosalyn closed her eyes, remembering.

After the judge handed down a sentence that included a chance at parole, she'd begun to tremble. Rage had rumbled and roiled inside her until it felt as if her body would split wide open. Then Zoe had turned.

And when their eyes had met, she'd suddenly snapped.

She'd bounded to her feet and lunged at Zoe, taking everyone, including the bailiffs, off guard. They might have expected Ashton to cause trouble, but not Rosalyn. Though it only took a second or two for the bailiff to react, that hesitation allowed Rosalyn to make it ten feet to the defense table.

She shoved Zoe, who had risen for the judge's decision.

Zoe fell backwards, hitting her head on the railing behind the table, and, as the bailiff pulled Rosalyn off, she saw a tiny trickle of blood seep from Zoe's ear.

*I deserve this.*

At first, Zoe had shown very few signs of injury—just a mild headache, according to the prison doctors. But, two days later, she'd collapsed in her cell. An autopsy confirmed that Zoe had a fractured skull and something called an epidural hematoma—bleeding in the brain. That bleeding had caused increased pressure inside the skull, and, over the course of time, death.

*Because of me.*

Rosalyn made a deal with the D.A., pleading guilty to manslaughter.

"I blame the district attorney and the judge." A vein pulsed in Ashton's forehead. "Why didn't the judge give her life without parole? If they'd done their jobs, you wouldn't have been driven to do what you did."

"You know why." Rosalyn sighed. "I know you're looking to absolve me of blame, but I *am* guilty."

"Then you're not the only one. It was me who brought

Blake Tyler and Zoe Wessex into our lives." Ashton looked at her with devastated eyes.

"And I lied to you. I didn't warn you when I should have." A tear slipped down Lola's cheek.

"*None* of us knew who Melanie really was." More than anything, Rosalyn wished she could take away their guilt. "Please don't cry for me. And don't stop living. Don't waste another minute of your lives—I know I certainly won't."

No one should feel sorry for her.

"Both of you begged me to make a victim's impact statement and I refused. I shouldn't have given up my chance to speak up for myself. I could have asked the judge for a harsher sentence, and I could have confronted Zoe with the anger I felt—like you did, Lola. You did your part. But I was still trying to protect 'Philip's widow'. I truly believe he would've wanted the judge to show Zoe some form of mercy. But by staying silent, I acted for Philip at the expense of my own needs—and that was something he would've never asked of me."

She knew in her heart her brother never intended for her to focus all her energy on keeping that promise. But she'd told herself Melanie was her responsibility. She'd neglected her friends. She'd neglected her work. She'd neglected *her husband*. All that time Ashton spent with Blake was as much her fault as his—she'd hardly been around because she was always fussing over Melanie. Not only that, her promise to Philip had kept her locked inside her own grief, stopped her from moving on with her life.

When the judge handed down Zoe's sentence, Rosalyn allowed herself to experience her own pain for the first time. And now, even though she was behind bars, she felt freer than she had since the day Philip died.

Free to live for herself again.

"I didn't want Zoe dead," she said. "But I *am* relieved to know she can never hurt anyone again. And as much as I loved

Philip, I'm not going to spend what's left of my life grieving. I'm going to enjoy each day—even the ones I spend in prison."

The guard motioned to her. It seemed it was already time for her to go back to her cell.

"I'll visit you often," Lola said, shakily.

Ashton's face was grim. He reached across the table, defiantly, and squeezed her hand before the guard could stop him. "I love you, Rosalyn."

"I love you, too." She held her husband's gaze as long as possible, living in the moment until the guard grew impatient and tapped her on the shoulder. "You'll see," she said, her chains clanking as she climbed to her feet, "four years will fly by in the blink of an eye."

# A LETTER FROM CAREY

Dear Reader,

I'm honored that you have taken time from your life to join my characters on their journey. Creating stories and then sharing them with you so that you can shine your own light on them, reading through a lens shaped by your own perceptions and imagination, is such a joy. I hope you enjoyed *The Widow Bride*!

If you'd like to be the first to know about my next book, please sign up via the following link. Your email address will never be shared and you can unsubscribe at any time.

*www.bookouture.com/carey-baldwin*

If you loved this story, I would be very grateful if you could leave a short review. Reviews are one of the best ways to help other readers discover my books. They don't need to be long or clever. You can make a big difference simply by leaving a line or two.

Building a relationship with readers is one of the best things about being a writer. I love hearing from you, so please stay in touch by connecting with me on Facebook and my website, and by following me on BookBub. I've posted the information below for your convenience.

Thank you very much for reading and don't forget to stay in touch!

# KEEP IN TOUCH WITH CAREY

www.CareyBaldwin.com

 facebook.com/CareyBaldwinAuthor

 x.com/CareyBaldwin

bookbub.com/authors/carey-baldwin

# ACKNOWLEDGMENTS

Thank you to my readers! You are the reason I write.

Thank you to my fantastic agent, Liza Dawson, the terrific Lynn Wu and everyone at Liza Dawson Associates. I want to thank my wonderful editors, Laura Deacon, Natalie Edwards, and Eve Hall who gave me brilliant insights into how to make the story better. Thank you to my eagle-eyed copyeditor, Donna Hillyer. Thank you, thank you, thank you, to publicists extraordinaire Kim, Noelle, Sarah, and Jess. Thank you to the directors and publishers as well as all the individuals in marketing, art, audio and the entire team at Bookouture who champion every book by every author they publish. Thank you for treating each of us with so much care.

Thank you to my dear friends and brainstorming, critiquing, beta-reading geniuses: Suzanne Baldree and Leigh LaValle. You are always there for me whether I need to cry, celebrate, or fix a plot hole. I don't know what I'd do without you. Nancy Allen and Kristi Belcamino, I treasure your friendship beyond words.

To my family: Bill, Shannon, Erik, Kayla, Lumi, Sarah, Junior, Olivia, Marlene and little Scout—I love you truly, dears!

# PUBLISHING TEAM

**Turning a manuscript into a book requires the efforts of many people. The publishing team at Bookouture would like to acknowledge everyone who contributed to this publication.**

### Audio
Alba Proko
Sinead O'Connor
Melissa Tran

### Commercial
Lauren Morrissette
Jil Thielen
Imogen Allport

### Cover design
The Brewster Project

### Data and analysis
Mark Alder
Mohamed Bussuri

### Editorial
Natalie Edwards
Sinead O'Connor